Ben's ruthlessness shocked Jethro Musseldine. Up until the assault on Little Rock, he had not known just how well-equipped the Rebels were. Now he knew. He had lost nearly a third of his army in Little Rock. Something had to be done to stop the rampaging of Ben Raines. The man was so . . . *godless.*

At Russelville, Arkansas, Musseldine made up his mind. He ordered his columns halted. "We shall fight the many-headed beast here," he announced. "We'll force the Great Satan to meet us *mano a mano!*"

Then he had to explain to his true believers exactly what that meant, for many of his followers weren't too swift when it came to gray matter.

"This will be the end of Ben Raines," Musseldine shouted to his wild-eyed followers. "This will be Ben Raines's last stand in America . . ."

Uh-huh. Yeah. Right.

When Ben heard that, he was reminded of that old joke about Custer's last thoughts: *Holy cow, where'd all these Indians come from?*

CHAOS
IN THE
ASHES

WILLIAM W. JOHNSTONE

PINNACLE BOOKS
Kensington Publishing Corp.
http://www.kensingtonbooks.com

PINNACLE BOOKS are published by

Kensington Publishing Corp.
119 West 40th Street
New York, NY 10018

All Kensington Titles, Imprints, and Distributed Lines are available
at special quantity discounts for bulk purchases for sales promo-
tions, premiums, fund-raising, and educational or institutional use.
Special book excerpts or customized printings can also be created
to fit specific needs. For details, write or phone the office of the
Kensington special sales manager: Kensington Publishing Corp.,
119 West 40th Street, New York, NY 10018, attn: Special Sales
Department, Phone: 1-800-221-2647.

Pinnacle and the P logo Reg. U.S. Pat. & TM Off.

ISBN-13: 978-0-7860-2080-5
ISBN-10: 0-7860-2080-6

First Printing: November 1996

10 9 8 7 6 5 4 3

Printed in the United States of America

Prologue

During the final days of the second millennium, the end came. It had been predicted; some even planned for it. Most didn't. Those who did plan were called survivalists—some were called militia—and they were much maligned by the press and by the government. The left-leaning liberal press belittled them and the very government to whom they were paying taxes portrayed them as evil, racist, and dangerous. A few were just that, but not most. The majority of those who practiced survivalism and who joined militias were decent men and women who had simply grown disgusted with big government. They were wolves, making plans to survive, while others around them were dewy-eyed lambs unknowingly waiting for the slaughter, despite the fact that they had been warned time and again that the lid was about to blow off. The lambs stood with their hands out, waiting for the government to run their lives, tell them what to do and when to do it, and give them something for nothing—paid for with tax-payers' money, of course.

Many survivalist groups were harassed by federal agents and vindictively punished. People were killed by federal agents; others watched as their possessions were seized or destroyed by agents of the federal government. But the movement could not be broken. It grew as the end approached, as did the hatred and fear many in the government and the press felt for the men and women who made up the various groups around the nation.

When the end came—and it was the end of civilization and order and reason world-wide—training and discipline saved many of the survivalists, or Constitutionalists, as many preferred to be called.

One of the quiet survivalists was a man called Ben Raines.

Ben belonged to no organized group, although federal agents had for years tried to prove he did. Like most Constitutionalists, he owned no illegal weapons, paid his taxes, obeyed the law, and lived a quiet and peaceful life. Because of his so-called radical views, he did receive the occasional visit from the feds, but like many other Americans who longed for a return to the true meaning of the constitution and a commonsense form of government, Ben learned to live with the creeping socialism and the uninvited intrusions into his privacy. However, he didn't have to like it and was quite vocal in his opposition of it.

That got Ben's name on the list compiled by federal enforcement agencies; the list containing the names of

Americans who had broken no laws but needed watching anyway.*

Real red, white, and blue democracy at work.

But in the end, the prying and the snooping didn't do the feds a bit of good . . . the whole goddamn world fell apart.

And it was the Constitutionalists and the Survivalists who convinced Ben Raines that he should be the one to lead the nation out of the ashes of destruction and chaos.

Ben reluctantly agreed, with conditions attached: the new government would bear little resemblance to the old government, for the old government had stopped working. It worked for many years, until Congress started screwing around with the Constitution and passing so many laws the average tax-paying citizens didn't have a clue as to what was going on.

It would not be that way in the new government.

The new government, at first, would be called the Tri-States.

Unlike the old government, the Tri-States would not attempt to be all things to all people all the time. That was and is impossible in a true democracy. Consitutionalists and Survivalists know that, to a very large degree, we all control our own destinies—or should. The government need not get involved, and in the Tri-States, the government would not get involved.

Ben Raines laid the groundwork for the new, common-sense government. When a society is based on common sense, there really isn't much need for lawyers.

*Author's note: that list does indeed exist.

In North America, when the end came, the ratio was something like one lawyer for every three hundred and ninety people—the highest in the world! The Tri-States had lawyers, of course, but the beauty of the Tri-States is that there aren't that *many* laws.

A common sense society means that if someone breaks into my house and I catch them at it, I am going to shoot them on the spot. And after I shoot them, I won't be arrested, won't be tried, won't go to jail, and can't be sued by the thief's family or by the thief, should he or she survive.

A common sense society means that if you buy an over-the-counter drug and eat the whole damn package and fall over dead, the manufacturer and the druggist can't be held liable for your stupidity.

A common sense society means that if someone gets drunk and has a wreck and kills himself and a whole bunch of other people, the families of the survivors can't sue the beer company or the person who sold the irresponsible nincompoop the beer. (It's called controlling one's own destiny.)

It takes a special type of person to live in a society based on common sense. It takes a person who has respect for the rights of others. For *all* the rights of others, regardless of race or religion or creed.

Ben Raines figured, and calculated correctly, that only two or three out of every ten Americans who survived the Great War could prosper and enjoy life in a free society. It was a radical change from the old form of government, where the government was constantly interfering in everybody's business, with new rules and regulations and complicated paperwork.

In the Tri-States, crime was virtually non-existent. The

main reason being, it just wasn't tolerated. In the Tri-States, not only was carrying weapons allowed, each citizen was *required* to have weapons, for everyone of age was a part of the Rebel Army. Once the government outside the Tri-States crawled to its knees and again started screwing around in the lives of its citizens, the press called the Tri-States a gun-powder society. As in so many cases, the press was only half right. The people who chose to live in the Tri-States did so willingly and happily. They were people who did not have to lock the doors to their homes at night or take the keys out of their car or live in fear of being mugged or assaulted. Any street in any town in the Tri-States was safe to walk upon any time of the day or night. There were no slums, no gangs, no drive-by shootings. There was full employment. In the Tri-States, everybody who was able worked. Or got out. There were no free rides. The old and the young and the infirm were cared for with the utmost compassion. Values and respect and morals were taught in school. In the Tri-States, morality was once more in vogue. Teenage pregnancies were rare and it wasn't due to schools handing out condoms to young people. That came about by like-minded parents and educators teaching children values and self-respect, beginning at a very early age. Reading was emphasized in the Tri-States.

Civil liberties types were appalled at what was going on in the Tri-States. It was such a quiet and happy place. Something must be wrong with a society where *everybody* is contented. Life isn't supposed to be that way. You're supposed to have discontent and dissent and troubles and woes and personal analysts and psychiatrists and head manipulators and so forth. Something must be drastically wrong with a society that wasn't wallowing in a plethora of misery.

Why are these people smiling?

Because they're happy, stupid!

But the government of the former United States of America just couldn't tolerate the contentment that was found in the Tri-States, and eventually moved against the society, finally over-running the residents of the Tri-States with sheer force of numbers. The main objective was to kill Ben Raines.

But Ben Raines was as hard to kill as the Tri-States philosophy.

After the fall of the Tri-States, Ben rebuilt his army of Rebels and moved against the government of the (once) United States; a government that had begun to turn on its citizens again, becoming everything that the old Tri-States was not; becoming exactly what it was before the Great War that nearly destroyed the world.

Ben and his Rebels began claiming territory out of the ashes of defeat and despair and destruction. First it was a small area called Base Camp One. Then it grew, until finally thirteen states adopted the philosophy of the old Tri-States.

The central government of what used to be known as the United States of America finally capitulated and held out the hand of peace to Ben and his Rebels.

Ben accepted the hand of friendship and cooperation and the two nations within a nation began working together . . . as much as liberal and conservative can ever work together.

But for years before the Great War, many people in America had been conditioned to expect the government to do nearly everything for them, including thinking.

All this freedom scared them.

What the hell do you mean, we control our own destinies? What the hell do you mean, tellin' me I have to work at a job I don't like? What is this common sense crap? I got a right, man. What do you mean, turn down my radio? I'll play my radio as loud as I want to. Screw you.

On the other side of the coin, there were those blue-lipped, narrow-minded types who simply could not tolerate any type of open society. If *they* didn't like it, *you* couldn't have it. Didn't matter if they lived in New York and you lived in Montana, *they* knew best. Period.

You may not read this book because *we* consider it nasty. You may not have an abortion because *we* don't think it's right. You may not own a gun because *we* are opposed to that. Like-minded people may not band together and form their own government because *we* won't let you. (However, *we* are perfectly within our rights to force our views on *you*.) On and on and on.

Gimme some money! Gimme a free ride! Gimme food! Take care of me from the womb to the tomb or we'll riot and burn and destroy.

Eventually, that's what happened.

And like Humpty Dumpty, it could not be put back together again.

Book One

If it be the pleasure of Heaven that my country shall require the poor offering of my life, the victim shall be ready, at the appointed hour of sacrifice, come when that hour may. But while I do live, let me have a country, and that a free country.

—John Adams

Chapter One

Ben was glad when he could no longer see the smoke from the fires of discontent. The big transport plane had entered Rebel-controlled territory. For hundreds of miles, the scene had been even worse than Cecil had described.

"We should never have left the country," Ben muttered. "I went against my own philosophy."

But he knew that even had he stayed, he could not have changed the course of events.

Ben dozed off and was awakened by the pilot's voice. "We'll be landing in about twenty minutes, General. The airport is secure."

"Landing into what?" Ben whispered.

Chaos. Rebellion. Upheaval. Mindless acts of violence and destruction. Civil war. Mobs of people running amok, after having reverted back to barbarism. Burning and looting and killing and raping. White against black.

Black against white. White against white. Black against black. Senseless brutality involving all races.

"Everything we fought for, destroyed," Ben whispered. "The nation in ruins."

Again.

Back to the ashes.

Ben looked at his reflection in the window. His hair was streaked with gray. He was middle-aged and, for a man his age, in superb physical condition—but now, for the moment, he felt old.

As the plane slowly descended, Ben allowed himself to wallow, briefly, in self-pity, something he almost never did. His personal team, Jersey, Corrie, Beth, Cooper, and the teenage girl he had adopted while in Europe, Anna, sat away from him. They knew that when Ben was in a lousy mood—as he was now and had been ever since receiving the communiqué from Cecil—it was best to leave him alone.

Ben's plane was the first one down, a dozen other huge transports coming in right behind his. Ben stood up and stretched the kinks out of his muscles and joints and deplaned. He spotted Cecil Jefferys standing on the edge of the tarmac and walked over to him. The men stood in silence for a moment, content to look at each other, as good and old friends will do. Ben had to struggle to hide his shock at Cecil's appearance. The black man's hair was now completely white, his face deeply lined.

Cecil put out his big hands and gripped Ben's shoulders in an unusual display of affection. "God, but it's good to see you, Ben."

"Same here, Cec."

"I've got a fresh pot of coffee, some food. We'll talk while we eat. Come on."

In a private room off the main terminal building in what had once been a major American airport, the men sat and talked and ate.

"What happened, Cec?"

"The whole damned country just fell apart, Ben. With practically no warning."

"President Blanton?"

Cec shook his head. "We don't know where he is. We don't know if he's alive or dead or hurt or what. We do know that most of his staff, his inner circle, are dead. We *think* he and his wife might have made it out. But we don't know for sure."

"The new capital?"

"In a shambles. Taken over by malcontents. It's bad, Ben. Real bad. We've lost about two thirds of the SUSA, including the old Base Camp One. But we deactivated the missiles there before we pulled out. They can't be launched. I doubt if these idiots can even find the silos, much less get into them. In all our years of war, Ben, I have *never* seen anything to equal this. The slackers, the malcontents, the give-me-something-for-nothing bunch, and all the rest must have been planning this for months—maybe years. And they've got some real brains behind this movement."

"Sure they have," Ben said sarcastically. "All those ultra-liberals we read the riot act to several years back. I should have seen this coming."

Cecil stared at him for a moment. "Ben, do you really believe . . . ?"

"I damn sure do."

"But Blanton was one of them!"

"*Was* is the key word, Cec. He changed. He and I became friends. Friends as much as we ever could be. Certain members of his old party just couldn't take that." Ben shook his head. "I should have seen this coming."

"Oh, hell, Ben! Nobody could have seen this coming. We've got the best intelligence network in the world, and we didn't see it coming. If what you're saying is true, then the old ultra-liberal wing of Blanton's party just sacrificed God only knows how many thousands of people."

"They don't care about that. To them, the end justifies the means. They want back in power. They don't give a damn how that comes to be."

"That's monstrous!"

"Yes, it certainly is. I preached for years that liberals were a greater threat to individual freedom than communism. Now tell me what happened."

Cecil drained his coffee mug and sighed. "People began peacefully gathering along our borders. One day there were five thousand, the next day a hundred thousand, the next day half a million. Then they started pouring across and rioting and looting. They came across our borders in human waves, thousands and thousands of men and women and children. Hell, Ben, we couldn't open fire on unarmed civilians and little kids. We used rubber bullets and gas but they kept coming; our people were overwhelmed by the solid crush of humanity. We were spread thin as it was and the rioters broke through in dozens of places and began circling, trying to trap our people. But now they had weapons—"

"Carefully planned out, wasn't it?"

"It damn sure was. Communications became impossible. Our people had to keep falling back, fighting a rear-guard action over hundreds of miles of border. All this happened in a day, Ben—one day. Blanton's military was trying to contain the rioters in their territory, but they were spread much thinner than we and were quickly overwhelmed. Once the rioters became armed, we started using deadly force. Our field reports show that we killed probably twenty-five thousand rioters and wounded that many more before we were finally able to stand and hold.''

Ben sighed and nodded his understanding. ''I'm leaving a token force in Europe. Bringing the rest of them home. But it's going to be weeks before we have all of our equipment back Stateside. We're just going to have to do the best we can until then.'' Ben smiled. ''Hell, Cec, we've fought worse odds.''

Cecil leaned back in his chair and rubbed his face. ''Jesus, ol' buddy, I'm tired.'' Then he smiled and it was the old Cecil once more. ''I've been out of the field for a long time. I don't see how you do it.''

Ben returned the smile. ''For the most part, I've never left the field. That's how I do it.''

Cecil cut his eyes to Jersey, Ben's bodyguard, standing silently by the door. The diminutive Jersey, all five feet of her, was as lethal as a spitting cobra. Trained in martial arts, she could kill with her hands, as well as being expert with gun, knife, or garrote. Everyone knew she was in love with Ben, but it was a love that was not to be, and Jersey knew and accepted that.

''I hate to hit you with this, Ben . . . I know it's early. But what's the agenda?''

Ben looked down at the map before him; the territory the Rebels had lost was highlighted, and it was huge.

"We start reclaiming our territory. Slow and easy. But this time we're going to be fighting a political war as well as a fire-fight. I hate to use the term, but we're going to have to win the hearts and minds—"

Cecil groaned and Ben laughed. "Sounds familiar, doesn't it?"

Cecil said, "I don't believe these people we'll be fighting, many of them, even want a government, Ben."

"Maybe so. But this nation can't exist without some form of government. We certainly can't have anarchy. And the liberals don't want that either . . . in the long run. But for now they're using anarchy for their own gain. We have a government, Cec. As long as there are people working together to make something better, to pull something useful out of the ashes, we have a government. But when we start our push, we're going to take it easy. We're going to talk to the people and listen to what they have to say. That's something that hasn't really happened since town meetings went out of style. Maybe we'll never be able to put this country back together again. Maybe we'll die as old men trying to do it. Maybe we'll die tomorrow trying to do it. But we've got to try. It can't be business as usual. We did something wrong, Cec. Blanton did something wrong. But our basic Tri-States philosophy works; we proved that. At least it works for us. But how about the millions of people who say they can't live under that type of open government? What about them? Is it that they *can't* live under our rules, or that they *won't* live under them? We won't be able to solve the problem until we understand it."

Cecil stared at him for a moment, then chuckled. The laughter took years from the man. "What is this, a new Ben Raines?"

"In a way, perhaps it is. Might be better, might be worse. We'll just have to see." He looked over at Jersey. "What do you have to say about it, Little Bit?"

"Well, the way I see it, we're going to kick them in the ass and then extend a hand to help them up."

Ben laughed. "That about sums it up. Now let's go see if it works."

Chapter Two

The transports never stopped except for maintenance. As the days drifted slowly into weeks, the Rebel battalions were gathering strength, back on American soil. Still Ben made no moves against those malcontents who now controlled—or thought they did—much of what used to be called the Southern United States of America. The SUSA. He would not move until he was up to full strength.

Ben had left three battalions in Europe for a time, to assist and advise the growing European forces: Batts 21, 16, and 17. He pulled everyone else back to the States.

Ships began docking at safe ports, unloading thousands of tons of equipment, including tanks and Hummers and helicopter gun ships and the souped-up P-51s that made up much of Ben's air force.

Ben was almost ready to move.

Ike McGowan's 2 Batt was the last one to leave Europe.

When the ex-SEAL's ship docked, a plane was ready to take him to Ben's HQ, now located in what used to be known as Alabama.

After shaking hands, the two men poured mugs of coffee and got down to business. "Is it as bad as the reports I've been getting, Ben?"

"Worse, Ike. We've got a lot of territory to reclaim. And it's going to be a nasty business. We're up against hundreds of thousands of malcontents—for want of a better word—and we've got fifteen battalions to do it with. We've got the Gulf to our south, the Atlantic to the east, and facing the enemy west and north. I've made contact with some of their leaders, but they refuse to negotiate any terms. No compromise. For one of the few times in my life, I'm willing to compromise and bend some, to prevent blood-shed, and the enemy won't hear of it."

"So we start kicking ass and taking names, right?"

Ben sighed. Ike could see that he was clearly troubled. "It's not that simple any more. I wish it was. But I can't go in and start killing kids. The malcontents know that. I wish I could think of a better word than that, for malcontent just doesn't fit many of these people. I am firmly convinced that many are really good, decent people . . . solidly opposed to the Tri-States philosophy."

"But they are also people who won't practice live and let live, Ben," Ike said softly.

"You're sure right about that. The same types of people who, a decade ago, supported gun control, more government interference in private lives, higher taxes for some totally worthless social programs, etc., etc."

"So what's the plan, Ben?"

Ben met Ike's eyes. "That's the problem. I don't have one."

Ben was stymied and he would be the first to admit it. He worked up and then rejected a dozen plans over the weeks while he waited for all his people and equipment to be made ready.

But when everything was ready, his people sitting on "Go," Ben still did not have a plan.

Mike Richards, the Rebels' Chief of Intelligence, had hit the road moments after his plane touched down right behind Ben's, and he and half a dozen of his spooks had vanished into the countryside.

Just as Ben was planning to tear his umpteenth plan to shreds, Mike casually strolled into the CP, pulled a mug of coffee, and sat down.

"So nice to see you," Ben said drily.

"Thanks," Mike said with a small smile. "Good to be back."

Ike walked in, shook hands with Mike, and then took a chair.

Mike took a sip of coffee, set the mug down, and said, "Billy Smithson is dead. What was the free state of Missouri is now in the hands of rabble."

"Damn!" Ben said. "That explains why we haven't been able to contact him."

"Both President Blanton and his wife were wounded. They're going to be all right, but it will be some time. They're in Canada . . . or what used to be Canada. Parts of that country blew up, too."

"Does Homer need any help?" Ike asked.

Mike shook his head. "No. They're safe and well-protected. But the Joint Chiefs are dead. All of them. National Security Council—such as it was—dead. Most senators and representatives were caught in session in the capital. They're dead. We have no government. None.''

"What started it, Mike?" Ben asked.

"It was a well-planned coup, engineered by the old left wing of the President's party. Many of whom were voted out of office a decade back ... but still stayed active in the shadows. Their plan was to control, to one degree or the other, everything east of the Mississippi River, and Simon Border and his forces most certainly control quite a bit of territory west of the river."

Mike left it at that, drained his coffee cup, and stood up, pulling himself another mug. He sat back down and exhaled wearily.

"You look hungry, Mike."

"I could eat."

Ben sent out for sandwiches.

Mike wolfed down two sandwiches, sipped his coffee, and leaned back in his chair. "Well, Harriet Hooter and her bunch helped plan the coup, but it backfired on them. The rabble turned on them. They couldn't control the mobs when they went on a rampage, as mobs always do. Some of the left-wing were killed in the first few hours of rioting. We don't know if Harriet and her immediate cronies are among the dead or not. The capital was sacked, looted, and burned by those mindless goddamn mobs of heathens. And they were of all colors. No placing the blame on any one group. Now the movement, if that's what you want to call it, has splintered into several dozen smaller groups, each group controlling a certain section of territory. And each group vowing to fight right alongside the other if need be.''

Mike paused for another sip of coffee and Ben asked, ''I was always under the impression that Simon Border was a big fan of Harriet Hooter and those that follow her; couldn't she have taken refuge with him?''

Mike sat his mug down on the desk. ''It's a possibility, providing she and the others could get to him. But they were all in Charleston when the riots began, and Border is headquartered in Colorado. Harriet thought she was going to just walk right into the New White House and take over. She didn't take into account a mob's mentality. And there's something else—my people have uncovered a coup within a coup. Border was playing both ends against the middle. For a couple of years now, he's had people roaming all over the nation, quietly talking with citizens. And when we pulled out for Europe, Simon's people really went to work. When they were through, they had convinced most of the more or less reasonable-thinking men and women to come over to his side. They left Harriet and her group of fruitcakes the rabble, the punks, the gangs, and the hardcore criminal element.''

Ben held up a hand. ''Let me see if I can finish it for you. Drink your coffee and relax. Simon knows it's going to take us some time to deal with the groups on the east side of the river. While we're doing that, he's going to be hard at work building up his army and defenses, right?''

''You got it.''

''And Simon Border's people helped arm and supply the rabble, right?''

''Give the man a ci-gar.''

''That no-good, hypocritical son of a bitch!''

Mike smiled. "Right again, boss."

Ben drummed his fingers on the desktop. "Scouts reports that since the takeover, those on the east side of the Mississippi River, most of them, have turned once clean, quiet little towns into nothing more than filthy squatters' camps."

"Right again, for the most part. There are a few who have maintained the towns and villages, but damn few. Most don't know how to keep the sewerage and water plants working, and don't know jack-crap about power plants. It's pretty dismal. We're just about back to ground zero, Ben."

"We won't be for long," Ben said, a grimness behind his words and a hard glint in his eyes.

As he had done so many times in the past, Ben began walking the long lines of Rebels, his team a couple of steps behind him. Anna walked Ben's Husky, Smoot, on a leash. Stretching out for hundreds of yards were fifteen battalions of Rebels and Therm's short 19 Batt.

Therm's wife, Rosebud, had clouded up like a thunderstorm when Ben finally relented and gave Therm a front-line command. Ben had quickly backed down from that and Therm, with a sigh, finally accepted the fact that he was going to be CO of a short battalion that handled all the tedious paperwork and logistics and the thousand and one other details that keep the machinery of war running smoothly.

Ben knew he had grossly underestimated both Simon Border and Harriet Hooter and her pack of screwballs. He silently vowed never to do that again.

Ben, as always, wore no insignia. He didn't have to.

Everybody knew who Ben Raines was. And he and his team were the only Rebels that wore the old French-style lizard BDUs.

There was little banter between Ben and the men and women who made up the Rebel Army—not this time. This time the Rebels had their backs against a wall and they all knew it. There was no doubt in anyone's mind that the Rebels would be anything except victorious in the upcoming fight—no one had ever defeated the Rebels —but, to a person, they knew this fight was going to be the worst they had ever fought—in more ways than one.

This was going to be a full-blown civil war.

But it was still not clear in Ben's mind why Simon Border did what he did. There were other ways he could have carved out his own little empire. Ben would not have made any effort to stop him, and Blanton's armed forces had been so under-strength he would have been unable to prevent it.

As Ben walked the long lines of Rebels and equipment, acknowledging a salute here, a wave there, and a nod here, he concluded that Simon must want to be king of America.

A roar of incoming planes brought Ben's attention back to the present. The recon planes were returning from another photo op. The pictures would be ready for viewing in minutes.

Ben turned to Corrie, a step behind him. "Have the battalions move to their staging area. All batt coms at my HQ."

Ben would be taking his 1 Batt and two other battalions and moving directly west, to reclaim the territory originally known as Base Camp One, then he would cut north and start the move up to the Missouri border.

The other battalions, in groups of three, would head straight north, staying east of the Mississippi River, eventually clearing out the squatters all the way up to the old SUSA's northern boundaries, from the Mississippi River running west to east.

Everything that was necessary had been packed up and moved out, ready for the road. In a bare office, Ben faced his commanders. "We've bombarded the squatters with leaflets for three days now. They certainly know we're coming. Scouts report that they finally got it through the squatters' heads that we mean it, and have begun moving many of the non-combatant women and kids out." Ben sighed audibly. "But many have stayed behind . . ."

A loud groan went up from the batt coms.

"I know, I know," Ben said. "That means no shelling, no softening up with mortars and artillery. We do it eyeball to eyeball, down and dirty. I know you all well, and I know I speak for everyone here when I say that none of us wants to hurt a child." He shook his head. "But this is war and that is certainly going to happen. Probably before we get past our first skirmish. There is nothing I can say here that will prevent it, or ease the personal pain when it happens. Ah . . ." He sighed. "Words fail me here. What can I say to you? That we're fighting for our land? Yes, we are. But probably many of the people we'll be up against lived here before we came along. And don't think I haven't thought about that. With the exception of the gangs of punks and the criminal element we'll be facing, there are no clearly defined good guys and bad guys; no black hats or white hats. We're all wearing gray, so to speak. I've spoken to Rebels who have told me they have brothers and sisters and aunts and uncles and cousins out there facing us. This is not going to be a pleasant campaign—for any of us. At least not until we cross that Mississippi River and face Simon Border and his forces. Then we can start kicking ass the Rebel way. Any questions?''

There were none.

''All right, people. Let's do it.''

Since the Rebels were deep inside their own territory, they hit no trouble spots the first day out. It was noon of the second day before the Scouts, ranging miles ahead of the main column, radioed back to get ready for some trouble.

Corrie grimaced at the speaker and lifted the mic. ''What sort of trouble, Far Eyes?''

''The kind we don't handle very well,'' the scout said. ''Hang on. I'm trying to sort all this out.''

''What the hell is she talking about?'' Ben asked. In the Rebel Army, any woman who could make it through the rugged training of special operations groups such as the Scouts became a part of that unit. But there was no slack cut because of gender, and no bullshit was tolerated from the men once that female proved her mettle. The Rebels had proven years back that women were just as effective as men in combat.

Ben and team were riding in a large, completely modified van that seated six comfortably. The van had been bullet-proofed. A truck carrying their equipment and supplies traveled behind them, but each team member did carry an emergency kit containing a three-day supply of food.

''I can't think of anything we don't do well,'' Ben

bitched. He reached up and unhooked a mic. "Far Eyes, this is Eagle. What are you talking about?"

"Protestors, sir. People have formed a human chain across the highway. The road is completely blocked with men, women, and children."

"Shit!" Ben said. He keyed the mic. "All right, Far Eyes. Back off until we get there."

"Ten-four, sir. With pleasure."

Ben occupied the captain's chair beside Cooper, the driver. Jersey and Corrie had the two captain's chairs behind them, and Beth and Anna were in the rear. The big custom-built van was crowded with gear, but not uncomfortably so.

"How far away are we from the Scouts' location, Corrie?"

"About twenty miles, boss."

Ben nodded, a sudden smile creasing his lips. Cooper glanced at him. "You think of something funny, boss?"

"Maybe. Just maybe, I've come up with a way to temporarily deal with some of these . . . situations. Without a lot of bloodshed. That is, no bloodshed if these squatters have any sense at all. We'll see."

"Boss," Corrie said, "all Scouts in all sectors are reporting protestors forming human chains across roads and bridges."

"Tell all forward units to hold what they've got until I meet with the people up ahead. Tell them they will have instructions within the hour." He looked back at his team. "Cross your fingers and wish me luck, gang."

The blonde-haired, pale-eyed Anna said, "Why not just shoot them, General Ben?"

"Let's give them a chance first, Anna," Ben told his newly adopted daughter. The team had quickly discovered that Anna, despite being only fifteen or sixteen (she wasn't sure which), was a fierce fighter who gave absolutely no quarter to an enemy.

"Bah!" Anna replied. "If these people are not our friends, then they must surely be our enemies. I do not see any middle ground."

"Hush," Ben told her.

Anna was quite lovely, and very mature for her age. She also had a figure that had caused more than one Rebel to walk into trees and poles while watching her. But Anna had a streak of savagery in her that Ben had not been able to rid her of.

Anna had been orphaned when she was a very small child, and had been on her own until captured by the Rebels in Hungary; in her early years she had to fight dogs for scraps of food. Dan Gray had remarked to Ben that while Anna was lovely and charming and highly intelligent, she was, at times, only a cut above a feral child.

Ben had not taken offense at the statement, for he knew what Dan said was true.

Anna loved to get in close with an enemy and use a knife—and she was very, very good with a blade. Anna was also fiercely loyal to Ben and the Rebels.

"Scouts have pulled back about a mile from the protestors," Corrie said. "They're just up ahead."

When they reached the Scouts, Cooper parked in the middle of the road and Ben and team got out. "Are these people armed?" Ben asked.

"No, sir. Not a weapon anywhere. And it isn't an ambush. We checked the area. It's clean."

"Let's go see these people," Ben said, climbing back into the van. "Lead the way, boys and girls."

"What do you have in mind?" Jersey asked.

Ben smiled. "You'll see."

Chapter Three

"It's the devil himself!" a woman cried out as Ben stepped from the van and walked toward the group.

"Idiots!" Jersey muttered.

Anna said something under her breath, in her native tongue. No one in the team knew what it was she said, but all knew it was highly uncomplimentary, directed at the gathering of malcontents in the road.

Ben faced the group, all chained together like galley slaves. "Are you people crazy, or do you have a death wish?" he asked the front row of men and women, who had chained themselves together across the two-lane highway in Alabama.

"Kill us if you must," a man told Ben. "But you will never stop our movement."

"And what movement is that?"

"The movement to reclaim America for all."

"Take other people's property and squat there, you mean?"

"You took the property of others with your vile Tri-States philosophy, did you not?"

"As a matter of fact, we didn't. Those who chose not to live under our laws were compensated for their property, and paid well for it, I might add."

Ben felt just a bit foolish, standing in the middle of the road, talking with people who were chained together. When none of the squatters responded to his defense of the old Tri-States, he turned to several Rebels standing with heavy bolt cutters and motioned them forward.

"Oh, my God!" a woman shrieked. "They're going to kill us all." Kids started crying.

"Nobody is going to hurt you, lady," Ben assured the woman. "We're just clearing the road so we can move on."

"You go on and do that," a man shouted. "But we're staying right here. We have homes and we've broken the land, getting ready to plant."

"OK," Ben said. "Stay."

Both Rebel and civilian were astonished at that. They stood and stared at Ben. The Rebels working the bolt cutters paused, then continued cutting the light chain.

"Do you mean that, General?" a woman asked.

"Sure. Believe it or not, I will try to avoid bloodshed. I don't care if you stay and work the land and grow a garden. We encourage all our residents to grow gardens. You didn't try to ambush us. You all appear to practice personal hygiene. The children with you are cared for and well-fed. So stay if you like. But you will be living under Rebel law, and that might take some getting used to."

When none of the civilians said anything, Ben smiled at the group, now free of their chains. "You think it's some sort of trick, don't you? Well, it isn't. But if you had fired on us, the ending to this little drama would have been much different. All right, how many in this group? Who is the leader? You have to have one. Come on."

A man pushed through the crowd and stepped forward. "I . . . ah, I guess I am, General."

"Tell me, why did you choose this particular place to stop?"

"Because the village didn't appear to have been occupied in years. We're not thieves or outlaws, General. We wanted to make sure we weren't taking someone else's property."

"What is, or was, your profession?"

"I was a schoolteacher, as was my wife. That's her right over there." He pointed to a very attractive lady.

"Fine. That's good. We need teachers. Corrie, have one of our PT's come in here *ASAP.*"

"Right."

"What's a PT?" the man asked.

"Political team," Ben informed him. "They'll update you all on Rebel law and what we do in our public schools."

"I hope you teach," the man's wife said, walking over to stand beside her husband.

"Oh, we do that, ma'am. Rest assured of that. In the SUSA, the students don't run the schools, the teachers do—"

The husband and wife both smiled.

"—and on occasion, the teachers do plant the board of education firmly against the butts of deserving students."

The smiles broadened.

"Sports are secondary in the SUSA. We have sports, of course, but education comes first."

The husband and wife sighed in anticipated contentment.

"The PTs will brief you all. OK?"

"It sounds like heaven to me," the woman said.

"It isn't, ma'am. I assure you of that. All we've done is brought everything back to a common sense form of government. And it will take some getting used to, believe me. So . . . get squared away and start teaching your kids. It'll be planting time shortly. Do you have seeds and equipment?"

"We have seeds. No modern equipment."

"We'll see that you're properly equipped to farm."

A man stepped out of the crowd. "May I say something, General?"

"Sure. Free speech is freer here than in any other place on the face of the earth."

The man smiled. "You and your Rebels are not at all like what we were told you would be. We were told by members of Representative Hooter's organization, and also by members of Simon Border's group, that you were right-wing savages. That you all lived by the gun and that if we came in here and tried to stay, we would all be slaughtered. The women raped and the men tortured."

Several of the Scouts burst out laughing at that, and soon all the Rebels standing close enough to hear were chuckling.

"Well, I hope you've seen that isn't true," Ben countered. He caught the eye of a little girl clinging to her mother's hand and Ben smiled at her. She smiled shyly.

He dug in his pocket, found a package of gum and offered her a stick.

"She doesn't know what that is, General," the mother said. "It's been years since any of us have seen a real package of gum."

The sadness of that statement hit Ben hard. In the SUSA, life had pretty much returned to normal. But outside the SUSA, it was grim. Ben slowly nodded his head and gave the gum to the mother. "Corrie, we'll break for lunch. Let's help these people get settled in. Get the medics up here."

The teachers' names were Frank and Lois. Frank told Ben there were about a hundred adults and about half that many kids in the group.

"About a dozen or so members of your group don't much like me, do they?" Ben asked.

"They hate you," Lois said.

"I am getting weary of the dirty looks. Let's confront them and hear their beefs."

Facing a small knot of men and women, Ben asked, "What's the matter with you people? I'm trying to help you and you're acting as though I'm some sort of monster."

"We don't like the Tri-States philosophy," one of the men finally said, after looking at the others in his group. "We think it's barbaric. The very idea of shooting someone just because he's trying to steal your car, or your lawnmower . . . that's hideous! Why not try love and compassion and reason? Instead of guns, why not build gymnasiums, with proper basketball courts. Now, *that's* the way to control crime."

Ben knew that to attempt to argue with that type of logic would be hopeless. Living under the Tri-States form of government, this small group of people would be either dead or moved away within a few months . . . probably the former.

"It works for us," Ben told the group. "And if you stay here, that's the law you will live under. You might get away with ignoring it for a time, but within a few months, we'll have reclaimed our territory. Then you'll have no choice in the matter. I can tell you right now, the best thing for you people to do is leave. I won't force you out—I won't have to do that. You'll screw up. It's just a matter of time. But let me make something very clear to you all: when you fuck up big-time in this society, you're apt to get seriously hurt or seriously dead. I'd give that some thought. If you decide to pull out— and I hope you do—we'll take you to our borders and give you food packets that will last for a week or so. The rules and laws of the SUSA are few, but they are set in granite. Your civil rights end at somebody's else property line or business. I'll wager you were all left-wing liberal democrats back before the Great War. And I never met a left-wing liberal democrat that could understand common sense if it was stuck up their ass with a Roto-Rooter. If you value your lives, I would strongly suggest you leave. And do so now."

"You will provide us with food and transportation?"

How typical, Ben thought. "I will do so gladly," he replied.

"Then we'll leave."

"Good."

After the group had marched off, Lois said, "General, there must have been half a million people who streamed across the borders of the SUSA. How are you going to reclaim your territory against that many people?"

"With conversation and reason and compromise whenever possible, as I did with you people. With force, when that fails. But make no mistake about it: we will reclaim our territory."

Lois looked at the Rebels standing close by, men and women in the absolute peak of physical condition, eyes and skin glowing with health. She sighed. "Is your philosophy worth all the killing, General?"

"It is to us," Ben replied.

For the first few days and perhaps fifty miles in all directions of the Rebel push, the Rebels used conversation, compromise, and diplomacy with the people. Not many shots were fired, but those shots that were fired convinced many of the squatters that if they didn't want to conform to the Rebel philosophy, and desired to stay healthy, they had best head on back to whence they came—and do it post haste. Those that didn't, and offered resistance, were buried.

"We're still deep in the south part of our own territory," Ben told his batt coms by radio late one afternoon. "For the most part, we're meeting people who want to work with us and stay and make a future for themselves and families. The criminal element and the punk gangs and other assorted rabble are still north and west of us, and in a few areas along the east coast. My Scouts have not yet reported any signs of the slaughter of our people, but we all know we'll find them sooner or later. Not something I'm looking forward to seeing."

Ben signed off and leaned back in the kitchen chair one of his people had found for him.

Where in the hell were the gangs of punks and thugs? he wondered. Thousands and thousands of people had poured across the borders. That was solid fact—confirmed.

Where the hell did they go?

Hiding somewhere.

But where?

Waiting.

For what?

There were lots of places for them to hide. But what would they be waiting for?

That was something that was baffling even to Ben's Chief of Intelligence, Mike Richards.

"Survivors from the rabble attack coming in," Corrie broke into his thoughts. "Scouts intercepted about a dozen families. ETA thirty minutes. Most of them are disabled or retired Rebels, boss. And some of them are in pretty bad shape."

"Have them taken directly to the MASH tent," Ben said, after fighting back the white-hot anger that filled him. He picked up his Thompson and walked outside, Jersey and Anna right with him.

"Bastards want to make war against disabled vets and non-combatant women and small kids," Ben muttered through nearly clenched teeth. "I'll give them war like nothing they've ever dreamed in their wildest nightmares."

Ben paced up and down until the survivors arrived, working off much of his rage.

His rage returned when the survivors were trucked into the camp.

The first man out of the deuce-and-a-half was a man who had been with Ben since the dream of the old Tri-States was first discussed. He'd fought with the Rebels for years, until being severely wounded and forced into retirement a few years back. He'd been homesteading up near the Tennessee border when the rabble came pouring across. Ben's rage came rushing back.

"Gene!" Ben said, shaking the man's one good hand. The other hand had been blown off several years back. Ben looked at the man. "What can I say?"

"Good to see you, General. We never expected anything like this. They came pouring across the borders like ants toward honey. They killed my youngest boy. Shot him down as he ran to the house to warn us we were being attacked. I had to leave him in the backyard. There was no time to get the body." There were tears in the man's eyes. He wiped them away with the back of his hand. "I don't know what happened to my oldest daughter, Marie, and her husband. They were fighting a rear-guard action so Rose and me could get away with the grandkids. I think they bought it, General."

Ben nodded his head, not trusting his voice to speak.

"Goddamn lousy trash and street crap," Gene continued. Then he smiled very grimly. "I circled around and caught me one of them." He lifted his left arm, showing Ben the double prosthesis hook where his hand used to be. "I used this on the son of a bitch. Didn't take him long to spill his guts—literally."

"Are you coming with us, Grandpa?" a young girl with a bloody bandage around her head called.

"I'll be along, sweetie," Gene told the child, smiling at her. "You go with the soldiers." He turned back to Ben. "She thinks her mother will be returning. I don't.

Anyway, General, there were four gangs that hit my place, among many other homes. Those other survivors told me what happened to them and their loved ones. Raped, tortured, mutilated. No racial crap here, General. They were a mixed bag. The leaders are Ray Brown, Carrie Walker, Tommy Monroe, Dave Holton. They were heading for our old Base Camp One. Going to hold it for somebody. The guy I caught said he didn't know who. And if he did know, it died with him."

"All right, Gene. Thanks. You go on over to the MASH tent. Get checked out."

"There's more, General. I'd like to tell you all of it."

"Sure, Gene. Sure. You want some coffee?"

The old Rebel shook his head. "No, thank you, sir. I can wait. It's gonna be a real bitch, sir. A lot of the people who came across the border are pretty decent people. Many of them helped us along the way, until the Rebel patrols found us. The people shared what food they had with us, comforted the young. They were told, by someone—that's a little vague—that the Rebels wouldn't open fire on them. Well, at first our people didn't. But then they had to. Many of those in the front wanted to turn back, but the punks and thugs and criminals were all in the rear, and when some of the decent types wanted to retreat, their own people, supposedly their own people, fired on them, forcing them on. The Rebels didn't kill and wound as many as first thought. Many of the men and women were shot in the back by the punks and thugs. The people were lied to, General. Many were told that you and President Blanton had reached an agreement to open up the borders of the SUSA, and that they'd be welcomed. They really got suckered." Gene's eyes found Anna and smiled. "Who's this, General?"

"That's a little waif I picked up over in Europe, Anna. I couldn't get rid of her, so I said 'what the hell,' and adopted her."

"Got a mean look in those pretty eyes, General."

"She's been on her own since age five, fighting to survive."

"That'll put some meanness in a person, for sure. I'll get on over to the medics. Doctor Chase with you?"

"No. That old grouch is about thirty or so miles behind this column."

Gene looked around him. "New faces. A lot of the old bunch is gone, General."

"Yes." Ben's reply was softly offered. "Yes, they are. Buried all over the world."

"Is it ever going to stop, General?"

"Truthfully, I doubt it. At least not in our lifetime. Too many people hate us."

Gene nodded his head in understanding and agreement. "We've got room for millions and millions of people here in the SUSA. But instead we've got thousands and thousands. We know our system works. How come so many others can't see it?"

"Don't get me started on that, Gene."

Gene smiled. "Yeah, I seem to recall you could get real worked up on that subject. Well, there's about twenty-five or so trucks 'bout an hour behind this one, General. Filled with old soldiers like me and what's left of their families. We've all agreed to go back into uniform for this fight. We're about company-sized, I reckon. Soon as we get patched up and plugged up, we'll wander on over to the quartermaster and draw some gear. You might say the Over-The-Hill-Gang is ridin' again."

"Glad to have you with us, Sergeant. We'll damn sure find a place for you."

"I figured you wouldn't kick up much of a fuss. This is gonna be a fight to the finish. And it damn sure isn't gonna be over in any hurry." He threw Ben a salute and limped off.

"One of the toughest and meanest guerrilla units back in my country was made up of older men," Anna said, watching Gene limp away. "They couldn't run as fast as we could, or march for as long, but the punks and thugs and creepers soon learned they could fight like hell."

"What happened to them?" Jersey asked.

"Last I heard they were still up in the mountains, fighting." She looked at Ben. "Where are you going to assign those old men, General Ben?"

"Wherever they wish, Anna."

"Pilots report our old Base Camp One area is crawling with crud," Corrie called to Ben. "Heatseekers show several thousand people."

"Our underground facilities?"

"They appear to be safe and secure to this point."

Certain areas in and around the old Base Camp One were honey-combed with underground chambers, the tunnels and bunkers filled with thousands of tons of supplies and equipment. Other areas contained carefully constructed and concealed underground storage tanks, where hundreds of thousands of gallons of fuel were stored (the Rebels had thousands of tons of equipment secretly cached all over the lower forty-eight).

"They have SAMs, they have SAMs," Corrie said, as

soon as the pilots' words crackled through her head-phones.

"Any planes hit?" Ben asked.

"Negative. No hits."

The souped-up version of the old P-51, now called the P-51E, which made up a large part of Ben's air force, usually came in right on the deck, rendering SAMs all but useless against them. The pilots came in so low, by the time the SAM was readied and fired, the planes were gone and out of range, flying at about 550 mph, tops. The pilots seemed to thrive on the danger of it, which did not come as any surprise to Ben. He thought all combat pilots to be half nuts anyway.

It would have amazed Ben to learn that most combat pilots thought themselves to be a hell of a lot safer where they were than where Ben was, and they thought Ben was half bonkers for taking the chances he took on the ground.

"Corrie, have we received any further word on President Blanton's condition?"

"Negative, boss."

"His staff?"

"Only that first confirmation that most of them were killed during the first hours of looting. It was rumored that a few got away. But that's still just a rumor."

Ben knew that Mike Richards had gotten a few people into the Charleston area. They had reported back that the city was a shambles. The looters and other equally vile and worthless street slime had gone crazy when all order had broken down.

"We'll call that a dead city," Ben had said, after hearing the dismal news about the sacking of the nation's capital. "When we rebuild the capital, it won't be there.

If I have anything to say about the rebuilding, and I strongly suspect I will, we'll build the new capital in the center of the nation—where it ought to be. And it won't be the crime or welfare capital of the damn world either. Not like it was before the Great War."

"Why weren't the looters shot on sight?" Anna had asked.

"If I had been in command, they would have been shot—on sight," Ben had responded.

But for now, Ben looked toward the west. He couldn't go slam-banging straight through to the old Base Camp One. Everything between here and there had to be cleaned out first. He wanted no major resistance forces at his back.

Ben turned to Corrie. "Get Jackie and Danjou up here ASAP. We've got some planning to do."

Chapter Four

"You stay north of us on 80 and drive straight across the state," Ben said to the commander of 12 Batt, Jackie Malone.

She nodded her head.

"Danjou, we'll give you time to get in place down south. You get on highway 98 and drive straight across. My 1 Batt will hook up with you here." He jabbed a finger at the map. "And we'll push across together."

The French-Canadian nodded his head.

"We'll be meeting the hardcore of resistance, so get me some prisoners. I want to find out everything I can about who is behind all this mess."

"General," Jackie said, "you know what Ike and Georgi and Buddy and Tina and Dan are going to do when they hear of this," she reminded him.

Ben smiled. "Let them scream all they like. Won't be a thing they can do about it. Except complain."

Buddy and Tina were Ben's kids. Buddy commanded

8 Batt, the special operations group, and Tina commanded 9 Batt. Ike had been with Ben since the beginning. Ben and the ex-Navy SEAL were just about the same age—Ike was second in command of the Rebel Army, commanding 2 Batt. Dan Gray was British, a former officer in the Special Air Service. Dan commanded 3 Batt. Georgi Striganov, CO of 5 Batt, a Russian, and Ben were once bitter enemies, until Ben and the Rebels kicked his butt and Georgi decided the best thing to do, if he wanted to stay alive, was to join with the Rebels. West, a former mercenary, was engaged to Tina; they would marry someday. West commanded 4 Batt. Pat O'Shea, a wild Irishman, commanded 10 Batt. Rebet was CO of 6 Batt. Raul Gomez headed 13 Batt. Buck Taylor was commanding officer of 15 Batt. Greenwalt was the CO of 11 Batt, and Jim Peters the commander of 14 Batt.

Batts 16, 17, and 21, commanded by Post, Harrison, and Stafford, had been left behind in Europe. But Ben was seriously thinking of pulling them back Stateside. He was waiting for a report from Mike Richards before he made that decision.

Rebel battalions were much larger than conventional military battalions, and they were self-sustaining, carrying with them artillery, armor, and fully equipped MASH units. When a Rebel battalion pulled out on the highway, their vehicles stretched for miles. It was an awesome sight to witness, from the HumVees to the massive sixty-ton main battle tanks.

Ben looked at Danjou and Jackie. "I don't want the other battalions to know what we're doing until we're in place. I don't want to have to listen to a lot of bitching about it. OK, let's roll. Danjou, give us a bump when you're in place. Let's do it, people.''

Scouts reported trouble as soon as they crossed the state line. The sniper fire was heavy and it forced the column to a halt.

"MBTs buttoned up and roll," Ben ordered. "Take them out."

The sixty-three-ton M1/M1A1 MBTs surged forward. With a top speed of 45 mph, it did not take them long to get into position. The Rebel armorers had reworked the guns on the tanks and the MBTs bristled with fire-power. The MBTs could run on diesel, gasoline, or aviation fuel. The armor was state-of-the-art, far superior to the ceramic and reaction-type armor used on the older models.

"Those houses to your left," a Scout told a tank commander. "Ten o'clock."

The MBTs swiveled their turrets, lowered their cannons, and the 120mm main guns began to roar, hurling out HE rounds. The houses began exploding as if made of matches.

"All Scouts on our three fronts reporting heavy sniper fire," Corrie told Ben. "Tanks are rolling."

"Any anti-tank missiles fired?"

"Negative."

Ben smiled, but it was devoid of humor. "Simon Border's people have all of them. He never had any real plans to defend the territory east of the Mississippi. He's sacrificing these people, giving his own followers time to beef up and dig in. Simon and Hooter fed these rabble a line of bullshit and they swallowed it. Everything

I initially prophesied is coming to be. Years ago I predicted that the country would first break up into small nations within a nation. That happened. After those small nations fell, the country would split up into several large nations. That is happening now."

"That's why so many people are frightened of you, boss," Beth said. "You've been dead accurate on the future of not just North America, but the world. The rumor now is you have a third eye."

Ben smiled. "All-seeing and all-knowing, huh? Me and Johnny Carson."

Cooper looked over at him. "Who is Johnny Carson?"

Simon Border looked at the road-weary and much bedraggled group before him. Harriet Hooter, Rita Rivers, and several others of Hooter's New Left party had made it across the river to safety. The rest were either dead or missing and presumed dead.

"I never thought the masses would turn on us," Harriet said, her voice numb with lingering disbelief and shock and weariness. "We were trying to help them. Our plan was to take from the have's and give to the have not's. I just never dreamed anything like this would happen."

"Of course, you didn't, my dear," Simon said. Like all practicing hypocrites, the lies flowed out of his mouth as easily as the truth. "But we have a place for you all here. The armies of the Democratic Front control nearly all of the western half of North America. Eventually, we plan to move against Ben Raines and once more reunite this nation, and bring it back to its former greatness. With your help, of course," he added with a smile.

"You can count on us," Rita River said. "My new main squeeze, Issac Africa, has written a rap song about the great Satan, Ben Raines. Would you like to hear it?"

"Ah . . . no, not at this time," Simon said quickly. He hated rap music and everything connected with it—including blacks—but he kept that concealed. "Some other time, perhaps. Issac Africa? Ah, yes. Isn't he the militant who now thinks he controls what was once the state of Missouri?"

"He doesn't think he controls it," Rita said proudly. "He *does* control it. Issac and his ANA—that's the Army of the New Africa—will show Ben Raines who is really the meanest cat on the block."

"Army of the New Africa," Simon muttered. "And this, ah, Issac person is the commanding general of the ANA?"

"Not really, but sort of. He's actually the Premier of New Africa. Mobutomamba is the head of the army."

"Mobutomamba? He's from Africa?" Simon questioned.

"Naw," Rita said. "He's from South Carolina. But he's descended from kings. His grandmother told him that."

"How interesting. Well, I wish them the best of luck in fighting Ben Raines." They are certainly going to need all the luck they can get, Simon silently added.

Although Simon Border despised Ben Raines and everything he stood for, he would never make the mistake of underestimating the man, or his Rebels.

Simon Border's face looked remarkably like a cottonmouth snake, and he was just about as dangerous. Simon played all angles: to some he was the great emancipator, to others he sat on the right side of God. Others saw him as the salvation of America. Before the Great War, Simon had been an advocate of wealth redistribution, womb-to-tomb health insurance for everybody (no matter that it would bankrupt the country), midnight basketball, a Bible in every home, death to any who practiced abortion. That was one side of the man. The other side was much darker. Of course, Simon was a racist, a hypocrite, a womanizer, a fraud, a snake-oil salesman disguised as a preacher, and a charlatan. He could be all things to all people at a second's notice.

But Simon really did think of himself as the savior of freedom—freedom as he narrowly defined the word, that is.

Simon shook his head. Mobutomamba? It was so sad. Another self-proclaimed descendant of kings who was going to get rudely dethroned when he butted heads with Ben Raines.

Simon cleared his head of those thoughts. He couldn't worry himself with the woes of others. Besides, this Mobutomamba sounded like some sort of nut . . .

He was sure right about that.

However, there was more than one type of nut. And whenever law and order breaks down, the nuts surface.

Just south of where Issac Africa and his band of fruitcakes were holding sway, there was another band of banana-cream pies who had risen up, proclaiming all of Arkansas as theirs . . .

Ben looked up from his map and blinked. "Who did you say was claiming all of Arkansas?"

"The Reverend Jethro Jim Bob Musseldine," Corrie said, struggling to keep from laughing.

"You have to be kidding!"

"No, sir," Corrie said, regaining her composure. "And he's reported to have a following of about ten thousand."

"Ten thousand!" Ben blurted.

"Yes, sir. And from the reports the Scouts are sending back, they are well-armed and spoiling for a fight."

Ben sighed. "What's his beef?"

Rebel artillery and Rebel snipers, using .50 caliber sniper rifles which had an accurate killing range of over a mile, had knocked all the fight out of the forward units of the rabble army and had advanced about ten miles inside what was once known as the state of Mississippi before picking a spot to bivouac for the night.

Corrie smiled. "He and his followers don't like your philosophy on hunting . . . among other things."

Ben had to think about that for a moment. He knew that over the years he had angered some people with his so-called stance on hunting. But Ben wasn't anti-hunting at all—he was anti-poaching. Ben did believe that there should be areas set aside for animals to live as God intended them to live, without fear of humankind, letting Mother Nature control the animal population through natural predators. But in the SUSA there were many, many areas wide open for hunting, millions of acres.

Ben decided it had to be the "other things." "What other things, Corrie?"

Corrie's smile widened. "Oh, he's anti-abortion, wants prayer in public schools . . . you want me to go on?"

Ben exhaled and shook his head. "The entire country has fallen apart. There isn't a stable government in all the fifty states, much less on the federal level, chaos and violence is the order of the day, and this idiot wants to start a war with me because I believe that abortion should be a personal choice and left up to the woman."

"He is also opposed to any type of legalized gambling and you're on record as saying that also is a personal choice."

"Wonderful," Ben said.

"The squirrels are coming out of the trees again, boss," Cooper said.

"They damn sure are, Coop."

The team wandered off for chow and Anna came to sit beside Ben. The girl had tailored her BDUs to fit snugly and had her blonde hair cut short. The spring night was pleasant and the bugs were few enough to be tolerated without insect repellant, but in a few weeks the mosquitos would be fierce. Anna propped her short-barreled 5.56 CAR against a porch railing and sat down.

"What are you thinking about, General Ben?" she asked as she petted Smoot.

"What a mess this country is in, Anna. And if it can ever be fixed."

"Like Humpty Dumpty?"

"Yes. Just like Humpty Dumpty."

"We had people like those we're now chasing in the old country, too, General Ben. They weren't much good for anything. Whiners and slackers and complainers and people who want something for nothing. I never had any use for them."

Ben wasn't at all sure he wanted to know what Anna did with those types of people. The girl had a savage streak in her, coupled with a solid streak of pragmatism. She was also very intelligent and surprisingly well-read, considering that she'd been on her own since about age five.

Anna cut her eyes to Ben and smiled, as if reading his mind, which, Ben thought with a small smile, she might well be able to do, since she sprang from the loins of gypsies. "No, General Ben, I didn't shoot them willy-nilly. But they did learn very quickly to stay far away from me and the people I ran with. We planted little hidden gardens to grow vegetables. Why couldn't they do the same? But no, they wanted us to do all the work and then they would try to steal from us or want us to give them the food we worked for. We shot them when we caught them stealing from us. But General Ben, food is life. Didn't we have the right to do that? I think so."

Ben wondered if Anna was trying to tell him something or just making conversation. If it was the former, he wasn't going to take the bait.

"I have read in books and magazines about this insurance people could buy for their homes and vehicles. The person pays so much money a month or a year so that if his possessions are stolen, the insurance people pay him to replace the goods. And then the amount of money he pays each month or year for the insurance goes up according to the value of goods stolen . . . which doesn't seem quite fair to me. But if the thief was caught, not much was ever done to him because the prisons were full, and if the authorities wanted to put one prisoner in jail, one had to be released. Wouldn't the authorities have been helped if law-abiding people were able to protect what was theirs without fear of being arrested or sued by lawyers?"

Ben had to agree. "Yes, we who adopt the Tri-States philosophy think so."

"So do I. But back when the world was whole, it didn't work that way very often, did it?"

Ben shook his head. "No. Not very often."

"Well, we shared what we grew with the old people, and why not? They were the ones who had worked all their lives, supporting the nation with their blood and muscle and sweat. The old have a right to live out their years in dignity and comfort. But the gangs of thugs and punks preyed on the old. We shot those types of people whenever we could find them. I used to dress up like an old woman, carrying a sack of potatoes or fruit or bread, and go limping and tottering down a street where my people waited in ambush. Pretty damn quick the punks and thugs learned to never come into the area we controlled. However, we did let them enter to remove the bodies." She stood up, grasping her CAR with one hand and Smoot's leash with the other. "Come on, Smoot. Let's take a walk. See you. General Ben."

Ben watched her go, then became conscious of eyes on him and turned his head. Doctor Lamar Chase, the Rebels' Chief of Medicine, was standing close by. "How long have you been standing there, Lamar?"

"Ever since Anna sat down. I damn sure wouldn't want that child for an enemy, Ben." He sat down in the camp chair Anna had just vacated.

"She's tough."

"*Tough!* She's ruthless."

Ben smiled.

"Ben? What are you going to do with these thousands and thousands of people who have invaded the SUSA? When we catch up with them, that is."

Lamar had just caught up the main column. He'd been late joining because of a morass of paperwork.

"I'm going to use reason with those who will listen."

"And those who won't?"

"You know the answer to that, Lamar."

The doctor watched Ben roll a cigarette and grimaced in disgust, but for once he didn't say anything about Ben's smoking habits. "Have you given any thought to reuniting the entire nation, Ben?"

"Yes, I have. Quite a lot of thought. But unless you want a return to the old form of government, which sure as hell didn't work, I don't see how we can do it."

"But what we set up didn't work either, Ben. Not for the whole."

"You know damn well it wasn't meant to, Lamar. You just want to argue."

Lamar was getting too old for the field, but he wouldn't admit it and would not voluntarily give it up, although nowadays he did little operating and had a staff and a driver to look after him. But he still ran the department with a iron fist. "I'm sure you've heard the theory that the men who drafted and signed the Declaration of Independence were divinely inspired?"

"Of course."

"Do you believe it?"

Ben shook his head. "I don't know, Lamar. Could be. Maybe so. Why?"

"Oh . . . I was just wondering how they might have handled this mess."

"They wouldn't have let the nation get into the mess in the first place," Ben said sourly, ignoring Lamar's smile, but knowing the doctor had aced him into this debate. "We wouldn't be in this mess if those assholes in government back during the last decade, and four decades before then, had adhered to the Constitution and applied a little common sense in the first damn place."

As it always happened when Ben started getting wound up, Rebels began gathering around. Chase had forgotten about that. He looked all around him and grumbled, "I am not going to sit through another of your harangues, Raines. I would rather watch paint dry." Then he noticed he was completely blocked in. "Shit!" the doctor said, and leaned back in the chair.

"OK, Lamar," Ben said, waving a hand at the Rebels gathered around. "You explain to them why America fell apart, why it went bankrupt, why federal law enforcement agencies became stooges for the government, in many cases no better than the old Nazi Gestapo. Tell us why the government allowed the IRS to become the most powerful agency in Washington, answerable to no one? You want me to reunite the entire nation? OK. Tell them how we can do that and still preserve our way of life. Come on, wise-ass, enlighten us." Ben folded his arms across his chest and smiled at Lamar.

"I swear you set this up, Raines."

"Me? You opened this conversation, not me."

Lamar looked all around him. "Go on back to your duties!" he shouted. "Go on, now, or I'll have you all lined up for a short-arm inspection."

Since about a fourth of the Rebels were women, they got a good laugh out of that. "You think that would really bother us?" one yelled.

"Oh, good Christ!" Lamar muttered.

Then the humor got a little raw as some of the women

began suggesting where to line the men up for the inspection.

"Make way, dammit!" Corrie shouted, shoving and pushing her way through the throngs of Rebels. "Ike on the horn, boss. And he is very unhappy."

Ben stood up. "I really hate to leave you like this, Lamar. I'd like to stay and hear your lecture. But . . ." He shrugged. "Duty calls."

"Now wait a minute, Raines! You can't leave me trapped in here!"

"Close ranks behind me!" Ben shouted.

As the Rebels closed ranks, trapping Lamar, the doctor yelled, "Raines, you insufferable jackass!"

Ben walked away, chuckling.

Chapter Five

"Goddammit, Ben!" Ike yelled over the miles. "What in the hell do you think you're doing, splitting your command? I thought we agreed that—"

Ben tuned him out until Ike paused for breath.

"Calm down, Ike. I'm not exactly alone, you know. I've got a battalion of troops, plus armor and artillery, plus Lt. Bonelli's people. Now stop yelling. Have you been meeting any resistance?"

"Very little, Ben. But we have found numerous places where our permanent residents were executed. Whole families wiped out."

"We've found the same thing. What do you hear from the others?"

"Same thing. The troops are pretty damned steamed about it and spoiling for a fight. But so far all we've run into is some scattered sniper fire."

"Cat and mouse, Ike."

"Yeah, that's the way I figure they're playing it. But what's their game?"

"I don't know." Ben paused, thinking fast. "Ike, stand by for a burst transmission."

"Ten-four, Ben."

"Corrie, order Scouts to start back-tracking us. I think the bastards are trying to put us in a bottle."

"Coming up from behind us, boss?"

"Coming from all directions may be more like it."

Ben taped a short message and it was compressed and sent out in burst to all batt coms.

All over the SUSA, Rebel units began shifting troops.

Lamar stepped into Ben's CP. "I've got to get back to my hospital convoy, Ben. I—"

"No time, Lamar," Ben interrupted. "I'm getting that old cold and familiar feeling. I think we're about to get hit. And hit hard. Get to cover and stay put."

Lamar visibly paled. "Ben, my people only have a couple of platoons traveling with them. And—" He bit that off.

"And what, Lamar?"

"Cecil is with the convoy."

"What!"

"He flew in a couple of days ago. Said he was tired of waiting around back at the assembly area. Said he wanted to be near the action."

"Jesus, Lamar—"

"Dammit, Ben," the doctor flared back. "The man is the elected President of the SUSA. He's my boss. Technically, he's your boss. I couldn't tell him no."

Ben turned to Corrie. She was already on the horn to the hospital convoy. "The convoy is under attack, boss! Rabble and punks coming at them from all directions."

"I should have stayed with them," Lamar muttered.

"Why?" Ben asked. "So you could get killed with them? Don't be an idiot." He looked around him. "Anna?"

"Right here, General Ben."

"Take Doctor Chase and Smoot and get to cover. Stay with them."

"Yes, sir."

"Batten down the hatches, people," Ben ordered. "It's about to get lively around here."

But before Anna, Chase and Smoot could get to cover, gunfire tore into the old house, knocking out what remained of the windowpanes and gouging great holes in the walls. Ben and the others hit the floor.

Cooper dragged his SAW over to the window and Ben shoved a can of 5.56 ammo his way; the can contained 200 rounds.

"Light up the sky," Ben shouted over the rattle of gunfire. "Let's see what we're up against."

Somewhere along the outer perimeters of the Rebel camp, a Big Thumper opened up, spitting out 40mm grenades. A .50-caliber machine gun was added to the roar and crash.

"All battalions under attack." Corrie's voice came over the rattle of combat.

"Figured this one out a little too late," Ben muttered, crawling to a window just as the night was lit with IF mortar rounds.

"Shoot anything not in BDU's," Ben shouted. He spotted half a dozen men running his way, clad in various articles of dress and carrying a variety of weapons. On his knees, he held the trigger back on his old .45 caliber Chicago Piano and blew a full magazine in their direction, fighting to hold the powerful old SMG level.

The line of men went down like bowling pins as the fat slugs tore into flesh and shattered bone. "Keep those flares going!" Ben shouted, ejecting the empty mag and slipping home a fresh one. "Keep the night bright."

Anna had stowed Lamar and Smoot in the windowless center bathroom of the home and now joined the fight.

"Goddammit, Raines!" Lamar shouted over the sounds of battle. "I'm a doctor, not a dog-sitter!"

"Where'd you put them?" Ben yelled.

"In the bathtub," the teenager returned the yell, grinning at her adopted father.

Two men suddenly appeared in the darkened hall of the home and Beth shifted the muzzle of her M-16 and blew them backwards. They landed in a lifeless sprawl of motionless arms and legs.

A man dove through a broken window, landing right on top of Jersey and knocking the weapon from her hands. Cussing a blue streak, the diminutive Jersey brought both hands hard over the man's ears. He screamed at the sudden pain in his head. Jersey jammed fingers into his eyes and then into his throat. She used her knife to finish it, driving the blade deep into the man's belly and twisting it up. Blood sprayed from his mouth.

"Yuck!" Jersey said, wiping off her blade and crawling over to her weapon.

Anna turned and gave several men a full magazine from her CAR just as Ben was tossing grenades into the night, the flash and boom of the Fire-Frags followed by shrieks of pain as shrapnel ripped into flesh.

Cooper was laying down a steady stream of fire with his SAW, stacking the bodies up outside the home.

"The rabble is falling back on all sides," Corrie said. "We've beaten off the first wave."

"Get the hospital convoy on the blower," Ben told her.

"Trying, boss. But they're not responding."

"Keep trying."

Lamar appeared in the darkened archway, holding Smoot's leash. Anna walked over and took the leash.

The room became quiet, everyone waiting for a response from the radio van with the hospital convoy.

Nothing.

Only static.

"Eagle to Mercy One, Eagle to Mercy One." Corrie repeated the call. "Come in, Mercy One."

Corrie cut her eyes to Ben. She shook her head.

Lamar opened his mouth and Ben held up a big hand. "There is nothing we can do until dawn, Lamar. We'd be easy targets on the road tonight. If they've been wiped, they've been wiped. But I'm sure some got away. They're just out of contact, that's all."

"Cecil—"

"I try not to think about that. But don't sell Cec short. He's a tough old bird. You're forgetting he's Special Forces trained. I pity the rabble who corners him this night."

"Where is that goddamn nigger president?" The hard voice sprang out of the darkness. "We killed everybody but him."

Cecil was belly-down in a weed and brush-filled ditch that ran alongside an old soybean field, about a hundred feet away from what was left of the burning, smoking rubble of the hospital convoy. He had a full canteen, his sidearm and M-16, and his knife for close work. Cecil had been out of the field for a long time, but brutal training dies hard. He was unhurt except for a cut on his upper left arm. Cecil waited and listened.

"Maybe we got bad information." The voices began drifting to him. "Maybe he wasn't with this convoy."

"Could be. Search the bodies again just to be sure."

Cecil watched as beams from flashlights began darting about like mad fireflies. *If I just had one full squad with me,* Cecil thought ruefully, *I could wipe out the whole damn worthless bunch of these bastards.*

Might as well wish for the moon, he thought, ceasing his wishful thinking.

Although he was well-hidden in a drainage ditch, with tall weeds all around, Cecil ducked as a harsh beam of light was cast out into the field to his right.

"That white-haired son-of-a-bitch ain't here. I'd know him anywheres."

Oh, really? Cecil thought. *Now how might that be?*

"I swore on my mother's eyes, I'd find that nigger bastard and kill him," the same man said. "The day he run me out of Louisiana. Him and that goddamned uppity Ben Raines. I swore I'd see them both dead someday."

Interesting, Cecil thought. *I wonder why we ran him out?*

"Just 'cause I wouldn't stop whuppin' my young'uns, they come 'round givin' me orders that I had to go. They took my young'uns. Ain't seen 'um since. Prob'ly wouldn't even know me now if'n I did run into 'um."

"Hell, Jeeter. They prob'ly Rebels by now. Fightin' agin us, you know?"

Ah, yes, Cecil thought. Jeeter. From down in that part

of the parish that Ben used to call the land that time forgot. White trash of the worst sort. *Tell it all, you miserable piece of shit. Tell your friend how you sexually abused your daughters, starting when they were about ten years old, you miserable bastard.*

"Man's got a rat to whup his kids," another voice added.

"Shore do," Jeeter said. "Well, hell, come on. Let's go. That nigger wasn't with this bunch. We'll rat-eo ahead and find out how Denver done with Raines' bunch."

"Shit!" a man said, his voice filled with contempt. "They done prob'ly kilt 'em all. These Rebels ain't shown me nothin' when it comes to fightin.' They ain't nothin' but a bunch of candy-asses, you ax me."

Cecil fought back an almost overwhelming urge to rise up and empty a full mag at the voices. He calmed down and willed himself to lay still in the ditch and watch as the men faded into the night.

Cecil waited for fifteen minutes, then slowly made his way toward the wrecked, looted and still smoking ruins of the convoy. He found a walkie-talkie and checked it—it still worked. The Rebels' repeater system was still functioning, so he could talk to damn near anywhere in the SUSA. Trying his best to ignore the bloody and mangled and sometimes charred bodies, he filled a pack with food and ammo and slipped away into the darkness. In the timber, he switched over to the emergency frequency and keyed the talk button.

"Eagle, Eagle. Come in, Eagle."

Miles away, Corrie was on it immediately. "This is the Eagle's Nest," she radioed, frantically motioning for Cooper to find Ben. "Come in."

"Eagle's Nest, this is—" Cecil grinned "—Ol' Black Joe. You copy this, Eagle's Nest?"

"Ol' Black Joe?" Ben said, running into the room. He laughed. "Well, he hasn't lost his sense of humor. Give me that mic, please, Corrie. Joe, this is Eagle. Report."

"Entire convoy wiped out. They took no prisoners. Supplies looted and vehicles, most of them, burned. The truck took some sort of hit in the rear, rocket I think, and tipped over—threw me out and into a ditch. I got overlooked by the rabble. It's our old friend Jeeter from the land that time forgot who seems to be heading up this pack of crap."

"I remember him. Are you hurt?"

"Negative. Just my pride. I'm going to rest for a time and eat a bite and then catch some Z's. Don't try to extricate me this night. Too dangerous. I'll see you in the morning."

Ben knew better than to ask for a position. "All right, Joe. That's ten-four. Hang tough."

"You got it. Joe out."

"That's a relief," Jersey said.

"Yes," Chase agreed. "But five percent of our field doctors and medical staff are dead, and a lot of valuable supplies with them. All the whole-blood we collected for this push, refrigeration units and all the OR tents and instruments." He met Ben's eyes and shook his head. "I have a real lousy feeling about all this, Ben. I have this feeling that conditions are going to get a lot worse before they begin to turn our way."

"I have a feeling that you just may be right, Lamar."

* * *

All battalions took hits the night the rabble and punks attacked. After the fire-fight, there were Rebel dead to be buried, and Rebel wounded to be patched up.

Batt 1 suffered five dead and twenty wounded, two of the wounded not expected to live.

At first light, 'Ol' Black Joe' made contact with Ben and Ben turned his 1 Batt around and headed back to the ambush site, Scouts ranging out in front of the long column.

They hit no resistance along the way. The rabble had no stomach for a daylight fight, and that disappointed the men and women of 1 Batt, for after the sneak attack of the past night, they were more than ready for a fight.

As the first Scouts approached, Cecil rose up out of the field and walked to the shoulder of the road. The Scouts did a visual on the man walking out of the field, determined it was the President of the SUSA, and immediately fell into defensive positions around him.

"Relax, boys and girls," Cecil's calm voice touched them. "No bogies around here. They're long gone. I've been scanning the area since before dawn."

The Scouts treated Cecil with the same respect they showed Ben Raines. Everyone knew the two men were as close as brothers and had been for years. Everyone knew that Cecil had been with Ben since the beginning of the old Tri-States dream, right after the Great War. A medic with the Scouts sat Cecil down and began checking him out.

"Orders, Mr. President. Doctor Chase told me to do this."

"I understand, son," Cecil said. "You have any pills in that kit for old age?"

"Wish I did, sir."

By the time the cut that Cecil had suffered was cleaned out and bandaged, the main column had arrived, the massive MBTs leading the way. Ben and Cecil shook hands, then stood and smiled at one another for a moment.

"It was close, Ben. Close." Cecil's eyes found Sergeant Major Gene Cousins, now fully decked out in Rebel BDUs. He waved him over. "What is this, Gene? Are you back in action?"

"Yes, sir."

"You feel up to snuff?"

"All the way, sir."

"How many old soldiers that can still cut the mustard you figure you could round up?"

Ben narrowed his eyes.

"Hell, sir . . . maybe five or six hundred if I could put the call out," Gene answered.

"Put it out. Right now. And as of now, you are my battalion sergeant major."

Gene grinned. "Yes, *sir!*"

Ben shook his head and stepped into it. "Cec, what the hell do you think you're doing?"

Cecil cut his eyes. "Getting back into it, Ben. It's personal now."

Chase had walked up. "Are you out of your mind, you old goat? You're in no shape for the field."

"The hell I'm not. As long as I take my pills, I'm in as good a shape as Ben . . . almost," he added with a grin. "And who are you to be calling me an old goat, you old goat!"

"Your designation would be 22 Batt, sir," Beth said, stepping between the President of the SUSA and the Rebel Chief of Medicine, jotting that down in a small notebook.

"Thank you, Beth. 22 Batt it is."

Chase threw up his hands in disgust, snorted, and walked away, back to the ruined convoy, to see if he could salvage anything.

"You're sure about this, Cec?" Ben asked.

"Positive."

Ben nodded. "All right. Corrie? Pull some armor and artillery up here. Assign a MASH unit and get some Scouts in here. He'll need a political team and an inter-rogation team. Notify Mike Richards so he can assign a couple of his spooks to 22 Batt."

"Yes, sir."

Ben turned back to Cecil. "I have a great XO in mind for you. And he's past due for a promotion. I can jump him a couple of grades."

"Oh?"

"Yes, Lt. Bonelli."

Cecil chuckled. "And that would get him out of your hair, right, Ben?"

"Why . . . Cecil! That never crossed my mind."

"What a terrible liar you are, Ben. You get worse as you get older. All right. I'll take him. Mix his people in with mine." He looked at Corrie. "Corrie, find me some good communications personnel."

"Right, sir. I know just the people."

Ben said, "Now, Cec, you take it easy until you get accustomed to the field. You've been out of it for a long time."

"I know. Hell, most of my people will be around my

age . . . or older. Just be sure we are well supplied with Geritol.''

"I think you look very distinguished, sir,'' Anna said.

Cecil grinned.

"Yes, your white hair really sets off that black beret,'' she added.

Cecil's grin faded.

"Gotcha!'' Ben said, and laughed at the crestfallen expression on his friend's face.

Chapter Six

Ben halted all forward movement of the battalions until Cecil's 22 Batt was set up and fully equipped and staffed. To say the least, 22 Batt was unusual. The youngest Rebel was nineteen, the oldest was seventy.

"Incredible," Doctor Chase said, after reading the last of the fitness reports on the personnel of 22 Batt and closing the folder. "I can truthfully say I have never seen anything with which to compare it. I should assign two MASH units to this battalion. We have an amputee who is battalion sergeant major. We have a one-eyed old fart who is at least seventy years old. One of the officers is the *grandfather* of one of my doctors. Half of 22 Batt is on some sort of medication for various ailments, and some of them have recurring bouts of gout, for Christ's sake. And these people are going into combat?"

"Pulling out in the morning," Ben told him. "They'll be about forty miles north of Jackie's 12 Batt, coming in just above the northernmost boundaries of the old Base Camp One. And don't sell them short, Lamar.''

"Oh, I know they can fight. Hell, I know all of them. For years. I've treated most of them at one time or the other. It's just a hell of a way to run a war, Raines.''

"It's personal now, Lamar. These men are out looking for blood. Some of them lost their entire families.'' He smiled. "Besides, it's as you said—Cecil is the elected President of the SUSA. I can't tell him what to do.''

"Right, Raines,'' Chase said sarcastically, cutting his eyes heavenward. "Sure.''

"Your people all set, Lamar?''

The doctor nodded his head. He started to speak when a runner walked into the room.

"General?''

"What is it?''

"Simon Border is on the horn. He wants to talk to you.''

Ben rose from the chair. "Well, now. How interesting. Want to come along, Lamar?''

"I'm not in the least interested in anything that nut has to say. But you watch yourself, Ben. He's slick. He's conned millions of people over the years.''

"Only those who wanted to be conned, Lamar,'' Ben countered.

Ben stepped inside the communications' truck and took the mic. "This is Ben Raines.''

"General Raines.'' The snake-oil smooth voice of Simon Border came over hundreds of miles. "We finally get a chance to chat.''

"What's on your mind, Simon?''

"Preventing a war.''

"You started this conflict, not I.''

"Nobody started it, Ben. The people became desperate, that's all. Desperate people are capable of anything. They were hungry, they wanted jobs. You refused to open your borders. That's all it was."

"Cut the shit, Simon. We have intelligence working just as you do. We've taken prisoners. We have the whole sorry story. So don't try one of your famous con jobs on me."

There was a long moment of silence, with only the faint hiss of static from the speaker. "Well, General Raines," Simon finally spoke. "Let me be the first to inform you of something you probably don't know—Homer Blanton has officially resigned the presidency—"

"That is news," Ben said to those in the truck and those waiting and listening outside. "If it's true."

"The government of the United States is no more. The United States of America is officially kaput. The nation is up for grabs, so to speak. Now then, you and I can either fight each other for the next decade, or longer, or we can attempt to work something out. What do you say?"

"I'm listening."

"Good. Very good. That is a start."

"Don't believe anything that Republican son-of-a-bitch has to say!" The braying voice of Rita Rivers came over the miles, loud and clear.

"Oh, my God!" Ben said. "She's still alive."

"The man is a fascist!" Harriet Hooter squalled.

Simon was deliberately leaving the mic open so Ben could hear it all.

"Harriet Hooter," Jersey said. "I don't think you could kill that woman with an axe."

"As you can see, Ben"—Simon's voice was calm—"you do have enemies."

"Simon, I've had enemies since the concept of the Tri-States philosophy was first discussed. Years before the Great War. What else is new?"

"Don't make any deals with that honky, racist Republican son-of-a-bitch!" Rita hollered.

"He's a tyrant!" Harriet shrieked. "He's a modern-day Vlad the Impaler."

"If you want to have any kind of conversation with me, Simon," Ben said, "get those two idiots out of your communications room."

A long moment passed. Ben thought the transmission had been broken. Finally, Simon came back on.

"Sorry about that, Ben. I had to have the two ladies forcibly removed . . ."

Ben smiled. He had a mental picture of that.

"Ben, do you think our two nations could co-exist?"

"What's happened to you, Simon? The last word I got is that you had sworn to destroy both me and the Tri-States concept of government."

"Those were hastily spoken words, Ben. I sincerely regret them. But yes, that was my plan. I will freely admit that was my plan up until a few weeks ago. But why should we both deplete our manpower and resources fighting each other in a bloody war that might not ever end? Why not try to co-exist?"

"What the hell is he up to?" Ben said. "He's done a complete one-eighty on me." He keyed the mic. "Simon, I'm game for anything that would save innocent lives. And I stress *innocent* lives."

"That's good, Ben. Fine. With those words, we have both taken the first step toward agreement."

"What boundary lines are we talking about here?"

"You keep your SUSA, Ben. I will not interfere with your retaking of that territory. Here are the coordinates my people have worked out . . ."

With the exception of Texas, Simon cut the nation directly in two parts. He would take the sixteen western states. The midwest, the north, and the northeast would be decided upon at a later date.

"Yeah, you bet," Ben muttered. "What the hell are you up to now, Simon?" He keyed the mic. "All right, Simon. We're in agreement so far. We'll talk more later."

"Very good, Ben. As of this moment, all hostilities between us are over, agreed?"

"Only if you give me your word you will cease immediately all support of the rabble who invaded our territory."

"You have my word on that, Ben. We'll talk again soon." Simon broke the transmission.

"Get all batt coms in here, Corrie. We'll delay the push-off until we've discussed this new twist."

"You really trust Simon Border to keep his word, Ben?" Cecil asked.

"I don't know, Cec. But if I have to fight, I'll take words over weapons any time. Let's see what the others have to say about it."

Ike opened the debate. "We know Simon Border had Billy Smithson killed," the ex-SEAL said. "His people killed off the Joint Chiefs. His people killed all the members of the National Security Council. His people tried to kill the President and the First Lady. We know

Simon Border masterminded and organized the assault against the SUSA. Now all of a sudden he runs up the white flag of truce and wants to make a deal. Why?"

"Perhaps the man finally recognized the futility of fighting us," Ben's son Buddy said. "We both have well-equipped and seasoned armies. Why continue the bloodshed when half a loaf is better than no loaf at all?"

"That's a good point, son," Ben said. "But consider this: Simon has never settled for anything less than one hundred percent. He despises our concept of government. He swore publicly to see me destroyed and then grind the Tri-States philosophy of government under the heel of his boot. *Maybe* he's changed. *Maybe* he's sincere. *Maybe* he really believes our two systems of government can exist side by side. Well . . . I personally think the man has something up his sleeve. But I also think we should give his plan a try. It's going to take us months to clear out the rabble and get our SUSA up and running again. If we can have Simon Border off our backs during that time, so much for the better. Cecil, the people elected you to run the government of the SUSA. What do you think?"

Cecil was thoughtful for a moment. "I think we should give it a very cautious try."

"Then that's it. Let's start clearing our territory."

Ben put out the word on short-wave radio and by dropping leaflets: *We are reclaiming our territory. Surrender and you may leave peacefully. Resist and you will be killed.*

Two days later, the Rebels slammed west and north like a mighty armed fist. When they hit roadblocks, the main battle tanks blew them apart, along with any defenders that were foolish enough to be standing behind them. The Rebels began retaking towns and villages in brutal hand-to-hand combat. By the end of the third day out, the Rebels had advanced more than fifty miles in all directions. They had killed and wounded hundreds and taken hundreds more prisoner. By the end of the first week, the Tri-States army had to stop their advance because so many Rebels were needed to guard prisoners, it was cutting into the effectiveness of the advance.

Ben was touring one prisoner camp with Ike, discussing what the hell to do with them.

"We demand to be taken care of, General Raines!" one prisoner shouted from behind the loose-strung wire. "We have rights, you know."

"Sometimes I hate that word almost as much as I did political correctness," Ben said.

"What the hell are we going to do with all these people, Ben?" Ike questioned. "We're all going to be on short rations if this keeps up. We just don't have the food to keep on feeding them much longer."

"We have rights! We have rights!" the prisoners began shouting.

Ben stood for a moment, looking at the chanting men and women. "Turn them loose."

"What?"

"Turn them loose with a warning that if they try to steal food or wage war against us, we'll shoot them on sight. Male or female. Makes no difference."

"I don't know, Ben," Ike said doubtfully.

Ben lifted his Thompson and blew a full magazine of .45 rounds into the air. The sound was enormous in the warm spring afternoon. The chanting stopped and the prisoners fell into a sullen silence.

"Bullhorn," Ben said. A guard produced one and Ben lifted the bullhorn to his lips and said, "Now that I have your attention, I have an announcement to make. I am ordering your immediate release—"

Ben waited until the cheering had died down.

"You will all be given five days' field rations and pointed north. Go that way and keep going until you are out of our territory. Don't even think of staying and squatting in the SUSA. You are not wanted here. Not if you insist on our feeding and housing you without you giving us something in return."

"What are you going to do if we stay, General?" a woman shouted. "Kill us?"

Ben didn't hesitate. "Yes," he said bluntly. "Unless you agree to obey the laws we have in force in the SUSA. Those of you who wish to stay and work and obey the law are welcome. We'll help you get started. You'll be welcome here. But that isn't going to happen; not with a large percentage of you. You people waged war against us. You wanted what we worked to build; but you wanted it given to you. You are not the type of people we want in the SUSA and we will not tolerate your presence. I don't know how I can be any blunter than that."

"Then . . . who is left to see to our rights and our needs?" a man called.

"Goddammit!" Ben lost his temper.

"Here it comes," Jersey muttered.

Ben lifted the bullhorn. "You take care of yourselves!" he roared. "You band together and form little communities. You work together to grow gardens and raise chickens and cattle and sheep and hogs. Get something through your thick skulls, people: the government of the United States of America no longer exists. It's gone. Finished. Done. Kaput. Through. Ended. The day of the free ride is over. In all likelihood, it will never return, not as you all have known it. It certainly will never happen in the SUSA. Now, for the first time in your lives, you control your own destinies. How you live is entirely up to you. If you want to work and get along with your neighbors—whatever color they might be— and obey the law and live under the few rules we have on the books in the SUSA, that's fine. Then by all means, stay, you'll be welcomed and given some help in getting started with your new way of life. Open those gates," Ben told a guard.

The barbed wire gates were opened and Ben pointed north, lifting the bullhorn. "For the rest of you bastards and bitches, that way—" he pointed "—is north. Get your field rations over there." He pointed to a line of trucks. "Then get on that road and keep on walking until you are out of our territory. You'll know when you reach the boundary—it's still littered with Rebel dead that you worthless trash had a hand in killing during your mindless rush for a free ride and a handout." Ben slung the bullhorn and slipped a fresh magazine into the Thompson, jacking a round into the slot. He lifted the bullhorn. "Now get the hell out of my sight. And you goddamn well better stay out of my sight. Move!"

Of the several hundred prisoners in this camp, most quietly shuffled over to the supply trucks and drew rations. They got on the highway and started walking north. Most did not look back. Ben's words had chilled them to the bone. About forty men and women stayed.

Ben walked over to the small group, his team right

with him. He carefully eyeballed each man and woman. "So you think you want to try life in a Rebel-controlled zone, huh? OK. That's fine." He looked at Beth. "Have a runner get a political officer over here. These people have a lot to learn in a very short time."

"Right, boss."

"What about the ones you just put on the road, Ben?" Ike questioned. "You want them followed?"

Ben shook his head as he handed the bullhorn to Cooper. "No. If they fuck up, we'll know about it."

"And if they do?"

Ben met his old friend's eyes. His expression was bleak and very easy to read. Those forty odd men and women who had elected to stay could read it, too. The silent message touched them all with a icy hand.

"Right," Ike said.

Two men and two women exchanged glances, shook their heads, stepped out of the group, and walked over to the supply trucks. They drew rations and started walking slowly north.

"Thirty-eight out of four hundred stayed," Corrie said. "That's just about right."

Statisticians had worked out that only about three out of every ten people could, or would, live under the laws that governed the SUSA.

Ben turned back to the group who had elected to stay. "The SUSA can be a very easy, peaceful, and laid-back place to live, folks. Or you can make it very a difficult and unpleasant place to live. That is solely up to you. The political officer will carefully explain the rules to you. You listen well and take his or her words to heart. Understanding and adhering to them is a matter of survival here. Now, people, you'll be starting fresh here. Just like the old French Foreign Legion, your past is forgiven and forgotten. I don't care what name you give for your permanent papers. But that will be the name you will live under and die with. Good luck to you all."

Ben turned to Corrie. "Bump all prison camps. Cut the rabble loose and head them north. You know what to say."

"Right, boss."

Ike smiled. "Some of those people are going to circle back and squat, Ben."

Ben nodded his head. "When they do, I hope they pick a very comfortable place to squat. They're going to be buried there."

Chapter Seven

Hundreds of families who had settled in the SUSA had been killed by the rampaging rabble. As the Rebels pushed further in all directions, they began finding more and more evidence of the mindless and wholesale slaughter of citizens. The rabble they now encountered were the hard-core. The Rebels found entire families, from the oldest to the youngest, killed execution-style, their family pets lying dead beside them.

As they rolled past the ruins that was once Meridian, Mississippi, Ben's mood became foul. As they approached the rubble that had been Jackson, Ben's orders came as no surprise to any Rebel.

"No more surrender talk. These are savages we're dealing with. Hit them first, hit them hard, and finish it."

As the Rebels approached the eastern edge of the old Base Camp One, the remaining bands of rabble finally realized the futility of any further resistance and began fleeing for their lives.

Ben and his 1 Batt rolled and rumbled onto the soil of the old Base Camp One. Ben ordered the long column halted and got out of the van to stand for a moment, looking out over fields that should have been long planted with corn and beans and cotton and milo. Weeds waved in the soft gentle breeze.

"This will tell you something about the caliber of people who invaded our land," he said, speaking to no one in particular. "No thought for the future. They just ate up everything we had stored and then wondered why there wasn't any more. These are the types of people the old liberal wing of the Democratic Party used to piss and moan about. They spent several trillion dollars of taxpayer money feeding and clothing and housing these worthless sacks of shit. That money would have been put to better use by stuffing it down a rat hole."

Anna had left the road to kneel down and dig up handfuls of the rich earth. "It's so rich," she said, rejoining the group. "It would grow anything. Why didn't the rabble plant food?"

"Because they're assholes," Ben said bluntly. "They want somebody else to do it for them: work the land, harvest the crops, and then give them the final product—cleaned and cooked and prepared, of course." He sighed. "Let's push on. See how much damage was done."

It was awful.

The leader of the four gangs that had occupied the town, Ray Brown, had lived in Ben's house. He had also killed Ben's dogs and thrown their bodies in a ditch that ran behind the house. Scouts had found what was left of the dogs and buried them before Ben arrived.

Ben's team watched him very carefully as he received the news about his pets. His facial expression did not change. But his eyes turned as cold as the sea.

"It will not be pleasant for Mr. Brown when we finally meet," was all Ben had to say about the matter.

"I hope Ray Brown has a high pain tolerance," Cooper whispered. "'Cause it's going to take him a long time to die."

"For a fact," Jersey agreed.

Ben looked at the graves of his beloved dogs for a moment, then turned away.

His team gave him a very wide berth. They had witnessed Ben once before as he beat a man to death with his fists . . . to a person, they knew what Ray Brown had waiting for him.

Most of the men and women who had left President Blanton earlier to take positions in the administration of the SUSA were dead. Rebels found their bodies in a shallow mass grave. The remains of the men and women were carefully removed, ID'ed, and reburied with honors.

Survivors of the attack began trickling in and the massive clean-up began.

Conservative estimates were that the residents of the SUSA had suffered about sixty percent casualties.

"Get the crops in the ground," Cecil ordered. "What we can plant this late, that is."

"Does this mean, I hope," Ben asked, "that you are disbanding your 22 Batt and stepping back into an administrative role?"

"No, it does not," Cecil quickly responded.

"I was afraid you'd say that."

"You know damn well we've still got a massive job ahead of us, Ben. We've got to hunt down and destroy at least hundreds and more than likely thousands of gang members. An entire nation is in shambles, and you know perfectly well that someday it's going to be up to us to try to put it back together again." He held up a hand, stopping Ben before Ben would deny he had any such plans. "Save it, Ben. I know you too well. Besides all that, we still have Simon Border and his army to deal with. And we'll have to fight them someday; you know that as well as I do. We really have no reserves left to fall back on. You're going to need every Rebel you can put in uniform."

Ben was forced to concede the point.

"Have you had any word about our people out west?" Ben asked Corrie. "We should have pockets of resistance out there."

"We've been unable to reach any of them," Corrie told him. "Mike Richards thinks Simon's army hunted them down and wiped them out."

"Did I hear my name mentioned?" Mike asked, strolling into Ben's office. Mike had been out of touch for several weeks, as was his custom.

He poured a mug of coffee from the ever-present pot and sat down. "Those aligned with us out west haven't been entirely wiped out," he said. "But not many are left. Simon cozied up to them at first. Then when they let their guard down, he moved in hard and brutal. Now Simon has started his gun-grab among the citizens. He's leaving some carefully selected citizens hunting rifles and shotguns, and that's it. No handguns, no semi-automatic rifles. But I can't figure out exactly where he stands politically."

"Neither can anybody else," Ben said. "For years I thought of him as a liberal's dream. But lately I've had to revise my thinking somewhat. I have a suspicion that Simon wants to be king of America."

"Well, if we move fast enough, before Simon finds and destroys all pockets of resistance, we will at least have some support from a percentage of the people once we kick it off."

"If we kick if off," Ben said, and that got him some startled looks.

Ben shrugged his shoulders. "There is always the possibility that Simon will keep his word, although I don't hold out much hope for that. I'd like to speak with Homer Blanton and get his input on this matter." Ben clarified that. "Homer is a career politician, I'm a soldier. Now that the man has his head screwed on straight, and has stopped listening to people with their heads in the clouds, he makes some sense. Personally, I'd like to see him return to the States, specifically here in the SUSA, and go to work for us."

"For Christ's sake, Ben!" Mike blurted. "Doing what?"

"As a diplomat, Mike. We're going to need some of those. Half the world is getting to its feet, while America has been knocked down flat—again. We're going to need people with Blanton's experience. We're going to try to reach him tonight."

"You mean that, Ben?" Blanton asked.

"I wouldn't have brought it up had I not meant it, Homer. We need you down here."

By the sound of his voice, Blanton had recovered from his near fatal wounds received during the coup.

"I can send an escort for you. You just say the word."

Blanton chuckled. "We've come a long way, haven't we, Ben?"

"Yes, we have. But we still have miles to go. How about it?"

"You've got a deal."

"Good!"

They worked out the details and then Ben smiled and leaned back in his chair. "The wound has been closed," he muttered. "Now the healing has begun."

Homer's wife still didn't like Ben very much, but at least raw hate was no longer shining through her eyes. She had spent several days touring the SUSA and had found, much to her surprise, it was nothing like what her goofy left-wing aides had, a couple of years back, convinced her it was.

"How about becoming our Secretary of State?" Cecil asked Homer. "But I have to warn you, we're starting from scratch."

Homer looked sad for a moment. "All my old friends who joined you?"

Ben sat silent as Cecil said, "Most of them are dead. We found many of them buried in a mass grave. They'd been executed."

"Their families?" the former First Lady asked.

"Killed with them."

"My God!" she said. "What manner of people are we dealing with here?"

Ben wanted very much to tell her: the same kinds of

people you pissed and moaned about for years. But he held his tongue for Homer's sake, and Homer knew it, quickly ducking his head to hide his smile.

After they had left the building, Ben and Chase stood in the hallway and talked for a moment.

Chase studied Ben's face for a few seconds and said, "I don't like that smile, Raines. It's one of your sneaky ones. What's going on in that devious mind of yours?"

Ben spread his hands. "Why, nothing, Lamar," he said innocently. "Nothing at all."

"You also tell lies, Raines. But perhaps I'm better off not knowing." He checked his watch. "I'm late. I have to leave for a few days. Make some inspections of outlying aid stations. Stay out of trouble, Raines."

"See you, Lamar."

Outside the building, standing with his team, Ben said, "Have our 1 Batt ready to pull out. Do it quietly and stay off the air with it. I want supplies for a sustained campaign. A full MASH unit with us. Everything on the QT, people."

"Cecil is going to hit the ceiling," Ben warned him.

"That's the beauty of it. Cecil is stuck here with Homer, showing him around and getting him settled in. His 22 Batt and Jackie and Danjou are here with their battalions protecting the area. Everyone else is gone. Now is the perfect time for us to slip off north and mix it up a little in Arkansas."

Corrie smiled. "You have a very sneaky mind, boss."

Ben laughed. "Sure, I do. Everybody knows that."

Anna looked at him. "This Ray Brown in Arkansas, General Ben?"

"So I hear, Anna."

"Thought so," she replied.

*   *   *

Cecil glared daggers at Ben, but there was nothing he could do about Ben's pulling out. As the elected president of the SUSA, it was his job to run the country, see to the many and much needed appointments, entertain dignitaries, and so forth. Ben was commander of the armed forces and could leave whenever he wanted to leave.

And he wanted to leave.

"You don't play fair, Ben," Cecil bitched.

"Right."

"This is sneaky."

"Ain't it the truth."

"Crap!" Cecil said in disgust. "How about this Jethro Jim Bob Musseldine and his army of ten thousand up in Arkansas?"

"What about him?"

"You're only taking one battalion, Ben."

"First of all, it hasn't been verified that Musseldine has anywhere near ten thousand men. So far, all we've been able to determine is that he's some sort of a nut and has about twenty-five hundred people in his army. Besides, air support is only forty-five minutes away, tops."

"You know I'm going to catch hell from Buddy and Tina about this."

"Oh, for a little while, maybe. They'll get over it."

Cecil stared at him for a moment. He shook his head, shrugged his shoulders, and sighed. "I give up, Ben. You're impossible. Have been ever since I met you. I should have guessed what you were doing years back, watching you put together the nucleus of 1 Batt. You filled the ranks with men and women who thrive on danger. You don't have a single person in the battalion—including the damn doctors—who is happy outside of combat. I don't know why I continue wasting my time."

"I don't either," Ben said with a laugh. "Why don't you quit warning me about it?"

Cecil grimaced. "I might as well. You're going to be out in the field until the day you die."

"I hope so."

"You will stay in touch?" Cecil asked, his tone decidedly sarcastic.

"Why, of course."

"Thank you for that."

Ben smiled and patted his arm. "Have fun now, ol' buddy."

Cecil watched him walk off, thinking: Why in the hell did I ever let that man talk me into politics?

In the gray light of dawn, Ben walked the ranks of his personal battalion. Cecil was correct—the men and women of 1 Batt loved walking the razor's edge. Another point that Cecil had nailed down was that Ben was very careful about replacements. He chose them personally, after a careful review of records and talking to other Rebels. Some of the men and women in 1 Batt were ex-Scouts and special operations people; men and women who had grown just a bit too old for the often times wild and wooly antics of those teams, but were perfect for 1 Batt.

Ben also allowed his people some latitude in dress. Dan Gray, the former British SAS officer, who was a stickler for discipline and uniform codes, often cast a very jaundiced eye at how some of the men and women of 1 Batt dressed. Some of them looked as though they had just stepped right out of Snoopy's World War I fantasies, with drooping handlebar moustaches, pony-tails, beards, and occasionally the awfulest combinations of uniforms one could imagine. But no one could cast aspersions at how they fought. The men and women of 1 Batt, from cooks to Scouts to tank commanders to medics, were the best of the best. And they were, to a person, one hundred and ten percent loyal to Ben Raines and the Tri-States philosophy.

Ben glanced at Corrie. "All right, Corrie. Let's do it."

"Kick ass time!" Jersey shouted, and hundreds of voices joined in.

1 Batt was on the prowl.

Chapter Eight

"He's done *what?*" Ike roared over the miles, his words rattling the speaker.

Cecil repeated his statement.

Dan jumped in. "Counting all the rabble that withdrew to Arkansas, Ben might well be up against thousands of hostiles."

"At least," Georgi Striganov stepped in.

"So what do we do?" Raul Gomez asked.

"Nothing," Tina broke in. "Because Dad is doing what he wants to do. You all know he's always been a lone wolf. He'll never change. You also know that if he gets in too deep, he'll call for back-up. Besides, lest we all forget, he is the boss."

"He's also hard-headed as a goat," Ike said.

"You're a fine one to talk, you illiterate Mississippi redneck ex-porpoise," Dan Gray needled his friend, knowing Ike would come back at him.

"SEAL!" Ike shouted at the man, correcting him for

about the ten thousandth time. "That's SEAL, you god-damn goofy limey." Then he told the Englishman to go pour a cup of tea and stick it where the sun don't shine.

Several hundred miles to the west, Corrie had the conversations on speaker in the van and everyone was laughing.

The laughter died away when Corrie, monitoring their battle frequency on her headset, said, "Trouble just up ahead, boss."

The column was about forty miles inside the Arkansas border, pushing up from the south.

"What do we have?" Ben asked.

"Several hundred rabble occupying the town. Far Eyes has had them under observation for about an hour. Light weapons and a few machine guns. No mortars or anti-tank weapons have been spotted. It appears the rabble killed the residents. There is evidence of a mass grave just outside the town."

"MBTs up and circle the town. Mortar crews up and get into position."

Corrie relayed the orders and the big sixty-three-ton monsters surged forward, other vehicles pulling off to the shoulder to let the tanks rumble past.

The small town, probably populated by no more than a thousand people before the Great War, had been reduced to about two-hundred-and-fifty new people since the SUSA became reality. They had worked hard, planted their crops and gardens, maintaining neat lawns and freshly painted and well-kept homes, and were starting a new life.

Now they were dead at the hands of rabble.

Cooper had driven up close to the town and Ben stood by the side of the van, giving the area a once-over through binoculars. The streets were littered with trash. Windows had been smashed from newly opened stores and shops. Ben was sure the few places of business had been looted. They always were.

Ben said, "Corrie, I'm certain this bunch of trash doesn't have the sense to operate a military radio. What CB channel are they on?"

"Nineteen," she answered promptly.

"That figures," Ben muttered. "All right, Corrie. Tell those idiots in the town to give it up."

"I already have. They said for you to kiss their ass."

Ben sighed. "The originality of that reply boggles the mind." He grimaced. "Take the damn town."

It wasn't much of a fight. After less than ten minutes of the strafing of heavy machine-gun fire from the Rebels, and few mortar rounds which landed in the streets, the rabble hoisted a white flag and began streaming out, their hands in the air.

But this time, Ben had a new twist to the taking of prisoners. Each person was photographed and fingerprinted and blood was drawn for DNA matching . . . should that person ever be foolish enough to return to the SUSA.

"We didn't hurt or kill nobody," a man said during questioning. His eyes were shifty and scared. "The town was empty when we got here."

"He's lying," a PSE operator told Ben.

"Sure, he is. But we can't prove it. No witnesses. All we can do is head them north."

"They all claim to have no knowledge of anyone named Ray Brown," Ben was told. "But one of them was wearing this ID bracelet. It belonged to Major Rogers, General. His wife's name is engraved on the back. He never took it off. His wife gave it to him just before she was killed. That was back when he was a lieutenant. When we were fighting in the northwest.''

When Jerre had been killed, Ben thought. Then shook off that sad memory.*

''Rogers was one of the bodies found in that mass grave back at Base Camp One, right?''

''Yes, sir.''

''Bring this man to me.''

''Right away, sir.''

Ben had set up a CP in an old house on the outskirts of town. The prisoner was led in and sat down in an old straight-backed chair.

''I ain't done nothin','' the man protested. ''Y'all ain't got no call to treat me this a-way.''

Ben held up the gold ID bracelet and let it speak silent volumes as it slowly twisted in his fingers.

Sweat broke out on the man's forehead.

''Where did you get this bracelet?''

''I . . . ah . . . swapped a feller for it.''

''You're a liar.''

The prisoner looked around him. Anna was squatting down, her back to a wall, sharpening her already razor-sharp knife. She looked up at him. Something in those very cold, pale young/old eyes was strangely frightening. Beth was staring at him. Cooper was standing behind the prisoner. Jersey was standing beside Ben, her dark eyes unreadable. Corrie was at the radio.

''What do I get for the truth?'' the man whispered.

''Your life,'' Ben told him.

The man nodded his head. ''That's fair, I reckon.

---

* *SURVIVAL IN THE ASHES*—Pinnacle Books.

Ray Brown's got at least three other gangs with him. All tole . . . maybe three to four thousand people when they all group up. They's Carrie Walker and her bunch. Tommy Monroe and his gang. And Dave Holton. I was with Tommy Monroe for a time. Joined up with him in Alabama. That's where I'm from original. Tommy's a bad one, General. Probably badder than Ray, you get right down to it. And he knows military tactics, too. Was a sergeant in the army for a time, he was."

"What kinds of weapons do the gangs have?"

"All kinds, General. Machine guns, surface-to-air missiles, mortars, rocket launchers. They ain't got no big guns or tanks, though. We tried to get them tanks started y'all had in the depot back south of here, but nobody could get 'em to crank."

Ben smiled. It would take any member of a tank crew about one minute to get them running again: a little matter of a missing part which rendered the tanks inoperable.

"Go on," Ben said.

"We was promised all sorts of stuff if we'd join up. Land to work, a nice home, a car or truck. A better life."

Ben stared at the man in disbelief. Same old song, different jukebox. The song was titled Something for Nothing. Ben sighed. "There are thousands of cars and trucks sitting idle all over the country. Stick a battery in one, fill it up with gasoline, and drive it off."

The man shrugged. "Why go to all that bother if someone else is gonna do it for you?"

Anna shook her head at that.

"Anyways, when I seen what Ray Brown done to your dogs, I 'bout puked. I've always like dogs; don't like to see no harm come to 'em. I knew right then and there I'd better haul my ass outta there. And I done 'er, too.

But on the way out, I come up on Tommy Monroe. He had him some prisoners. Him and his people had raped the women—some of 'em no more than children—and they used 'em bad, too. Tommy, he just lined up the folks and shot 'em dead. He tossed me that there gold bracelet he took off a man's wrist. That's how I come by it. And that's the truth."

Ben looked over at Corrie and she nodded her head. She was wearing a headset and was monitoring what the PSE operator in the next room was saying. The prisoner was telling the truth.

"How'd you get up here?" Ben asked.

"Started out walkin'. These old boys come along in cars and trucks and give me a ride. Then y'all showed up."

"And you plan to do what?"

"Drift, I reckon."

"You have no plans, no thoughts of the future?"

The man shrugged his shoulders. "I quit high school in the ninth grade. Finally got me a job drivin' a pulpwood truck. But I couldn't stay out of trouble. I like to drink. I was in jail when the Great War blew everything to hell and gone. Then it was just hand to mouth for a long time. I'll just bum around, I reckon."

"Do it outside of Rebel-controlled territory," Ben told him.

"You can count on that." Some fire returned to the man's eyes. He glared at Ben for a moment. "Who the hell do you think you are, General? You ain't got no right to tell me I *got* to work."

"And you have no right to expect us to feed you and house you and clothe you and see to your medical needs while you lay up on your ass and do nothing," Ben countered.

"That's the way it used to be."

"No more."

"I can see that plain."

"All right. You can go," Ben told him. "Hit the trail. North. And keep going until you're out of our territory. Then you can keep going north, or turn east or west; makes no difference to me. Just get gone."

"You're a cold, mean son-of-a-bitch, Ben Raines."

"I've been called worse."

"I 'spect you have." The man stood up and stared at Ben for a few seconds. "You'll never make your rules work nationwide, Ben Raines. The American people won't stand for it."

"I have no plans for the entire nation."

"Lemme ax you this, General: so you get all set up here again. All your rules and such. What are you gonna do when hundreds of thousands, maybe millions of folks, come floodin' 'crost your borders again? Shoot 'em all?"

"It might come to that. But I hope not."

"Then y'all better get ready to fight for the rest of your lives. They's millions of folks around that ain't got no jobs and ain't got no hope of ever gettin' none. And they ain't gonna live under your laws, General."

"Then they've got a real problem."

"I ain't never, ever, seen no one like you, General."

"Thank you."

The man blinked. Shook his head. "Can I go now?"

"Please do."

Ben sat quietly for a time after the man had left, the only voice in the room that of Corrie, touching base with the other battalions in the field.

She finally told the team working the main communication truck to take it. She took off her headset and leaned back. "They're all reporting the same thing, boss. Wherever they go, hundreds of people just milling around. Not doing anything, just looking for something to eat. Walking around in rags, picking through the rubble, living in filth. We're going to have some real health problems before long."

"Probably billions of chickens wandering around, laying eggs everywhere," Ben said, just barely hanging on to his temper. "Untold thousands of cattle and hogs and sheep. Can't these goddamn people do *anything* for themselves? We started from scratch, why can't they?"

Corrie waited until Ben had ceased his angry muttering. She smiled and said, "However, there is one small bit of news you'd better know now."

Ben cut his eyes. "I don't know whether I want to hear it. But go ahead."

"Remember you said that leaving that little con artist Emil Hite in Europe was the one bright spot in our returning to the States?"

Ben sighed. "All right, Corrie. What has that little bastard done now?"

"Nick Stafford just radioed Cecil at Base Camp One. Seems that Emil Hite has just proclaimed himself to be the SUSA's ambassador to Hungary."

Ben put his forehead down on the cool surface of the old table he was using for a desk. He didn't know whether to laugh or cry. "Ask Cecil to please recall our, ah . . . new ambassador and bring him home."

"Where do you want him assigned?"

"How about the moon?"

"Not feasible at this time."

"How about assigning him to Thermopolis?"

"Rosebud said she'd shoot him."

"Emil or Therm?"

"Both of them."

Ben raised his head and smiled. "Then assign him to Cecil's 22 Batt."

"Cecil is your best friend!"

"That's what friends are for."

Corrie was busy for a few moments, the speaker turned off so Ben could not hear the transmissions. "Cecil says he'll be happy to recall Emil. But he is strictly your baby."

"How about assigning both Emil and Cooper to a two-man observation post in the Rockies?" Jersey suggested.

"Now, now, my little cactus flower," Cooper said.

Jersey tossed him the bird. "Screw you, Cooper!"

"You have just put into words my one burning desire, you lovely little Apache princess." Cooper was moving toward the door before the words left his mouth, Jersey right behind him. Fortunately for Cooper, he could always outrun Jersey. But this day, when he had outdistanced the shorter-legged Jersey, he made the mistake of hiding in an old two-hole outhouse. The outhouse had just recently been abandoned as a secondary relief station and the pit was still rather fragrant.

Jersey began rocking the old privy, with Cooper screaming like a banshee, and finally turned it over. Cooper fell a few feet. Into the pit.

It was quite an operation getting Cooper out, involving the use of a Hummer with a winch and the Rebels all wearing gas masks.

Jersey made herself scarce. She *knew* Cooper was going to get her for this.

"You like snakes in your sleeping bag, Jersey?" Ben asked with a smile.

"I really didn't mean for him to fall into the shit pit," Jersey said.

"How about a dead skunk in your sleeping bag?" Corrie asked her.

"It was an accident, I tell you!"

"He'll probably put dead mice in your canteens," Anna suggested.

"Look, you guys," Jersey moaned. "Cooper has an inventive enough mind. He doesn't need any help from you. Just keep your suggestions to yourselves, huh?"

But Cooper was all forgiving and sweet (after he took several showers), and that made Jersey even more nervous.

"He's plotting to get you," Ben said with a smile.

"Yeah, when you least expect it," Beth said.

"This is going to be something to see," Corrie remarked.

"I can hardly wait," Anna said.

"Will you for Christ's sake do something, Cooper!" Jersey yelled at him.

But Cooper would only smile and say, "All is forgiven, my little desert blossom."

"In a pig's ass, it is," Jersey snarled at him.

"This is a lot more fun than actually doing something," Cooper told Ben one evening after chow.

"Are you going to pull something on her?"

Cooper shook his head. "No. But Jersey *thinks* I am. That's why it's so much fun."

As the column slowly advanced north, in a zig-zag route, taking various highways, they began to see signs of a massive and hurried exodus by the punks and rabble. But still no signs of Jethro Jim Bob Musseldine or his army.

"Do they even exist?" Ben asked one late afternoon, as the Rebels were making camp for the evening.

"If they do, they're staying off the radio," Corrie said. "I have a hunch they're using CBs in a very limited way. We've intercepted nothing."

Ben sipped his coffee and then said, "I swear I've felt eyes on me."

"Me, too," Jersey agreed.

"Oh, hell, Jersey," Ben told her. "That's Cooper, lusting after your body."

Cooper waggled his eyebrows and grinned, nodding his head in agreement.

Jersey gave him a dirty look.

Corrie held up a hand for silence. She listened, and then said, "Scouts have made contact with Musseldine's people. We are being warned to turn back now or die."

"Wonderful," Cooper said.

Beth yawned at the warning.

Anna spat on the ground in contempt.

Ben drank his coffee and said nothing.

"Boss," Corrie said. "I have contact with Musseldine."

Ben took the mic. "Musseldine?"

"What do you want, Raines?"

"We need to talk, Musseldine. Before we start butting heads in a needless war."

"I have only this to say to you, Raines: leave our territory at once or die."

"You're an idiot, Musseldine." Ben tossed the mic back to Corrie and went off to find the mess tent.

Chapter Nine

Rebel tanks blew the roadblock and guards apart at first light, sending various body parts flying all over the place.

Musseldine's men returned fire, mostly in the form of small arms. The bullets clanged off the tanks and went whining away into the warm and humid summer air.

"FO's have their positions spotted," Corrie said, standing beside Ben.

"Mortars," Ben said.

Mortar crews began laying down a devastating walk-in of 81 and 60mm rounds. Musseldine's forward positions soon fell silent. The Rebels advanced to find shattered bodies and smashed weapons.

"Stupid," Ben said, looking down at one foxhole, and at what was left of several men after a 60mm round had landed directly in their midst. "So far as we know, these people aren't thieves or murderers or criminals of any type. Why won't they at least sit down with me and talk this thing out?''

No one said anything because they all knew that Ben was not expecting any reply.

"Corrie, see if you can make contact with this Musseldine. Arrange a meeting. This bloodshed is not necessary.''

The column was about thirty-five miles south of the ruins of Little Rock, on highway 167.

"Boss, Musseldine wants to know if you are ready to surrender.'' Corrie asked, struggling to hide her smile.

Ben looked at her, then took off his helmet and scratched his head. "Bring me one those prisoners. I've got to find out something more about this squirrel.''

"Right, boss. Ah . . . there is something you should know . . .''

Ben arched an eyebrow.

"Every man we captured was carrying a Bible.''

"Oh, me,'' Ben said. "I really hope we aren't dealing with a bunch of religious nuts.''

"I wouldn't want to bet against it,'' Beth said.

"We'll soon know.''

The prisoner's eyes shone with the light of a fanatic. "We are the Army of the Salvation, the Sword, and the Hand of the Lord!'' the man shouted at Ben. "And you, sir, are an abomination.''

"Is that a fact?''

"Yes! You are the Great Satan! And Brother Musseldine has decreed that you must be destroyed.''

"Sorry if I don't wish you luck.'' Ben was beginning to put it all together. "And what church did he pastor before the Great War?''

"The Church of the Salvation, the Sword, and the Hand of the Lord, of course."

"Naturally. How silly of me to ask."

"God is on our side!"

How many men had mouthed that same phrase over the long and bloody centuries? How many had died with those words on their lips? How many really believed it?

"This bloodshed is not necessary," Ben told the man. "I believe we can talk this matter through and reach some sort of settlement."

"Never!" the man shouted, startling everybody standing close-by. "The Rebels are the scourge of the earth and must be destroyed!"

"This guy's not totin' a full load, boss," Cooper said. "He's about two bricks shy."

"Degenerate!" the man shouted at Cooper, the veins in his neck standing out. He was red-faced and sweating. "Filthy follower of the Great Satan!"

"Where in the hell do all these dodos come from?" Jersey asked.

"Whore!" the prisoner shouted at her. "Dirty harlot of the devil!"

"Get this crackpot out of here," Ben ordered, before Jersey could butt-stroke him with her rifle. The man was led away, shouting Biblical phrases, more or less.

"Boss, Musseldine says he has nothing to say to you," Corrie said. "He says we all have the mark of the beast on us."

"*Revelation.*" Ben sighed. "I'm sorry to say that we're dealing with religious fanatics—true believers. There probably won't be any compromise from these people. They are one hundred percent right, and everybody else is one hundred percent wrong. There is no middle ground with them." Ben expelled air, his face grim.

"For the sake of peace, I'd back out and give them the state," Ben said. "But that wouldn't satisfy them for long—nothing ever does. They want it all."

"That's just half the story, boss," Corrie said. "Communications has just begun to pick up transmissions out of Missouri between Issac Africa and some general who calls himself Mobutomamba."

Ben blinked. "What the hell was that last name?"

Corrie smiled. "Mobutomamba. According to our intel, this Issac Africa has four divisions of troops. Their divisions are about three times the size of our battalions. First division is commanded by General Mobutomamba. The other commanders are Colonel Cugumba, Colonel Kenyata, and Colonel Zandar."

"You have got to be kidding!"

Everyone started laughing at the expression on Ben's face.

Ben looked at one of his sergeants. "Do you know anything about this Issac Africa, Lewis?"

"No, sir. That's a new one on me. But I do know this damn Zandar nut. He's a bad one. He was in prison when the Great War hit the globe. He was oh, maybe nineteen or twenty at the time. A black militant who belonged to a terrorist group that had declared war on all whites. He killed a white police officer who had pulled him over for speeding. He had just started his prison term when the balloon went up."

"You knew him personally, Lewis?"

"I went to high school with the son-of-a-bitch in Cleveland. Until he dropped out in his junior year. He came from a real good family. Upper, upper middle class.

That's the shame of it all. Hell, he wasn't oppressed. He had money, clothes, car, good looks. Sharp as a tack. He was accepted by everybody. Well-liked for a time. I don't know what turned him around. He showed up at school one day wearing robes and beads and those silly goddamn hats. He started preaching hate. And it went downhill from that point. I stayed the hell away from him.''

"Thank you, Lewis."

The sergeant nodded. "I came over to tell you we came out clean in this little fight. No dead or wounded. But those prisoners we took are nuts, General. What do you want to do with them? They're driving my people crazy."

Ben chuckled at the expression on Lewis' face. "I'll have a chopper come in and take them back to Base Camp One for more interrogation. We're going to hold here until we can find out exactly what the hell we're up against with this Musseldine character."

"Right, sir."

"Death to the Philistines!" the faint shout came from the prisoner compound.

"This war just keeps getting weirder and weirder," Ben muttered.

Back at Base Camp One, the newly appointed Secretary of State of the Southern United States of America settled right in and went to work. Since there wasn't as yet a lot to do on the international scene, Homer started helping Cecil with the administrative duties of running the SUSA.

Blanton's wife, older now and a hell of lot more tactful

(and wiser in the ways of the world) than when she'd first met Ben Raines, began making plans to start teaching at a local college as soon as it reopened. The first thing she noticed (with a slight smile) was that the textbooks were not in the least politically correct—they were accurate. The textbooks detailed events as they happened, not as some had wished they had occurred, and portrayed people in their order of importance, favoring no ethnic or political group.

Mrs. Blanton's eyes had widened considerably since the Great War blew the entire world apart a decade back, and widened even more since the assassination attempt. She understood (finally) what Ben and the others had done. For as he had told her, or tried to tell her some months back: "Look lady, six thousand years ago, the Jews had a working government, a written language, schools, etc. At the same time, my European ancestors were sitting around in caves, grunting at one another and painting themselves blue. We all had to start somewhere. Every race of beings had their order of advancement. I'm not going to whitewash history— no racial slur intended—just to satisfy some ethnic group. In the SUSA, we'll teach what actually happened, not what some group *wished* had happened."

At the time, she thought Ben to be racist.

She saw now that her thinking could not have been further from the truth.

"We've got three battalions of Rebels left in Eastern Europe," Cecil told Blanton. "What is your thinking on leaving them there?"

Older now, and much more the statesman, Homer sat back and gave that some thought. "Let's leave them there for the time being as advisors and administrators only," he finally said. "I don't want them in any combat role. And I sure as hell don't want us to get bogged down over there. We've got too many problems here in North America to resolve before we can take on the world."

Cecil smiled. "You and Ben really aren't that far apart in thinking."

Blanton returned the smile. "Not anymore, at least. But he had to kick me in the ass to make me realize that."

Cecil laughed. And yet another friendship was born out of misunderstanding.

Far to the north of Ben's position, Issac Africa read the dispatch with great interest and growing anger. Simon Border was up to something—but what? According to the dispatch, Rita Rivers couldn't figure it out either. But that came as no surprise to Issac. Rita was ugly as a mud fence, but a great fuck. However, she didn't have the common sense Allah gave a goose.

And neither did Harriet Hooter.

Both of them together couldn't change a light bulb.

Issac crumbled the note and tossed it. Rita and Harriet had no more stroke. Politically, they were finished. Therefore, Issac had no more use for Rita. Simon Border would make a place for both of them in his organization, but it would be positions of no importance.

Issac's main concern now was that goddamn Ben Raines. Issac knew that once Ben got pissed off, he would squash that loony-tunes honky redneck Musseldine like a bug.

Then Issac would be next.

Issac was under no illusions about that, either.

No army anywhere in the world had ever defeated the Rebels, including the U.S. Armed Forces. Issac had a lot of troops; the Rebels had more and they were much better equipped. The Rebels had rocket-assisted artillery that could lay back twenty miles and hit the targets with scary accuracy.

So what was the best course of action?

Issac knew, but it galled him to even think about it. Compromise.

But would Raines even talk about a compromise?

One way to find out.

He headed for his communications building. If he could just buy a little time, perhaps he could build up his army so strong that even Raines might have second thoughts about attacking him.

It was worth a try.

What had once been the thriving city of Little Rock was a shambles, almost exactly as the Rebels had left it after bringing it down in their relentless quest to rid the earth of gangs and thugs and punks and the hated Night People.

There was one difference now: the rabble were squatting amid the ruins.

"Why?" Anna asked, upon sighting the men and women and kids. "With all the land and homes theirs for the taking, with cows and chickens and pigs and goats and sheep by the hundreds of thousands, why are they picking through the trash, always on the verge of starvation?"

Ben didn't reply. His eyes were sweeping the area

ahead. Something was all out of whack here but he couldn't immediately bring it into focus.

"Hold it up right here, Coop," Ben said.

Cooper stopped the van. "What's wrong, boss?"

"I don't know. Corrie, order tanks buttoned up and forward. Everybody get ready for a fight. I think we've been suckered."

"How?" Cooper asked.

"Just a hunch, Coop. Just a hunch. See how the women are staying between us and kids at all times? See how both the men and women are all dressed in long coats? Hell, it must be ninety degrees out there. They're hiding weapons. Back us up behind the tanks."

But Ben's warning came too late. The so-called "rabble" suddenly dropped behind carefully worked out and previously chosen defensive positions and opened fire on the Rebels.

A battle tank was coming up fast, trying to get between the van and the attackers, but it was just a few seconds too late. A mortar round exploded in front of the van, rocking the heavy vehicle and pocking the bullet-proof windshield. Light machine-gun fire hammered against the grill and the radiator began pouring out clouds of steam.

"Out the back!" Ben yelled. "Grab what you can and get the hell out of this tin coffin before it blows."

Ben and his team quickly exited out the rear of the van with just seconds to spare. A rocket slammed into the side of the van and the vehicle exploded in flames. The force of the explosion knocked Ben and team to the street, momentarily stunned, but otherwise unhurt. They scrambled to their boots and raced for cover.

"Talk about walking into an ambush with our eyes

wide open,'' Ben panted, as he crouched down behind what was left of a brick store-front wall.

"Nobody picked up on it, Boss," Jersey said. "These people are better than we thought."

Ben brushed the dust off his Thompson and nodded his head. "Yeah. But we do have a slight problem, gang."

His team looked at him over the rattle of weapons.

"We're cut off," Ben said.

Chapter Ten

Musseldine's people tried a frontal against Ben and team. It was suicide. The guns of the MBTs opened up and chopped them to the pavement of the littered street.

"Cooper, you and Anna take the rear," Ben ordered.

Cooper grabbed his SAW and a can of ammo and he and Anna got into position.

Ben was thankful now that he had sent Smoot back to Base Camp One, getting the Husky out of harm's way.

A long burst of heavy machine-gun fire kept the heads of Ben and team down for half a minute.

"They'll be working closer under that cover," Ben shouted over the roar of combat. "Coming out of the alleys from side and rear. Get ready for it."

Several of Musseldine's people rushed the side, making it over the piles of brick and junk that were once the building.

Anna caught one in mid-jump and gave him a burst from her CAR, the .223 rounds stitching him from groin to neck. He fell in a lifeless lump at her boots.

Cooper made a one-handed catch of a thrown grenade and tossed the pineapple back with about one second left on the fuse. "Down!" he yelled, just as the grenade blew. The pineapple exploded about two feet off the ground and the shrapnel from it peppered several of Musseldine's fighters.

"Are they brave or just stupid?" Jersey called over the painful shrieking of the horribly wounded.

"They're religious fanatics," Ben replied. "And that makes them doubly dangerous."

Then there was no time for talk as Musseldine's people charged Ben's position.

But two more main battle tanks had joined the fracas, and they opened up with .50 caliber machine guns and M-60 machine guns, laying down a devastating half circle of fire around Ben's position. Musseldine's people went down like broken bowling pins, flopping and kicking and screaming their lives away on the littered and now blood-soaked street and alleys.

"We have a narrow window to our left," Corrie called. "But it'll be closing in a matter of seconds."

"Let's take it!" Ben shouted. "Go, people, go! Follow me!" Ben was over the wall and running before anyone could stop him.

The few seconds of the safety net closed as Musseldine's people shifted around.

Ben came face to face with a burly and bearded man, a wild light shining in his eyes. Ben stuck the muzzle of the old Thompson in the man's face and pulled the trigger. The man's head exploded in a shower of blood and brains and bone, all of it splattering the brick wall behind him.

Ben and team ducked into a building as the window of opportunity was completely sealed off.

A woman came running and shrieking toward Jersey, shouting something about saving babies from the devil's knife of abortion and calling Jersey a whore of evil.

"Oh, fuck you!" Jersey said, then shut her up permanently with half a mag of .223 rounds.

"What kind of nuts are we fighting?" Jersey panted. "Abortions?"

Ben shoved a fresh mag into the belly of the Thompson. "A wing of the old religious right—the extremist branch of it. The nuts are really coming out of the woodwork now."

"All the years we've been fighting the punks and warlords and street crap and Night People, they've been in deep cover, training," Cooper remarked, keeping an eye on the street from his position behind a blown-out window.

"You got it, Coop," Ben agreed.

"And I thought we had some real piss-heads in my country," Anna said.

Ben smiled at the now grimy-faced teenager. Even the dirt and gunsmoke and dust of battle could not hide the young woman's astonishing beauty.

Ben looked up as a roaring came to his ears.

"They're all over us!" Beth shouted, rising to meet the charging crush of Musseldine's fanatics as they came streaming in through a hole in the concrete block wall.

Then it was hand-to-hand in a bloody no-quarter fight to the finish.

* * *

Thousands of miles away, at his mansion in Africa, Bruno Bottger smiled and leaned back in his chair. The recently arrived and decoded reports from his spies in North America were pleasing to his eyes. Ben Raines and his Rebels were fighting for their very existence in the States. Bruno's people had done their jobs well, infiltrating Simon Border's organization, infiltrating Jethro Musseldine's army, and working hard to bring down Homer Blanton's administration.

Everything was going exactly as planned and right on schedule.

The native men and women and children in the territory that Bruno's army now controlled in Africa had been either killed or cowed to the point where they were no longer any threat.

All those found with AIDS had been exterminated shortly after Bruno had arrived. Everyone was tested (those that refused the tests or tried to run were shot), and anyone who tested positive for HIV had been gassed or shot and their bodies burned. Entire tribes had been wiped from the face of the earth.

The Nazi flag now flew over thousands and thousands of acres of Africa. Gold mines and diamond mines were now solidly under Nazi control. Some of the richest farmland in the world was now producing crops for the men and women and children of the New Reich.

Bruno Bottger closed his eyes and his smile widened in satisfaction.

Ah! he thought. *Life is good.*

* * *

None of the hundreds of roaming gangs of rabble, none of the self-proclaimed warlords, nor the armies of Issac Africa or Jethro Musseldine worried Simon Border. The rabble and the warlords had no real organization and Africa and Musseldine were both idiots. Ben Raines would deal with all of them in his usual manner.

It was Ben Raines that worried Simon.

Simon Border trusted Ben even less than Ben trusted Simon.

Simon had no intention of allowing Ben and his Southern United States of America to flourish. And Simon knew that Ben was probably well aware of that.

It was just a matter of time before their armies would clash.

Ben emptied a magazine of .45s into the knot of screaming fanatics and then slammed the butt of the Thompson against a head and heard the skull bone pop under the impact. Jersey had emptied her M-16 and was now using an entrenching tool from her pack; the blood was flying with each savage slash from the sharpened blade. Anna was using a machete and had already sent several heads slopping to the dirty floor, unblinking and frozen eyes wide open in death shock. Corrie was swinging her CAR like a club, with devastating results. Cooper and Beth remained at their positions, keeping others of Musseldine's army at bay outside the ruined building.

Troops and MBTs finally smashed through to Ben's

position and the assault from Musseldine's men and women was broken . . . for the time being.

Every member of the team was cut and bleeding from minor wounds, but none suffered any serious injury. Tough body armor and helmets had saved them all from being badly wounded.

"Get out of these ruins," Ben ordered, brushing away a medic who had rushed up and started fussing over him. "The city is a deathtrap. Everybody out of here."

The Rebels began pulling back until they were clear of the ruins of Little Rock.

There, Ben let the medics go to work on him.

"We sure got suckered into that one," Ben remarked, as the aid man finished cleaning out a cut on his cheek. He gave Ben a shot to dull the pain before he started stitching up the two-inch long knife slash. While the medicine was taking hold, he gave Ben a tetanus shot and then started closing the cut.

A Scout walked up. "We know now what kind of weapons these nuts have and what kind they don't have," he reported. "They have only a few rocket launchers. But they have plenty of heavy machine guns and enough mortars to cause us some grief."

Ben nodded his head.

"Hold still!" the medic said.

"Sorry," Ben muttered.

"The men and women of Musseldine's army are highly disciplined and reasonably well-trained in military tactics," the Scout continued. "We're not dealing with amateurs. But only a few wore any type of body armor and they appear to have no universal dress code."

"But they're damn good guerrilla fighters," Ben

replied, his words slightly slurred due to the deadening of part of his face.

"They are that," the Scout agreed, a grimness behind his words. "We took some hits."

"Give it to me."

"Eighteen dead. Twenty-five wounded. Five of them not expected to make it."

"Corrie, order replacements up from the ready pool."

"Right, boss. I've got a big nine-passenger wagon on the way up from Base Camp One. It's one of the last made before the Great War. Our people just finished bullet-proofing it and adding some electronic gear."

"Cecil order that wagon found and updated?"

"Right. He thought our van sucked—his words."

Ben smiled, then sobered. "All right, people. Let's bury our dead and start making some plans to teach a hard lesson to Mr. Musseldine and his army of fruit-cakes."

The first lesson came in the form of heavy artillery from Ben's massive self-propelled 155's. They began dropping in every type of round in their arsenal, including tactical CS gas. When Musseldine's people came staggering out of their holes, Rebel snipers, many of them using specially built .50 caliber rifles, lined them up in the cross-hairs and killed them. Closer in, the MBTs were slinging out anti-personnel and HE rounds. Then Ben ordered the P-51E's in, loaded with napalm.

When it came to warfare, Ben was not a nice person.

Ben's Rebels circled the city, pounding it and surrounding areas with land-based artillery and air attacks for two days and nights without a break. When Ben finally ordered a halt to the bombardment, there was little left of what had once been the capital of Arkansas. The city was a smoking, burning ruin, stinking of death and the lingering residue of CS gas.

"Scouts in," Ben ordered.

"It's a dead city," they reported back.

"Let's go," Ben told his team, climbing into the big four-wheel drive vehicle just up from Base Camp One. The original seats had been pulled out and six individual seats installed. A hole had been cut into the roof and a ring mount with a machine gun had been added to the strengthened roof of the big wagon. The wagon didn't get much in the way of gas mileage, but it was comfortable and well-armored.

With two MBTs leading, Ben once more entered the city.

A deadly stillness greeted the Rebels, punctuated only by the crackling of an occasional fire, as the napalm-ignited flames ate into old and smashed wood.

"Pull over there," Ben said to Cooper, pointing to a Scout checkpoint. He lowered the window. "Prisoners?" he asked the young Scout.

" 'Bout a dozen so far, General. They're a pretty sad-looking bunch. Held 'bout a half mile further down. On your right. Interrogation teams are there now."

Cooper parked at the interrogation site and Ben and team got out, walking over to the one-story building that had, miraculously, escaped the barrage virtually unscathed. An officer from the psychological warfare and interrogation unit had just stepped outside as Ben drove up.

"All the fight got knocked out of this little bunch,

General," the officer said with a smile. "Forty-eight hours of continuous artillery bombardment and air strikes will do that. According to them, we trapped about three thousand of Musseldine's people in the city. After the ambush, they apparently relaxed, thinking we had pulled out. The artillery and air strikes really came as quite a surprise. The CS gas drove a lot of them out of their holes and the incoming got them. Those that were near the outskirts got wasted by our snipers."

"Children?" Ben asked softly.

The officer hesitated for a moment. "Some kids were among the group, sir."

"Shit!" The oath exploded from Ben's mouth.

"That ought to tell you what kind of people they are, sir. Bringing kids into a battle zone."

"But the children are still dead."

"Yes, sir."

"Suffer the little children unto me," Ben muttered under his breath.

"Sir?"

Ben waved that off. "Nothing. Just talking to myself. Any word on where Musseldine's HQ might be located?"

"He doesn't have a permanent HQ. That's been confirmed. He's constantly moving from one location to another. But his people are spread out from west to east at the top of the state."

"I certainly know that part of the country. Were you with us at that time?"

"Yes, sir. I was in another part of the nation. But I heard about it."

A few years back, Ben had been captured by a bunch of wackos. For several weeks after his escape, he had waged a devastating guerrilla war against those who had taken him prisoner.

"Boss?" Corrie called. "Pilots report large groups of people heading north. They're spreading out all over the top part of the state. Visuals confirm it is Musseldine's people. Men, women, and children."

"Do not fire on them," Ben ordered. "Make that perfectly clear. Do not fire on them. I don't want any more children harmed."

"Right, boss." Corrie quickly relayed the orders.

When she had done that, Ben asked, "Any word on the whereabouts of Ray Brown?"

"Negative."

"He'll surface," Ben muttered. "And when he does, I'll be there." Ben was unaware of the psychological warfare officer looking at him strangely. "And then," Ben added, "I'll see just how well he can die."

"This thing with Ray Brown sounds personal, sir," the officer said.

Ben looked at him. The officer thought he had never seen such deadly coldness in a gaze. "Very personal," Ben said, then walked over to the wagon and got in.

"Where to, boss?" Cooper asked, when everybody was in their seats.

"North. Let's settle this thing with Musseldine. Tell the battalion to fall in, Corrie. Scouts out."

"You may never find this Ray Brown person, General Ben," Anna said.

"I'll find him," Ben replied. "Whether it takes one month or ten years, I will find him. And whether he surrenders or I capture him . . . I'll kill him."

Chapter Eleven

Ben's ruthlessness shocked Jethro Musseldine. Up until the assault on Little Rock, he had not known just how well-equipped the Rebels were. Now he knew there was not a single weapon of war the Rebels did not possess . . . nor would Ben Raines hesitate to use any of them.

As his people advanced north, Musseldine dejectedly assessed his situation. He had lost nearly a third of his army in Little Rock. Musseldine was certain that somehow he had failed God, and this was his punishment.

Perhaps God didn't really want him to fight Ben Raines after all. Could that be it? Was this a sign from Above? No, Musseldine rejected that . . . absolutely not . . . Well . . . maybe it was. Jethro wasn't all that certain that God had instructed him personally to fight the Great Satan called Ben Raines. That vision might have been brought on by indigestion; he had eaten a whole berry pie that evening before retiring.

But for sure something had to be done to stop the rampaging of Ben Raines and his Rebels. The man was so . . . well, *godless*.

Jethro was on a mission . . . a crusade. When the nation was restored, there simply had to be prayer in public schools, as well as Bible classes beginning in the first grade. Abortion must be halted at all costs. Any mention of evolution would be forbidden. And non-believers would be cast out and stoned . . . that's what the Bible said must happen.

Well, it sort of said that . . . depended on one's inter-pretation.

At Russellville, Arkansas (what was left of it), Mussel-dine had made up his mind. He ordered his columns halted.

"We shall fight the many-headed beast here," he announced.

He ordered his people to form a line stretching from Russellville east to Searcy (what was left of it).

"We'll force the Great Satan to meet us *mano a mano!..*"

Then he had to explain to many of his true believers exactly what that meant, for many of his followers just weren't that swift when it came to meshing together gray matter.

"This will be the end of Ben Raines," Musseldine shouted to his wild-eyed followers. "This will be Ben Raines's last stand in America . . ."

Uh-huh. Yeah. Right.

When Ben heard that, he was reminded of that old joke about Custer's last thoughts: *Holy Cow, where'd all these fuckin' Indians come from?*

* * *

"Well, it's not that bad a place to make a stand," Ben said, looking at a map. Intelligence had quickly picked up on the signals from Musseldine's camp. "He's got the Arkansas River and this lake to his west, and the White River to his east. That would slow us down some if we wanted to do an end-around. How about these little towns around the area?"

"When the gangs of rabble came in, most of the people fled," a Scout told him. "Many of them headed into the Ouachita Mountains to wait it out. We've made contact them and advised them to keep their heads down until the smoke clears."

"The children with Musclehead's people?"

The Scout smiled but did not correct Ben. "We have confirmed that he has ordered them moved north, out of harm's way. Intel has intercepted a number of messages to that effect."

"I want one last try at talking to this man," Ben said. "Corrie, see if you can contact this Jethro Musclebrain."

"Musseldine, boss."

"Right. Whatever."

After a few moments, she said, "Musseldine on the blower, boss."

Ben took the mic. "Jethro, Ben Raines here. We don't have to be enemies. This fighting can come to a halt right now. It's all up to you."

"You mean, surrender, Raines?"

"No. Just quit fighting and go home. Keep your weapons. Let's live in peace. How about it?"

"You're trying to trick me!" Musseldine screamed.

"No, I'm not. No trick. We can end the fighting and you and your people can just go home."

"It's a dirty trick! That's what it is. It's a filthy, rotten trick."

Ben sighed. "Musselbone, it's no trick. We can work together and co-exist in peace. Set up your private schools and teach religion. I don't care. You can have a church on every corner if that is what you wish. Forbid abortions in your towns. I won't interfere with that and neither will any of my people—"

"I abhor a liar. And that's what you are, Raines. You are not an honorable man."

"What the hell does it take to convince this nut?" Ben muttered. He looked at Corrie. "I want every weapon that is capable of delivering tear gas and pepper gas made ready."

"They're ready, boss. Helicopters circling now, two minutes away. All troops have been issued tear gas and pepper gas canisters."

"Fine." He lifted the mic. "Musselfoot, are you there? Let's sit down and talk this thing out. We can live in peace."

"Liar, liar, pants on fire!" Jethro screamed.

Ben stared at the speaker and shook his head.

Jethro started preaching to Ben.

"Oh, shit!" Ben said. "I'm offering him peace and he's giving us a sermon."

Musseldine was ranting and raving and gulping air, running his words together as if he had suddenly been transported to the Plain of Shinar and was standing in the center of the Tower of Babel. Then he started speaking in tongues.

"What the hell is that?" Anna blurted.

"He's got the spirit," Ben told her.

"I hope it's not contagious," Anna replied.

Ben keyed the mic. "Musselhead," he said wearily.

Anna giggled. "Mussel*dine,* General Ben."

"Right. Whatever." He lifted the mic. "Are you receiving this?"

"Ummgomalottagoogooda."

"Muskethead, get a grip on things. Speak English. This is important. I've trying to save lives here."

"SlopgooyumgoochyJerryLeeandElvistoo."

"Shall we have the artillery start dropping in the gas?" Anna asked. "Please?"

"Hell, no," Ben said. "We can't interrupt a religious ceremony. That would be unconstitutional. I think." He pressed the talk button. "Muscatel, are you back to earth yet?"

"Gammaboggiewoogierockumsockumgomango!"

"He sounds like Emil Hite," Jersey remarked.

"Emil makes more sense than that." Ben frowned. "Most of the time, that is."

"FOs report Musseldine's people, all up and down the line, are standing up, boss," Corrie said. "They're dancing and waving their arms and appear to be speaking in tongues."

"This is not good," Ben said. "Tell all forward observers to get into protective gear and start falling back."

"Slay the infidels!" Musseldine shouted, rattling the speaker.

"Now he's beginning to make some sense," Ben said. "Well, sort of."

"Drive the godless Philistines into the sea!"

"What sea?" Cooper asked. "Nearest body of water around here is that pond over there."

Ben spoke into the mic. "Musselman? Can you hear me?"

"Whopbopaloomabopbamboom!"

"If you could put guitar and drums behind that, it'd be real catchy," Jersey said with a straight face.

He couldn't help it. Ben burst out laughing.

"I hear the sounds of the many-headed beast rising out of the fiery, smoking depths of hell!" Jethro shouted.

"I kind of wish we'd stayed in Europe," Beth said. "At least that war made some sense."

Ben wiped laughter tears from his eyes. "This may work out to our advantage, if he can really get his people all worked up. Have everybody stand by to throw gas. I think that nut is going to do something really stupid."

"Gird your loins!" Musseldine screamed orders to his people. "We have Michael with us and . . . ah, John Wayne, too."

"Now I *know* he's going to do something really dumb. Everybody into protective gear. Shake out those gas masks."

"Prepare to slay the dragon!"

"Is that us?" Cooper asked.

"That's us," Ben told him.

"Blow, bugle, blow!" Musseldine screamed.

"Here it comes," Ben said.

"Charge!" Musseldine shouted.

Ben looked at the speaker. "Did that fool say what I think he said?"

"I believe he said 'charge', boss," Corrie said.

"That's what I thought."

Corrie's radio squawked. "General, there are hundreds of those crazy sons-of-bitches charging us up here!

Many of them have forgotten their weapons and are charging us with empty hands. They're shouting in some strange language."

"They're all speaking in tongues." Ben grabbed the mic. "Get out of there. I'm sending in gas. Eagle to air leader. Get in there and drop those gas canisters. Cover the land. Mortar and artillery . . . start putting the gas to them."

Over the speaker, they could hear the faint shouts and wild speaking in tongues from the charging troops of Musseldine.

Ben slipped on his mask as the first canisters of gas were hurled into the air.

"Hell of a way to fight a war," Ben muttered.

There were no casualties on the Rebel side and very few among the soldiers of Musseldine. While Musseldine's people were staggering around, blind and incapacitated from the gas, the Rebels disarmed those who had remembered to bring their weapons along on the wild charge. Some of Musseldine's people escaped, but not enough of them to cause any worry for Ben.

After the medics flooded Jethro's eyes and he could once more see, Ben had him brought to his temporary CP. He waved him to a chair. "Jethro, are you still dancing with angels on the head of a pin, or do you now have both feet firmly on the ground?"

"I am quite lucid," Jethro said stiffly.

"Marvelous. Should you decide to go off again, speaking with the angels, warn me so I can clear out."

"I am not gripped by the spirit very often."

"Good. I'm very relieved to hear that. Where are you from, Jethro?"

"Fayetteville."

"And your, ah, followers?"

"From all over the state."

Ben stared at the man. Really a nice-looking fellow, now that the light of fanaticism had faded from his eyes. Ben guessed him to be about his age. "Jethro, what would you do if I told you to go home?"

Musseldine blinked. "Why . . . go home, I guess. I mean, you have our weapons. We're defenseless."

"We'll return the weapons to you."

Musseldine looked startled. "You will?"

"Yes, I will. As long as you will swear with your hand on the Bible that you and your people will never ever again use them against us."

Musseldine slowly nodded his head. "All right. Yes. I will agree to that."

"That's fine. Now then, are you fully convinced that I am not the Great Satan?"

Musseldine flushed. "Ah, yes, General. I guess I, ah, got a little carried away with that."

"Somewhat," Ben said, very drily.

"But I remain adamantly opposed to abortion."

"That's your right, Jethro. And you certainly have the right to speak out against it. Just don't try to physically stop someone from seeking an abortion should they choose to get one. The other side also has rights."

"Yes. I understand that."

"I hope you do, Jethro. Look, I don't care if you teach religion in your private schools. I'm personally opposed to private elementary and high schools . . . in many areas I don't believe they teach reality. But I see now that if the SUSA is to survive, I'm going to have to bend a little. And I'm amenable to that. We're all going to have to do some bending and readjusting."

"That's fair," Musseldine said.

"You want some coffee?"

"That would be nice, General."

Ben had coffee brought in. After sugaring his, Ben said, "I pose no danger to you and your people, Jethro. But we both have a real threat facing us from the west."

"Simon Border," Jethro said quickly.

"You got it."

"I understand that you have reached some sort of agreement with him."

The man might be half nuts at times, Ben thought, but he has a good intelligence network. "That's true. If he'll stand by his word."

Jethro took a sip of coffee. "That's good. Real coffee. Well, General, I wouldn't count on Border doing that. I don't trust him at all. He professes to be a liberal. But I think what he wants is to be king of America."

Ben smiled. Just before the Great War knocked the world flat on its back, the word liberal had become one of the most hated word in the English language. Social programs and blatant political pork, pushed through Congress, had very nearly bankrupted the nation, caused taxes to soar, and in many cases had politically and bitterly divided family and friends. "Oh, I don't trust him, Jethro. That's just one of the reasons why you and your people will return home fully armed. I'll be counting on your help when push finally comes to shove."

"In the form of Simon Border and his army?"

"Among others, yes. But mainly Simon. We'll clean out the gangs of punks first."

"You can count on us, General."

Ben wondered if, when Jethro and his people were needed the most, the man would once more start hearing heavenly voices? But Ben knew he didn't have much choice in the matter. The Rebels were spread much too thin as it was, and desperately needed all the allies they could get.

Ben opened the map case and took out a map of Arkansas. "When I leave here, I'm going to drive straight up to the Missouri line and contact this Issac Africa. I'm told he wants to talk and perhaps work something out. Maybe we can, if the deal is anywhere fair. But he's not going to like what I have to say to him."

"I've met him, General. The man despises all whites." He looked at Ben for a moment. "Just as you should despise me for the ambush against your people in Little Rock."

Ben shook his head. "I don't work that way, Jethro. One of my closest friends and commanders is a Russian named Georgi Striganov. Georgi and I butted heads all over the U.S. for a time. Now he's as much a part of the Rebels as I am. You and I had our battles, now it's over and we'll work together."

Ben smiled and Jethro returned the smile. "You were saying something about this Issac person?"

"Yes. I tried to work something out with him. But I soon gave that up as hopeless. I tried to point out that all-white and all-black states have been tried several times since the Great War. They all failed. He says his won't fail."

Ben nodded. "If that is the course he chooses to take, I can assure him it will fail. I'll place a full embargo against his state. He'll receive no help or trade from the SUSA. I won't be a party to wild, unreasonable hatred. And that's what it seems Issac Africa thrives on."

"Do you blame many of the blacks for feeling as they do?"

"Yes, I do," Ben replied without hesitation. "There is no place for racial hatred any more. No room for it. Racial hatred and racial divisiveness doesn't exist in the SUSA. We won't tolerate it. We're all Americans here. Our society is based on common sense; that's why so many people can't live there. The words nigger, honky, spic, slope, kike, wop, dago, greaser, beaner, and all the other derogatory words are not used in the SUSA. Our young kids have never heard them. You know how we work, Jethro. I don't have to explain it to you. Take your people and go home. Tend your crops and gardens and open your shops and mind your own business and keep your powder dry. You're part of the SUSA now. We stick together."

Musseldine smiled. "Count on it, General. Say, sure you wouldn't like to attend our Sunday services, Ben?"

"I think I'll pass, Jethro. Like the old country song goes: Me and Jesus got our own thing going."

Musseldine laughed, saluted, and left the CP.

Beth walked into the room that Ben was using for an office. She held a clipboard in one hand. Ben spotted it and groaned. He knew she was going to put some bad news on him.

"We just received a lot of reports from Scouts working outside the SUSA, boss. It's chaos out there. All semblance of order and reason have broken down in approximately twenty states, midwest, north, east, and a couple of states in the far west. We don't know what is happening in the far northeast. But California is a killing ground. Nearly everything we accomplished over the years—outside of the SUSA—has gone right down the toilet.''

Ben sat down, leaned back, and smiled. "By all means, Beth, don't spare my feelings. Give it to me straight.''

She smiled at the easy sarcasm. "Simon Border and his Democratic Front are managing to keep the lid on in the states they control. But little brush wars have begun to spring up in what was called Missouri. Mostly black against white and so forth. Michigan is an open battleground, and so is New York State.''

"Jesus, we're back where we started!''

"That's about right, boss. Except for here in the SUSA and the area under the control of Simon Border. It's a total breakdown everywhere else.''

"In the rubble of New York City?''

"Thousands of people are living there. The Scouts can't get on the island to really check it out. We don't know how the hell the people there are living.''

Ben sighed. "They're not living. They're existing. How about Night People?''

Beth hesitated. "Well . . . intel thinks there has been a heavy resurgence of those creepie bastards and bitches.''

"Damn! You have any more cheery news?''

She laughed. "That's it. For now.''

Ben thanked her and leaned back, putting his boots up on the battered old dining table he was using for a desk. Nearly everything the Rebels had accomplished over the long and bloody years had been either destroyed or damaged. In essence, they were almost right back where they had started.

"So we start all over," Ben muttered. "Why the hell not? We've done it before.''

Chapter Twelve

Ben and his people waited until Ike and a couple of other battalions had cleaned out their sectors in the SUSA and then pulled them over to his TO. Ike brought Buddy and his 8 Batt and Dan and his 3 Batt.

"I've got some things to say to this Issac Africa," Ben told his people. "But I wanted you batt coms here when I did." He looked at Corrie. "OK, Corrie. Let's get the man on the horn."

"General Raines," the voice sprang from the speaker. "Issac Africa here. I hope you're not planning on doing anything foolish, like attacking me."

Ben was silent for a few heartbeats, then said, "No, Issac. I have no plans at this time to attack you." Ben's son, Buddy, arched an eyebrow at that statement. "I'm going to leave you alone and let all the hate you have destroy you. That is, if all those black and white and brown and tan guerrilla groups you have all around you don't do it first."

"They won't," Issac came right back. "I took this land just like you and your Rebels seized all of the territory you now claim, General."

"You're about half right, Issac. We took the land. But we didn't drive out or kill all the blacks as you did the whites. Many of them stayed to work right alongside us. But you and your followers are all alone, Issac. All you have is each other and your unreasonable hatred for anyone not of your color. The SUSA is not going to trade with you, Issac. And I won't give you a shipping route to any port we control. Neither will Simon Border. So that means anything you grow or manufacture, you either eat and use or it rots and rusts. You might try some northeastern ports, but they're not going to be open for some years in the future. No, Issac, you won't last. But I'm not going to waste my time and put my people at risk fighting you. Not unless you make some hostile move against us. I don't believe I have anything else I care to discuss with you, Issac."

Issac was cursing as Ben handed the mic to Corrie and she switched the frequency, stilling the wild profanity.

"He might last several years, Ben," Ike cautioned.

"He might. But I suspect not. Intel reports dozens of small guerrilla bands nipping and biting at his people from all sides." Ben smiled. "Many of those guerrilla bands supported and equipped by us, of course."

Buddy smiled at his father's words and cut his eyes to Ike. Ike sighed and handed Buddy a silver dollar. Ben watched the exchange and said, "One of these days, Ike, you're going to learn not to gamble with my son."

"I believe that time has come, Ben. I'm a slow learner. So what's next for us?"

Ben walked over to a window—minus the glass and boarded up—and stared out through the cracks for a moment. When he turned to face the group, his expression was serious. "It's become obvious to me, and I suspect to all of you, that the SUSA cannot continue as a separate nation within a nation. Isolationism just won't work. Oh, it was a grand plan, and it worked for a time. However, too many forces and factions are against us for us to stand entirely alone. Somehow, someway, we've got to attempt to heal the entire nation . . ."

Ben watched as the expression on Ike's face changed to one of disgust and he dug in his BDU pocket and handed Buddy another silver dollar.

". . . if we don't do that, we're going to be fighting at our borders forever."

"Shit!" Ike said.

"You have a better plan, Ike?" Ben asked.

Ike shook his head. "Unfortunately, no. But Ben, my God, what a massive undertaking."

"I know, Ike, I know. And we're going to have probably as many failures as we do successes. But if we don't try, we're going to be in combat for the rest of our lives and the SUSA will fall from neglect . . . among other reasons. Our kids and their kids and their kids will know nothing but war. I just don't see any other route to take."

"Father," Buddy said. "We can't help people who won't help themselves. You know that."

"But we have to try, boy. For one thing, I don't want history recording us as making no effort toward restoring North America in its entirety. I personally don't think we'll be able to do it. But when we lay down for the last time, we can go out knowing that we tried."

Dan said, "So the plan is to take the country—that portion not controlled by Simon Border—and do it village by village, county by county, and start re-education programs for the masses?"

"That's about it, Dan. We go in and prop up the people. And if they fall after we do that . . ." Ben shrugged his shoulders. "I don't know what we'll do."

"Oh, many of them will fall," Buddy said matter-of-factly. "After we take them by their little hands and show them what to do and give them the materials and some help, and then pull out, probably about half of them will fall right on their faces. Because the government won't be there to pick them up and dust them off and prop them up again. Father, you know damn well—we've proven it—that only about a quarter of the population of North America can live under a common-sense form of government. The rest either can't or won't. I want to go on record as saying this is going to be a colossal waste of time and effort."

Ben's face hardened. "Well then, boy, I'll ask you the same question I asked Ike: Do you have a better plan?"

"No," the young man replied. "I do not." He held up a hand, silencing Ben before he could speak. "I understand *why* you're doing this, Father. Noble thoughts not withstanding. You've had our medical people working around the clock producing vaccines. We're going to inoculate the masses to keep epidemics from occurring . . ."

"Why not just inoculate the Rebels and our supporters, and allow the epidemics to take out those worthless people?" Anna suggested.

"I agree with Anna," Buddy said quickly.

"Jesus Christ!" Ben flared. "And people call me cold and unfeeling."

Dan and Ike exchanged glances and faded back, silently leaving the house, as did Ben's team, letting father and son and adopted daughter verbally have at each other. The only team member who stayed in the room was Jersey. The devil couldn't have moved her from Ben's side.

"Doctor Chase is on the way in," Corrie told the group. "He's bringing in our share of the vaccines. Buddy and Anna will not change the boss's mind."

"You can bet on that," Beth said.

"And your opinion of the plan, Beth?" Ike asked.

"It's a practical plan, General," Beth replied. "One we've tried before in a limited way. We failed then and will probably fail now. But we will get to a certain percentage of the population. And a certain percentage will, once propped up, stand on their own two feet and succeed."

"I know you have the stats all worked out, Beth," Dan said. "So what are they?"

"About thirty percent, maybe as high as thirty-five percent, of the population—that we get to, that is—will stand with us and work to restore the nation. The rest will whine and bitch and piss and complain about everything. They'll moan about civil rights and constitutional rights and gun control and this, that, and the other thing, and about how they're not appreciated and eventually they'll drop out and wander off. But nothing they do, or fail to do, will ever be their fault. It will always be the fault of someone or something else— usually society. But in the main I agree with the boss. We've got to try."

Anna came out of the house and up to the group. "General Ben has a temper, doesn't he?" she asked.

Ike chuckled at the expression on Anna's face. "Is Buddy still alive?"

"Buddy decided to go along with the plan," the teenager said, "but I still think it's stupid." She looked up at the sounds of planes as they began their airport approach. "Who is that?"

"Doctor Lamar Chase," Ike said. "Now the fun begins."

Lamar took a sip of his whiskey and smiled. "Ben Raines, the great humanitarian. Quite a difference from the fire-breathing dragon I recall from years back. Kill 'em all except six, and save them for pallbearers."

"You disagree with what I propose, Lamar?"

The men were alone in the den of the house.

"Oh, no, Ben. Not at all. I think it's a grand plan. If you can pull it off, it'll be the happening of the new millennium. How about Issac Africa and his people? Do they get inoculated, too?"

"If they want it. But they won't. Issac will convince the majority of his followers that it's some sort of trick. Issac was one of those who preached that the CIA deliberately started AIDS to wipe out the black people in Africa."

"Are you putting me on?"

"No."

Chase shook his head in disgust.

"Did you bring everything we need, Lamar?"

"Oh, yes. And I can be resupplied with no problem, by air drop if necessary. Our people down south have been working around the clock cranking out vaccines. How about this Jethro Musseldine and his people?"

"I've sent medics over there with vaccines. They'll rejoin us after we've taken, or retaken, I should say, the airport in Memphis. What will this be, the third goddamn time? I'm getting where I know that airport better than my own house."

Chase lifted his glass. "To success."

"I'll sure drink to that."

Three full battalions of Rebels on the move was a sight to behold. Dozens of tanks and both towed and self-propelled artillery. Several hundred deuce-and-a-halves, HumVees, Jeeps, APCs and Bradley Fighting Vehicles, and huge tanker trucks. The column stretched out for miles.

The long column headed northeast, toward the ruins of Memphis. They crossed the river and to a person were shocked at what they found.

"There must five or six thousand people living in the rubble," Scouts reported back. "Probably more than that. What in the hell is the matter with these people?"

"As if we didn't know," Ben muttered. "Let's go check it out, Coop."

"It's God's will," one man dressed in nothing more than rags said to Ben on the outskirts of the city. "All is lost. The mighty have fallen. We are doomed to wander forever like the lost children until the end comes."

"You're a blathering idiot," Ben told him. "Drive on, Cooper."

"Help us!" a man cried out as the big wagon drove

slowly past him, standing with a group of men and women and kids. "We're starving."

"Stop," Ben said. He got out, his team with him, and walked over to the man. "Did you say you were starving?"

"Yes, sir. Please give us food."

Ben was speechless; it was one of the few times in his life he was struck dumb for a moment. He couldn't believe what he was hearing. He pointed to a vacant lot about a hundred feet away. "You see those feathered fowl pecking at the ground over there?"

"Yes, sir. I do."

"Those are chickens, you nitwit. Of the male and female variety. There are eggs over there in nests. Chickens are also very good to eat. Go gather the eggs and kill and cook the chickens. But not all of them. Keep some alive to produce more eggs and allow some of the eggs to hatch. Little chickies pop out of the shells. Little chickies grow up to be big chickies. Do I have to write it all down for you?"

"You're a very insulting man," a woman mouthed off, walking up to the team. "Who are you, anyway?"

"They must have just come in from the dark side of the moon," Jersey muttered.

"Ben Raines."

Those two words stilled the group for a moment. They stood and stared at him.

Finally the woman said, "If that is true, then you have an obligation to help us."

Ben blinked a couple of times. "I do?"

"Of course. You have plenty, we have nothing. You must share."

Ben stared at the woman. Took off his beret.

Scratched his head a couple of times. He began walking around in small circles, muttering some highly profane words. He stopped with his back to his team and said, "Somebody better handle this, for I am rapidly losing grip on what little temper I have left."

Jersey stepped up to the woman, all five feet of her, the butt of her CAR resting on one hip, and said, "What the hell's the matter with you, lady? Are you some kind of fuckin' fruitcake?"

The older and taller woman stared down at the diminutive Rebel. "I am a professor of philosophy, young lady. And I am not accustomed to being spoken to in such a manner."

"Oh, yeah?" Jersey got all up in the woman's face, standing on her tippy-toes to do so. "Well, philosophize this, Miss Hoity-Toity—we are not obligated to do a damn thing to help you. Why don't you try living dangerously for a change and help yourselves?"

"I should slap your face!"

Jersey smiled. Sort of. "When you try that, lady, you best make sure your heart belongs to God. 'Cause your gimlet ass is damn sure gonna belong to me!"

Ben turned to see the older woman's reaction to that. When the words came, they came as no surprise to him.

The stringy-haired, grimy-faced woman drew herself up, her eyes flashing. "You damn right-wing, war-loving, gun nuts are to blame for all that's happened to the good decent people of America," she hissed. The words sprang past her lips like venom from a spitting cobra. She turned to glare at Ben. "If you hadn't insisted on your barbaric nation none of this would be happening. We were on our way back to a full democracy, but you had to break away."

Ben had his temper under control by now and he walked over to the woman. "A full democracy, lady? No. I don't know what it was you had, but it sure as hell was not a democracy. Even Homer Blanton—who is now the SUSA's secretary of state—admitted that it wasn't working. And as far as you being hungry, lady . . . don't talk to me about hunger when this country is overrun with chickens and cattle and sheep and hogs."

"I am a vegetarian, General," she announced primly. "I do not eat the flesh of living creatures."

Ben leaned down, put his nose about an inch from hers (which was running, he observed) and roared, "Then eat weeds, goddamnit!"

Ben raised no objections when Lamar began setting up his MASH tents and lining the people up for shots and physicals. "Just don't give that damn philosophy professor any shots that were developed from eggs or sheep shit or calf brains, Lamar," he said sourly. "She'd rather infect an entire nation."

Doing his best to keep from laughing in Ben's face, Lamar turned his back on Ben and busied himself with paperwork.

"How'd that goddamned woman ever get down here from Vassar or Harvard or Princeton, or wherever the hell it was she spewed her nonsense?" Ben asked.

His entire team burst out laughing at him. Lamar could no longer contain his own high humor and he started cackling and howling.

Ben endured the laughter stoically. When it had died away, he asked, "What is that woman's name? Did anybody find out?"

"Janet House-Lewiston," Beth said, wiping her eyes. "With a hyphen."

"One of those types," Ben muttered. "Where's her husband?"

"She doesn't have one," Corrie said.

Ben looked at her. "Now I am confused. I'm not at all *surprised* to learn she doesn't have a husband, just confused. If she's not married, what is the hyphen for?"

"House was her father's name," Jersey said. "Lewiston was her mother's name."

Ben sighed. Rubbed his temples with his fingertips. "Where is that woman now?"

"She's helping over at one of our inoculation tents," Lamar told him, pointing. "Over there. She was a nurse for a few years before she got her PhD. and turned toward an academic life."

Ben muttered something under his breath and glowered darkly in the direction Lamar had pointed.

Suddenly, from that direction, shouts and laughter rang out.

"I'm sure that's her causing all that commotion," Ben said. "She probably found a cockroach and wants to make a pet out of it."

His team grinned but said nothing. They all knew that Ben was very ecology-minded and tender-hearted toward animals; but there was a limit to everything, especially when one professed to be starving.

Ben watched as a woman left the MASH tent where the shouting and laughter had originated and began walking toward the tents where Doctor Chase and Ben were headquartered. Ben did not recognize the woman. But as she drew closer, he could see that she was a very attractive lady. Closer still, he could see that she was about forty, with light brown hair, cut short, and possessing a very shapely figure. There had been a time when Ben knew every member of the Rebels by their first name. But no more; those days were long past. Now there were thousands of Rebels.

The woman walked up to where Ben was sitting in a canvas camp chair. He looked at her. Her face was familiar, but he could not dredge up a name. Green eyes, very pretty in a mature way, filled out her BDUs nicely.

"General Raines, may I have a word with you?"

"Sure. Go ahead." Ben did not notice as his team began backing up, putting some distance between the boss and themselves. Chase smiled, ducked his head, and continued working at his papers.

"General, there is this perfectly horrid little man who suddenly appeared at the tent where I was assisting the doctors—"

Ben stared at the woman. Oh, no. No way. It couldn't be her.

"—he claims to be a general in your army. The people with him are just as confusing as he is—"

Ben sat up straight in the chair. My God, it was her! The grimy-faced, stringy-haired woman had metamorphosed from a moth to a butterfly. It was what's -her-name. Amazing what a bath and clean clothes could do.

"The man is horrible, General. I insist that you do something with him immediately. He is disrupting a very vital function."

Ben ceased his visual inspection of the lady's physical attributes and stood up as his mind began putting together all that she had said.

"A little man?" he questioned.

"Yes."

"Claiming to be a general?"

"Yes. He's dressed like something out of *Beau Geste*. I certainly hope he isn't a general."

"He isn't. Lady, do you always have to be the bearer of bad news?"

"I beg your pardon?" Janet questioned. She stepped closer, looking up at Ben. She really was quite pretty. And smelled good, too. Unlike a couple of hours back when she smelled like sheep dip. "Do you actually know this obnoxious person?"

"Unfortunately, yes."

"My general!" The shout came from some distance away.

"Oh, shit!" Ben muttered.

"Watch out, boss," Jersey called. "Here comes Emil."

"It looks like a band of escaped loonies with him," Beth added.

"What's this?" Lamar asked, looking up from his paperwork, his half-glasses on the bridge of his nose.

Emil Hite ran up, lost his footing as he tripped on a brick, and went sailing onto the table Chase was using for a desk. Chase went over backwards in his chair just as the folding table collapsed. Emil landed on his feet, off balance, and went lurching into Janet House-Lewiston, who fell against Ben, all three of them landing on the ground, Ben on the bottom, with Janet on top of him. All in all, it was not an unpleasant experience for Ben.

Emil bounced to his feet. "My general!" the little con artist shouted, saluting in the French fashion, palm out. "I have arrived."

With Janet still on top of him, Ben said, "Yes, Emil. I can see that."

"Now that we are here," Emil said. "Where would you like me and my people to go?"

With Janet struggling to get off him, it was with great effort that Ben refrained from telling Emil the first thing that popped into his mind.

Chapter Thirteen

Jersey and Beth got Janet off of Ben, standing her up, and Cooper helped Ben to his boots. Ben stood glaring down at Emil, the hard look bouncing off the smaller man. The little con artist was very hard to insult or intimidate.

"Did I and my followers arrive at an inopportune time, General?" Emil asked.

Ben almost told him that *anytime* Emil arrived was inopportune for somebody. He bit back the thought, looking at the colorfully dressed Emil and his small band of followers. When Emil had first joined the Rebels, his following had been large, Ben recalled. Whatever else he was, Emil and his group had suffered their share of dead and wounded over the years. No one could fault them for lack of courage. "The first thing you do, Emil, is get out of those clothes and into BDUs. When that is done, you report to Dan Gray for orders. Understood?"

"Yes, my general!" Emil saluted, turned around, and

almost fell down. He recovered nicely and he and his group trotted off.

"My God!" Janet said. "Where did you find him?"

Ben turned and smiled at the woman. "Actually, he found me, some years back. Emil means well."

"Blivet," Jersey said, before walking off a few yards. Lamar was on his hands and knees, trying to collect all his papers before the breeze sent them flying, Anna helping him. Cooper was trying to figure out how to re-set the folding table.

"Blivet?" Janet questioned.

Ben laughed. "That's an old military expression. It means ten pounds of shit in a five-pound bag. Pretty well sums up Emil Hite. He grows on you."

"Like gangrene," Lamar grumbled.

Ben righted a camp chair and waved to it. "Sit down, Ms. House-Lewiston."

Janet hesitated, then sat. Lamar had retrieved his papers and gone into the big squad tent. Janet said, "I want to tell you something, General . . ."

Ben sat down and waited.

Janet said, "I think . . . well, it's a fine thing you and your Rebels are doing for these people."

"It's a matter of health priorities, Ms. House-Lewiston. We don't want an epidemic on our hands." Although that might be one way of taking care of the problem, Ben thought, and was shocked by his thinking.

Janet looked at him for a moment. "No purely humanitarian gesture on your part at all, General?"

"Not one tiny bit, Ms. H.L. Except for the very young and the very old."

Janet was silent for a moment. "What happens when you run out of vaccine?"

"A lot of people are going to get sick and croak, Ms. H.L."

"Oh, for heaven's sake. Will you please call me Janet?"

"Certainly, Janet."

"Thank you. Will you have enough vaccine, General?"

"Not with us. Not for all the diseases that people have to be inoculated against. But we'll be resupplied within a couple of hours after calling for it. We aren't that many air miles from Base Camp One."

"I've heard all about your Base Camp One."

"I just bet you have. And I'll also bet that not ten percent of what you heard is true."

She smiled and Ben took notice of it. The smile wiped years from the woman's face and it was a very pretty face.

Janet visually took in what some had described to her as cruel features and cold, hard eyes. Ben's eyes were unreadable, and his features could sometimes be hard. But not cruel. Unless he wanted them to mirror that.

Ben continued, "The estimates of people who survived the initial attack and the plague that followed it were understated drastically. As were the number of cities destroyed," he added sarcastically. "Thanks to a very elaborate scheme we only uncovered about a year ago."

Janet had no comment on that, although she knew perfectly well what Ben was talking about, having been a staunch supporter of Harriet Hooter and her liberal left party. "How many people do you think now inhabit North America?"

"Millions. Getting an accurate count is going to be

damn near impossible for awhile. But if I had to take a guess ... I'd say about a hundred million. It seems we're constantly having to revise that figure."

"A hundred million," Janet whispered. "When the Great War came the population was approximately two hundred-sixty-five million in the United States."

"That's right."

"And only about thirty-five percent of those of voting age chose to vote in the last nationally held election," Beth the statistician spoke up. "That should have told Washington what the majority of Americans thought of politicians."

Ben smiled. If Janet wanted to match stats for stats with Beth, she was going to be in for quite a surprise. But Janet noticed the smile on Ben's lips and very astutely picked up on its meaning.

Corrie called, "Boss? Scouts in the city are reporting a very familiar smell."

Ben knew what she meant. He nodded his head in understanding and looked over at Janet. "Have you had any disappearances among your group?"

"Why ... as a matter of fact, yes. But among the homeless, people come and go all the time. Sometimes they return, sometimes not. Why?"

Ben stood up. "Get 1 Batt assembled, Corrie. It's time to go headhunting."

"Right, boss."

Ike was on his way to Nashville, Dan to Knoxville, and Buddy was back with his special operations group.

As usual, Ben and his 1 Batt were doing what they liked best: lone-wolfing it.

"Headhunting?" Janet questioned, tugging at Ben's shirt sleeve.

"You've got creeps living in the rubble of the city, Janet. Night People. Cannibals. That's why some of your group didn't return."

She visibly paled at the thought. "I . . . I thought all that was just a myth."

"Not hardly." Ben looked at Jersey, who had slipped on body armor and was standing close. "You ready, Little Bit?"

She smiled. "We finally get to go to work. Kick ass time!"

Janet shook her head at Jersey's words.

The rubble of downtown Memphis stood stark and silent before them. But to a person, the Rebels could feel eyes on them; feel the white-hot hate directed at them from the unseen eyes.

"Watch out for those manhole covers," Ben said. "The bastards do like to pop up out of them." He looked over at Janet, who had insisted upon coming along with the team, despite Ben's warnings that it wasn't safe and it was going to be bloody and brutal. "Excuse me. *Person*-hole covers."

Janet sighed.

"I like killing creepies," Anna said.

Janet cut her eyes to the teenager. "Child, these people can't help themselves. I'm sure they all came from single-parent homes and many were abused as children. They were also deprived of the childhood toys that others around them had in abundance. They probably were unable to receive adequate hot lunches in school and that affected their ability to learn. This is their way of striking back at what they perceive as an uncaring society.''

Anna stared at the woman. Unwrapped a piece of gum and stuck it in her mouth, chewing for a moment. ''Horseshit!'' she said, then walked off a few yards.

Ben smiled at the brief exchange.

''That is a very impudent child,'' Janet said.

''You and Anna should talk later on,'' Ben told her. ''She could tell you something about a lousy childhood. And something about a fierce drive to better herself without being on the public dole. She's a damn good soldier, too.'' Ben turned and walked into the ground floor of what used to be one of Memphis's largest department stores. His team followed him.

Janet hurried to keep up. She was unarmed, since she didn't believe in the individual owning or carrying of guns, or the use of them against human beings or animals.

''That woman is a ding-a-ling,'' Anna whispered to Ben.

''She's politically liberal,'' Ben returned the whisper.

''Ding-a-ling,'' Anna insisted.

Ben smiled and walked deeper into the darkness of the ground floor of the multi-storied old building.

A very faint odor reached his nostrils as he passed a door that led to a downstairs storage area. Ben paused, sniffed around the edges of the closed door, then stepped back, pointing at the door. Cooper and Beth took grenades from their battle harness and stood ready as Ben put his hand on the doorknob.

''Whatever in the world are you going to do?'' Janet asked.

''Make boom-boom,'' Anna told her.

"There may be innocent people down there!"

"If they are, they're being prepared for serving as appetizers," Jersey told her. "Now get the hell out of the way."

"Pull the pins," Ben said, then jerked open the door.

The fire-frag grenades were tossed into the darkness. Ben slammed the door closed and jumped behind cover, jerking Janet to the floor behind a counter with him.

The door blew off its hinges and brought with it the agonizing cries of men and women whose flesh had just been shredded and peppered with shrapnel. Cooper used his Squad Automatic Weapon to spray the shrieking and stinking darkness below. The howling stopped and only the smell remained.

In the rubble of what was once downtown Memphis, a battleground suddenly erupted as creeps opened fire on the Rebels.

Cooper bi-podded his SAW and bellied down, an extra can of ammunition beside him, as the others took up tight defensive positions in the old department store.

"That was horribly brutal," Janet said to Ben.

"Write your Congressman," Ben told her. "Excuse me—Congress-*person.*"

"All units now coming under attack," Corrie reported. "Rebels at the MASH stations holding."

"Let us rock and roll," Ben said with a smile.

Janet looked at him and shook her head.

The ground floor of the littered and rubbled old department store turned into a battle zone as robed creeps literally began coming out of the woodwork, pouring onto the floor in stinking screaming bunches.

Ben and his team, working out of a defensive circle,

laid down a blistering wall of fire that stopped the charging creeps hot and dying in their own blood.

Janet lay on the dirty and littered floor, both hands over her ears.

Ben and Beth began tossing grenades while Corrie, Cooper, Jersey, and Anna poured on the fire-power from weapons set on full automatic.

The attack broke off as suddenly as it began.

"Out, out, out!" Ben yelled. "Corrie, advise all units to fall back. Get out of the downtown district."

When all units were clear, Ben said, "Now call in air strikes. HE and napalm. Blow it up and burn it down."

"You don't mean that!" Janet said.

"Watch me," Ben replied.

In their stinking lairs, in basements and other underground caverns all over the city, the Night People waited, knowing full well what was coming at them next. They knew Ben Raines's tactics as well as he knew theirs.

The Rebels backed off, threw a thin and gappy defensive circle around the city, with the Mississippi as one stop-gap, and let the P-51E's and the attack helicopters have a field day.

When the planes and choppers would finish a run, Ben would order his tanks and SP and towed artillery to hammer the city. The air bombardment went on all day and the ground artillery all night, until what had been left of Memphis was in total ruins or on fire.

Ben then stationed snipers all over the city to shoot down any creep who might crawl out from under the ruins. If a hole leading underground was found, the Rebels dropped satchel charges down it or blew up any wall or half-building close by, forever sealing the tunnel.

"There were street gangs of young people in that city," Janet said, putting accusing green eyes on Ben.

"Not anymore," Ben told her.

When the Rebels pulled into Memphis, much of the city was rubble. This time when they pulled out of Memphis, they left behind them a downtown that was in smoking ruins. They left the airport runways and the tower intact. Ben armed several hundred of the survivors he'd found on the outskirts and they immediately began cleaning up and clearing out a subdivision and small mall just south of the city.

"Forget the city," Ben told the group. "We've got to go back to the land if we're ever going to pull this nation out of the ashes of ruin. You'll be in constant communication with Base Camp One and resupplied as you need it. Good luck."

Much to Ben's surprise, Janet House-Lewiston elected to go with the Rebels.

"It's the safest I've felt in a long time," she told him. "And you may take that as a compliment if you wish."

But before the Rebels pulled out, Ben had received some sobering and sad news from Cecil.

"Mexico and Central America just blew wide open, Ben. South America is in chaos. Civil war is raging in every country south of our borders. It'll take Europe years to get back on its feet, and God only knows how it will end south of us. Here in the SUSA, I have issued emergency currency and declared the old dollar worthless. Every one of our residents who held those old dollars was reimbursed. But that will stop the outlaws from using the money they stole here. We're not quite back to where we started from. I can see some light at the end of the tunnel. And Ben, I recalled our troops from Europe. We need them here in case of another attack. The Europeans said they could take it from this point and wished us good luck and thanks."

"Fine with me, Cec. It'll be good to have them home. As for the luck, we're going to need all we can get."

"There is more, Ben. Those three American reporters you got along with so well in Europe are back. They left here yesterday by resupply convoy. Should be catching up with you in a couple of days."

"Cassie Phillips, Nils Wilson, and Frank Service?"

"That's them."

"That's fine with me, but who are they reporting for?"

"Our newspapers down here," Cecil said with a laugh.

"Sounds good. Any word on Simon Border's boy, Bobby Day?"

"He's back with Simon. He's working on Simon's newspaper, *The Voice Of Reason.*"

"Shit! Voice of reason, my aching ass."

Cecil laughed.

"You have any more good news you want to share, Cec?"

"I believe that's enough for one day, buddy. Ol' Black Joe out."

"Ol' Black Joe?" Janet questioned, standing close to Ben.

"It's Cecil's idea of a joke. He finds it amusing."

"It's macabre."

Ben shrugged that away. He had found that if Janet even had a sense of humor, she kept it well-hidden. Ben had discovered years back that most left-wing liberals were the most humorless people on the face of the earth . . . at least to his way of thinking.

The long Rebel column took Highway 51 out of Memphis, heading toward Kentucky, traveling slowly, carefully checking each town and village along the way. The gangs that had invaded the SUSA had seemingly dropped off the face of the earth. Ray Brown, Carrie Walker, Tommy Monroe, and Dave Holton would not hesitate to attack lightly armed civilians, but they wanted nothing to do with Ben Raines. They, and every member of their gangs, knew that Ben would kill them with no more emotion than if he'd squashed a roach. Scouts had been unable to find a trace of the gangs.

But Mike Richards, head of Rebel intel, had learned something that really came as no big surprise to Ben.

"The gangs are working, albeit indirectly, for Simon Border," Mike reported one hot summer's day. "I know we suspected it all along, but now I have concrete proof."

"And their main objective is to kill me," Ben finished it.

"That's it, Ben. With you out of the way, Simon's thinking is the Rebels would fall apart."

"That just proves what a fool he is. He can't seem to realize that the Rebel movement is far more than mere flesh and blood. It's a philosophy that will never die. Killing me would accomplish nothing. Hell, it would make me a martyr."

1 Batt was bivouacked near what was left of the town of Union City, just a few miles south of the Kentucky border. The gangs of punks and thugs and rabble had hit the town hard, leaving much of it in ruin. No resident had returned. It was a silent ghost town, utterly devoid of life. The Rebels could not find any evidence of a mass grave, so they had to assume the people had just fled when the gangs poured across the border.

Mike had nothing to add to Ben's last statement. He

sipped his coffee in silence. But Ben knew the man had something on his mind. Mike would get to it, sooner or later.

After eating a sandwich and working on another cup of coffee, Mike finally said, "Ben, don't you think it's time you got out of the field?"

Ben smiled and said nothing.

"Ben, you're a middle-aged man. You're the Commanding General of the most powerful army on the face of the earth. CGs don't lead combat patrols."

Ben had risen to walk over to the ever-present coffee pot. He turned and looked at Mike. "Is this your idea, Mike?"

"Not entirely. A lot of the troops would like to see you slow down."

Ben laughed. "Oh, yeah. Right. Well, I bet you I can name most of those so-called 'troops.' Ike, Cecil, Danjou, West, Nick, Georgi, Buck—"

Mike held up a hand. "OK, OK. So you can name them. But they do have a valid point."

"Mike, Georgi is the same age I am. Ike is about the same age. Dan isn't far behind us. Hell, we're all getting older. You're no spring chicken."

"I'm not the supreme commander, Ben."

"Cecil is the elected supreme commander, Mike."

"On paper." Mike tossed the very true words at Ben. "The troops follow you, Ben. They always have, they always will. And you can't argue that."

Ben made no attempt to argue it. He knew it was true. "Mike . . . I'm not a politician. Never have been, never will be. I'm too blunt. I don't like to tell lies and try to fool the people. I'm a soldier. I'm happy in the field. I'd be miserable out of it. When I become a liability in the field, nobody will have to tell me. I'll voluntarily remove myself. End of discussion. I hope."

Mike nodded his head in understanding and lifted his coffee mug in a salute.

After a moment, Ben asked, "Where the hell did all the people go, Mike?"

"Good question. My personal thought on the matter is that they scattered in small groups. They've living on cold rations and keeping their heads down until they see which way the wind is going to blow."

"Millions of them?"

"Who really knows how many people survived the Great War and the time after it? Our own people are having to revise our figures every week. And how many people were killed by the rabble and the punks while we were over in Europe?"

"They've got to be networking some way."

"Short quick bursts on CBs, probably. Hell, Ben, they know a power play is going on between you and Simon Border. Even those who are aligned with us don't want to get caught up in the middle of it. The others—the majority of them—have sensed that you're planning on pulling this nation back together and they don't want any part of Rebel rule." Mike looked long at Ben. "A hard question, Ben?"

"Go ahead."

"Are we really going to try to heal the entire nation? And if so, what happens to the SUSA?"

Several seconds passed before Ben answered. And when he did, it wasn't what any Rebel wanted to hear. "I don't know, Mike. I just don't know."

Chapter Fourteen

Slowly, slowly the Rebels were driving the punks and thugs and the looking-for-something-for-nothing crowd out of the territory known as the SUSA. Most went voluntarily, but more than a few elected to fight. Those who went under their own steam crossed the borders with their lives. Those who chose to fight were buried (when enough of their bodies could be found) in unmarked graves and forgotten. One by one, the batt coms began radioing in that their sectors were clear.

Now Ben had some hard decisions to make. He flew back to Base Camp One and met with former President Blanton and Cecil. Ben was never one to beat around the bush. "Decision time, folks. Do we try to heal the entire nation? Can we? Will it work?"

"That part of the nation not under the control of Simon Border, you mean?" Cecil asked.

"For the time being, yes. But sooner or later we'll have to fight him."

"Cecil has discussed this subject with me many times in the weeks you've been gone," Homer said. He smiled. "It may surprise you to learn that I take a more conservative stance than Cecil on this issue. My reply would be a very cautious yes. Selected states only. The rest would have to wait."

That startled Ben. He stared at the former president of the United States, at one time, the most liberal president ever elected.

Homer said, "It is my opinion that the cost in Rebel lives would be too great."

Ben cut his eyes to Cecil. "And you, Cec?"

Cecil nodded his head in at least partial agreement with Blanton. "Homer and I did agree that the final decision should be yours, Ben. I've already sensed that you want to start a clean-up. But do it slowly and stay out of Simon Border's territory. Let's don't try to bring any more states into the SUSA, but just prop up the ones east of the river and see if they can stand alone. During that time, we'll be finishing up getting our own house in order and keeping a careful eye to the west."

Ben slowly nodded his head. "All right. It's a go, then. But I want you both to realize that it is going to take two or three years."

"Or longer," Cecil said.

"And during that restoration period," Homer said, "I can be spending some time in Europe, strengthening our ties over there. We just might have to ask for their help, for a change."

Ben said, "China remains an unknown. So does Russia." He paused and smiled a soldier's smile. "Israel has taken care of the militant Arab movement. At least that part of the world is relatively quiet."

"The grave usually is," Homer said, very, very drily. "But we all knew that was coming."

Ben said, "When I heard what had taken place over there, it reminded me of a bumper sticker I saw some years back: Nuke their ass and take the gas."

"And they did." Cecil put an end to that.

"Cecil has something else to say to you, Ben," Homer said, cutting his eyes to Cecil.

"Oh?"

Cecil said, "I know you'll never leave the field, Ben. And I also know that my dream of getting back into the field was just a dream. My job is here. But I will keep my 22 Batt intact, here. As other Rebels get hurt or have to retire from the field, I'll use them as replacements for 22 Batt. It's a strange way to run an army, but, hell, the Rebels aren't known for doing things the conventional way."

"Give some thought to this, gentlemen," Ben said. "Sooner or later, we're going to have to deal with Bruno Bottger. Simon Border is an asshole, true enough. But Bottger is the real threat to world stability. We know now that he controls the entire southern half of Africa. His factories, manufacturing the machinery of war, are running around the clock, seven days a week." Ben again smiled, but this time it was a savage curving of the lips. "However, I have a plan to slow him down; drop a few flies in his ointment, so to speak."

Both Homer and Cecil leaned forward, Homer asking, "Want to share it with us?"

"I thought you'd never ask."

* * *

In a very remote corner of Base Camp One, carefully guarded from any unwelcome eyes, three hundred African-American volunteers from the Rebel army were going back to school. They were going to learn some of the languages and dialects, customs and dress of their ancestors. They were studying the topographies of Africa. When they "graduated," so to speak, they were also going to be experts in the use of explosives, sabotage, all manner of weapons, guerrilla warfare, and the politics of democracy.

Every mission had to have a code name to work under. A black company commander who had volunteered for the assignment, and who also possessed a wicked sense of humor, came up with a suggestion: Ebony.

Project Ebony was born.

From Kentucky to the Carolina coast, the Rebels were poised to start the push north. Ben had lined them up numerically, with his 1 Batt in far western Kentucky, and Buck Taylor's 15 Batt's right flank overlooking the Atlantic Ocean. Ben had placed Therm's 19 Batt in the center of the line, about two miles to the rear, right behind Pat O'Shea's 10 Batt. Therm's short battalion, which would be the central hub of all communications and logistics, was protected by two full companies of combat-hardened Rebels, beefed up by tanks and helicopter gunships.

Finally Ben had, after giving the matter a lot of thought, named Emil Hite as recreational director of the SUSA.

"What the hell is a recreational director supposed to do, Ben?" Cecil had asked.

"He's going to inspect playground equipment all over the SUSA."

"Do you know how long it's going to take Emil to figure out this is a bullshit job?"

"Long enough for me to get several hundred miles to the north," Ben replied. "I hope."

"And in the meantime, I'm stuck with him."

Ben laughed. "That's what friends are for."

"Seems like we did this once before," Ben muttered, just moments before push-off time. "I wonder how many more times we'll have to do it?"

Corrie knew he did not expect a reply.

Ben glanced at his watch. 0557.

Everyone except Corrie was in the wagon. She stood by Ben's side, ready to radio the orders to move out.

0558.

The air was filled with the stink of fumes from rumbling engines.

The Rebels waited.

0559.

"Far Eyes reports no opposition for twenty-five miles straight in," Corrie reported. "South to north and west to east."

Ben glanced at his watch. "Let's do it, Corrie."

"What they found were fires," Corrie said softly.

Ben looked at her. "Say again?"

"Fires, boss. The retreating punks are setting everything they can on fire."

"Son-of-a-bitch!" Ben cussed. "Corrie, get every available plane and chopper we have up here ASAP. Odd-numbered battalions strip down to shelter tarps, light arms, field rations, and all the ammo they can stagger with. We've got to get behind those punks. The armor assigned to those battalions will make the push with the even-numbered battalions . . . and not ahead of them. Get cracking, Corrie."

Ben looked at Jersey, sitting in the wagon. "How do you feel about jumping, Jersey?" he kidded her, knowing full well how much she disliked it.

"Shit!" Jersey said.

The push-off was delayed until noon, when all odd-numbered battalions, or portions of them, could be boarded and in the air. As many as possible of those Rebels who were jump-qualified (and that was just about all of them) chuted up and made ready to go out the door, while smaller planes flew ahead and dropped ground controllers and pathfinders to set up the DZs and secure them.

Back at the various staging areas, which in Ben's case had been moved south to an old military base, it was organized chaos. The officers were yelling at the sergeants and the sergeants yelled at everybody, including the officers.

"It's President Jefferys on the blower for you, Boss," Corrie yelled at Ben. She had to yell to be heard over the roar of plane engines.

"Tell him I don't have the time right now. I'll get back to him in about two hours." Ben smiled. "By that time we'll be on the ground," he muttered.

"President Jefferys says if you jump in with your battalion, he's going to have you court-martialed," Corrie shouted.

"Tell him to go shit in his hat!" Ben yelled. "Come on, Corrie. Get your gear on and let's go!"

"I'm going to tell the President to go shit in his hat?" Corrie muttered. "Yeah. Sure I am."

Once airborne, it did not take long to reach the DZ.

Equipment checked and static lines hooked, Ben moved toward the open door, waiting for the light to pop on. The rush of cold air quickly dried the sweat on his body.

Ben looked at Jersey, standing right behind him. He grinned at her. She solemnly nodded her head. Jersey was not at all thrilled about jumping out of airplanes.

Ben knew he was getting just a bit too old for this. And he was well aware that once a person reached forty years of age, there were only two kinds of jumps: those that hurt a little and those that hurt a lot.

The red light blinked on.

"Stand in the door!" the jumpmaster yelled.

Ben shuffled to the open door. He would be the first one out.

Seconds ticked past. The green light blinked on.

The jumpmaster slapped Ben on the leg. "Go, General!"

Ben stepped out into a thousand or so feet of big empty. The static line jerked his chute out and Ben grunted from the opening shock. He looked up to see if his chute was full and no panels blown. The ground was coming up fast. Seemed to him back when he made his first jump, the ground didn't come up at him this fast. He had time for a quick smile. Of course, that had been thirty years back. He spilled a little air to avoid landing in trees, and with his feet together he let his equipment bag drop from the fifteen-foot tether and then made contact with the ground, relaxing and rolling. It had been a perfect drop. He still hurt. He was getting too damn old for this. He popped his harness and was on his feet, working fast to gather up his chute and then get his gear together.

As he almost always did when weight was a factor, Ben had left his old Thompson behind and was carrying an M-16—a CAR. The weapon was lighter and so was the ammo, so he could carry more of it.

Ben looked all around him. Everyone was down and appeared to be OK.

The Combat Control Team, or Ground Controllers (still called pathfinders by some) had come out of hiding and joined up with the main body.

"Find the enemy and let's get this dance started," Ben said to Corrie.

Corrie radioed the orders and the Combat Control Team and Scouts took off at a trot.

"Goddamnit, Jersey!" Cooper yelled. "Hold still. I'm trying to get you untangled."

Ben looked at the scene a dozen yards away and laughed. Jersey was on the ground, all tangled up in the silk, the shroud cords and the risers, cussing a blue streak.

Ben helped clear Jersey and get the tiny Rebel to her boots. "Shit!" Jersey hollered. "I *hate* jumpin' out of airplanes!"

"Gather around me!" Ben shouted. "Corrie, tell that platoon leader if he doesn't stop blowing that goddamn whistle the only way he's going to be able to blow it is when he farts!"

Corrie relayed the orders, changing the terminology just a little bit.

The whistle stopped. Abruptly.

"Anybody hurt?" Ben yelled.

A few scratches, a few bruises, one sore back (he landed out of position, feet wide apart), and one twisted ankle.

"Pilots reporting the enemy about four miles south of our position," Corrie said. "A large group in various types of vehicles. Traveling northeast, heading our way on Highway 45 and the old parkway. What was left of Mayfield is burning."

Ben looked at a map. "They won't try to invade Missouri, and they can't cross the river at Cairo or Paducah; those bridges are out." He placed a finger on the map. "That's where they'll try to cross. We need as many of those vehicles as we can salvage, so let's do this ambush right."

The terrain was perfect, rolling hills and brush that had not been cut back in years. The battalion got into place, with snipers carefully positioned to take out the drivers first.

"This bunch is led by a woman," Scouts radioed. "We grabbed a couple of stragglers and they were more than willing to talk to us."

"I just bet they were," Ben muttered. He did not ask if the stragglers were still alive.

"Name is Carrie Walker." The Scout began winding down his verbal report. "And she is a bad one. ETA your position is two minutes."

In the cold impersonal words of a written report,

the ambush would be: Highly successful with maximum casualties inflicted upon enemy with minimum injuries to Rebel forces.

In other words, the Rebels shot the shit out of the punks.

The punks and thugs and street slime had not seen the planes as they approached the DZ, for the pilots had flown miles out of their way to avoid flying over the area controlled by Carrie Walker's gang, coming up to the DZ from the west, instead of the south. The punks saw a couple of planes returning, but that meant nothing to them.

They drove unsuspecting into a deadly ambush.

The Rebels took out the drivers first, and when the punks began jumping out of the cars and trucks in a wild panic, the Rebels cut them down, coldly and efficiently. For the most part, the Rebels finished it, then and there. They did not have the medical people nor supplies to adequately treat many wounded—other than their own—so it was much more humane to end it permanently rather than let any mortally wounded linger for hours in terrible pain.

Carrie Walker was only slightly injured, when her driver had his brains splattered all over the upholstery, the car had slewed off the road and into a ditch. Carrie's head had hit the dashboard, cutting her forehead and knocking her goofy for a few minutes.

She now found herself with her hands tied behind her back, facing Ben Raines.

Carrie was an attractive woman, in her mid-thirties. But her eyes were cold and cruel and her mouth set in what appeared to be a permanent snarl. She glared defiantly at Ben.

"We'll skip the social amenities," Ben told her. "I know who you are and you know who I am. And I imagine you've got a pretty good idea what is going to happen to you. Do you have anything to say?"

"Fuck you, Ben Raines!"

"Not terribly original." Ben leaned back in the old kitchen chair in the dusty living room of an abandoned farmhouse and looked at the woman. "Oh, come on, Carrie. You mean you're not going to tell me about your tragic childhood, or how you don't know right from wrong, or how you were molested by your cousin as a child, or how you were traumatized by a police officer when you were a teenager, or some such shit as that?"

She spat at Ben, the spittle landing on the scarred old table he was using as a desk. "If I did, would that make much difference to you?"

"Not a bit, Carrie. Because I don't buy any of it. Never have, never will."

"Me and my gang sure fucked up your little playhouse down south, didn't we?" she asked proudly.

"Oh, for a very brief time. We'll get back to normal before long. But you'll be dead and in the ground. So what did you accomplish?"

It slowly began to dawn on the gang leader that Ben was going to have her shot. Ben watched her face change as the realization struck home. Carrie jumped as a volley of shots rang out a few hundred yards to the left of the old house. She said, "Hey, man! That was . . ." Her voice failed her.

"Some of your followers, Carrie. I've declared martial law. Resist us in any way, commit crimes against the general populace, and you die. Those leaflets were dropped all over the nation, weeks ago. You can read. You knew we were coming."

"Say, uh, you wouldn't, like, uh, maybe gimme one more chance, would you?"

"No. We've questioned several of your gang. I know your history."

"Look here, General," the woman whose life's work had been one of all manners of crimes against society blurted, as she began to panic. "I got rights, you know? I mean, like, man, I got a right to a lawyer and a trial and all that shit. If I'm convicted, I got a right to appeal the sentence."

Ben slowly shook his head. "You have nothing, Carrie. You have only what I choose to give you, and I am not in a very charitable frame of mind. You see, I lost a lot of good friends down in Base Camp One. I understand you personally castrated one Rebel officer and left him to bleed to death."

She sighed. "I could give you names, General. I mean . . ."

"I know all the names, Carrie." Ben read from a clipboard. "Ray Brown, Tommy Monroe, Dave Holton, Sandy Allen, Dale Jones, Hal and Robin Ford, Karen Carr, Fred LaBelle, Beth Aleman, Jack Brittain, Les Justice, Thad Keel, Foster Payne, Craig Franklin . . . Do you want me to continue?"

"How? I mean, like, there ain't no law. No computers workin.' How'd you get all those names?"

But Ben would only smile at her. Sort of. "We have religious people with us, Carrie. Do you want to speak to a minister, a priest, or a rabbi?"

"Fuck, no."

Ben held out his hand and Beth gave him another

clipboard. He glanced at it for a moment, then lifted his eyes to hers. "Some of your people were more than happy to speak to us, Carrie. You have tortured innocent civilians in ways that would be the envy of the Spanish Inquisition. You've murdered entire families and laughed and bragged about doing it. The list of things that you've done is disgusting and perverted and evil. Do you deny any of it?"

"Would that do me any good?"

"No."

"Then . . . *fuck you, Ben Raines!*" she screamed. "Hell, no. I don't deny any of it. I had a hell of a lot of fun. So go ahead, shoot me. I don't give a damn."

"OK," Ben said.

Chapter Fifteen

The men and women of 1 Batt waited until the trucks carrying the earth movers arrived, and then watched as the bodies of the Walker gang, including Carrie, were buried in a mass grave. The chaplains with the battalion played hi-lo with a deck of cards to see who would get the duty of speaking a few words over the grave.

The rabbi lost.

"Shit!" he said, then composed himself. "I'll say a silent prayer."

"Make it brief," Ben told him.

"Thank you."

The transports caught up with the Rebels who had jumped in and the Rebels headed north for a day's fast run, then started spreading out west to east, blocking all major arteries with troops and armor, throwing up a line that stretched for several hundred miles. The easternmost odd-numbered battalion cut due south and met up with the easternmost even-numbered battalion who had turned north. There were gaps in the line, big ones, some of them running for miles, but the gaps were open meadows, swamp and marsh land, nearly impenetrable forests thick with underbrush, rocky ravines, and a couple of mountain ranges. Those areas were patrolled by helicopter gun ships and fixed-wing planes.

With no way to cross the Mississippi River, the punks found themselves in a box. A very deadly box.

The Rebels waited.

The three reporters, Nils, Cassie, and Frank, had driven up to the southern front, along with Janet House-Lewiston. They were stopped at Ike's 2 Batt HQ and not allowed to go any further. Ike patiently explained to Janet why that had to be.

"Why don't you call for them to surrender?" she asked, wondering why Cassie, Nils, and Frank suddenly rolled their eyes in disbelief.

"They had their chance to do that," Ike told her. "They had several weeks to do that."

Janet's eyes narrowed. "What are you saying, Ike?"

"I'm saying, lady, that we don't take many prisoners. Not after they've been offered surrender terms time and again, and continue to fight us and go on raping and torturing and murdering civilians."

Janet took a deep breath and Ike sighed patiently. "But these gang members aren't Night People. They aren't cannibals. They're human beings who took a wrong turn, that's all. They deserve a chance at life."

"Stay out of matters that don't concern you, lady," Ike warned her.

"But this does concern me! This should be the concern of all decent human beings everywhere. I overheard someone saying that after the ambush, General Raines had prisoners. If he can take prisoners, why can't you?''

Ike stared at her for a moment. "Ben doesn't have them anymore, lady."

"What do you mean? I distinctly heard that soldier—" She stopped mid-sentence as she finally grasped Ike's coldly spoken words. Her mouth dropped open in shock.

"Close your mouth, lady," Ike told her. "It's summertime. You might swallow a bug."

Janet quickly closed her mouth and glared at Ike. She finally found her voice. "Are you telling me that General Raines actually *executed* those people?"

"That's right, lady."

"That is . . . *monstrous!*"

"No, lady. That's justice." Ike turned and walked away.

Janet whirled around to face the reporters. "Do you people condone this . . . this barbarism?"

Nils Wilson shrugged his shoulders. "I had a buddy used to say that when in Rome, do as the Rumanians do."

The three reporters walked away, leaving Janet trying to figure that one out.

The Rebels began nailing the lid on the box. Each day, the Rebels would move forward several miles, closing the gap, squeezing tighter and tighter.

Many of the trapped punks panicked and tried to break free. Rebel snipers, using custom-made .50 caliber sniper rifles, stopped them dead . . . literally. Others were caught out in the open by helicopter gunships and chopped up by machine gun and cannon fire.

At night, Rebel Scouts and special operations people went head-hunting, with silenced weapons, knives, and garottes. At first they brought back ears as proof of their kills, until Ben got word of it and told them to knock it off.

A few thugs were taken prisoner and allowed to live— a very few. And then only after they had cooperated fully with the Rebel questioners. The prisoners named many names and told of many atrocities committed.

The Rebels also learned that many gang leaders and their followers had slipped out of the state before the Rebels sprung their ambushes and closed the box, including Ray Brown and his large gang of punks. The Rebels had trapped and were about to eliminate several thousand gang members, but many of the top leaders had slipped out and gotten away.

Corrie glanced at Ben's face one morning and reached for her mic. She knew Ben had lost his patience with the thugs remaining in the box.

"Finish it," Ben said.

Had there been any liberal media types around, they would have called it carnage. Political middle-of-the-roaders and conservatives would have called it justice. The murderers and rapists and child molesters and assorted thugs and street slime caught in the box were dealt with swiftly and with typical Rebel efficiency. Janet House-Lewiston was shocked right down to her toes.

"Mass graves!" she wailed. "That isn't Christian."

"Neither were the crimes they committed," a Rebel told her.

*   *   *

Simon Border looked at the dispatch just handed him and frowned. The SUSA had been cleared, for the most part, of criminals. It had taken the Rebels approximately four months to do it. Simon had been certain it would had take them at least a couple of years to accomplish that.

"Are we next?" one of Simon's generals asked.

Simon shook his head. "No. Ben Raines will keep his word as long as I keep mine. Whatever else he may be, the man is honorable. He won't attack us without provocation. And I don't intend to provoke him." Simon smiled and added, "Yet."

"The man is a barbarian," one of Simon's church elders said. "He and his Rebels are worse than the Vikings. Only the Lord God Almighty knows what they do with women when they sweep through a village."

"They rape and pillage and burn," another of Simon's church elders said. "They're savages."

"Amen, Brother Carl," another church leader said.

Simon knew better, but he let his people talk. This coming Sunday morning, all over the territory Simon controlled, his ministers would be denouncing Ben Raines and the Rebels from pulpits, verbally whipping the congregation into a frenzy against Ben Raines, spreading lies and half-truths all mingled with the word of God.

Just as Ben Raines had succeeded in setting up his SUSA, Simon had succeeded in establishing his own form of government west of the Mississippi. And it was all in accordance with the teachings found right in the

Bible . . . in how Simon and his elders interpreted the Bible, that is.

In Simon Border's country, there were no abortion clinics, for abortion was not allowed for any reason. There were no offensive books; all reading material first had to be approved by a blue-nosed, tight-lipped, and narrow-minded censorship board. Nothing but G-rated movies were allowed to be shown in the few theaters open and on the TV stations. Music was heavily censored; only the classics were allowed, with a few exceptions, and that included music played in one's home. Homosexuality was punishable by death. Any man or woman who strayed into the fleshy adventures of promiscuity had his or her head shaved, was stood up and pointed out in church, and was shunned for an appropriate time. School days began and ended with a lengthy prayer, and Bible study was a course that every student took, in every grade. Divorce was frowned upon and actual divorces were rare indeed. Church attendance was mandatory, every Sunday and Sunday evening, and on Wednesday nights the services could run for hours, with the preachers ranting and raving and sometimes speaking in tongues (depending upon the church). Men worked, the women stayed home and took care of the children, cooking the meals and cleaning the house, subservient to the men at all times. (God said that was the way it should be, said so right in the Bible—sort of.) Women were not allowed to wear any type of revealing clothing and when swimming, men were separated from the women. When a husband and wife made love, only the missionary position was allowed (although just how Simon enforced that was a mystery to all outside his territory). Grunting and groaning and moaning and shrieking out one's joy in the act was not allowed (people were urged to keep an ear open for any violation of the rule by their neighbors).

"Fucking sedately, I suppose that would be called," Ben said, after reading the rules set forth by Simon Border.

In Simon Border territory, newspapers reported only good things—unless Mrs. Jones was caught fucking Mr. Smith. Such an abomination had to be reported so all the good people would know. For shame, for shame!

The religious far right had finally succeeded in setting up their own restrictive form of government.

"If your mommie is a commie, turn her in," Ben said with a smile, after finishing his reading of just how Simon Border ran his government.

"What the hell is the missionary position?" Jersey asked, looking up from the lengthy rules and regulations that residents of Simon Border's territory had to follow.

"I will be only too glad to show you," Cooper said quickly.

Jersey cut her dark eyes to Cooper. "Forget it, Coop. I'll figure it out."

"Man on top, woman on the bottom," Ben said, before Cooper could get himself in trouble.

Jersey looked at him. "That's it?"

"The singing of 'Onward Christian Soldiers' is optional, I suppose," Ben said with a smile.

"Raines, you are disgraceful," Doctor Chase said, entering the old house where Ben had set up his CP. "You should be ashamed of yourself."

"Oh, I am, Lamar. I am. What do you want?"

"Fresh vaccines will be here in a couple of hours. Have you decided when we start the next push?"

"Might as well do it in the morning," Ben said, standing up and stretching. "Let's see how the people outside the SUSA receive us."

Ben's battalion crossed over into Southern Illinois. They were not met with open arms by the survivors, but then no one shot at them, either. For the first twenty or so miles, anyway.

"The punks came through here and stripped our gardens of everything," a local told Ben. "Took everything me and the wife had canned for the winter."

"We'll see that you get rations to last you through the winter," Ben told him. "Our field rations might not be the tastiest things in the world, but they will keep you alive."

The man was looking over that part of the convoy he could see. "You got all kinds of folks in your army, General. We were told you were operating some kind of racist place down south."

"Whoever told you that lied. Racism isn't allowed in the SUSA. You have a trade before the Great War?"

"I did whatever was necessary to feed the bulldog, General. I'm a good farmer. I can weld, lay brick, and I'm a good mechanic. Why do you ask?"

"We've got millions of acres of the most fertile land in the world just waiting for a plow. Down in the SUSA, we have electricity, running water, proper sewerage, newspapers, radio and TV, a valid currency, shops and stores. And we don't have many rules and regulations.

We're a common sense society. You know what I mean by that?''

"Sure. Man puts up a 'No Trespassing' sign on his property, stay the hell off of it. Man has a closed gate, that means he wants to keep it closed. If it's locked, don't climb over it unless you want the shit shot out you." He smiled. "That about the meat of it, General?"

Ben laughed. "I believe you hit the high points, yes. You interested in relocating?"

"Damn right!"

"You know some others who might be interested?"

"Just about everybody I know."

"Get them together. How about a meeting tomorrow morning?"

"Suits me. Where?"

"Over where we'll be bivouacked. We won't be hard to find."

The man looked at the miles-long column. "Sure won't," he muttered.

"See you in the morning," Ben said. He smiled as the man walked away. "I'll repopulate the SUSA while I'm helping the good folks who live outside of our boundaries."

"You mean," Corrie said, "you'll move the cream of the crop down to the SUSA and leave the rest."

"Why, Corrie." Ben feigned great indignation. "You would actually accuse me of doing something underhanded like that?"

Ben smiled as his team roared with laughter.

Chapter Sixteen

"In the SUSA," Ben told the gathering of men and women, some one hundred or more, "you control your own destiny to a very large degree. Much more so than the old government, Republican or Democrat, would ever let you. In the SUSA, the government is not your nanny, nor will it ever be. We have very few rules and regulations. Because we have so few government agencies, our taxes are very low, and the tax system is very simple. We don't have police—not like you're accustomed to having. And we damn sure don't have secret police, prowling around in your lives. We don't have anything that even vaguely resembles the FBI, the Secret Service, the ATF, Postal Inspectors, investigators from OSHA, HUD, IRS, or POOP, CRAP, or FART . . ."

Ben waited until the applause and laughter had died down.

"There is no bloated bureaucracy in the SUSA. Agents from the government will not be sneaking and snooping around your property checking to see if you have some sort of assault rifle with a bayonet lug—because you damn sure will have at least one—and it will be fully automatic. Every adult living in the SUSA is part of the home guard and is expected to help defend the SUSA if or when the time comes. If that is something you do not wish to be a part of, then you may leave this meeting now and I respect your decision."

Four men and four women got up and walked away.

Ben said, "In the SUSA, our laws are based on common sense. That's why it is so difficult for some to understand life there. If you're constantly sticking your lip into someone else's business, you won't make it there. If you choose to ignore warning signs posted on someone's property, don't try life in the SUSA, because somebody will bury you there. If you get drunk and get behind the wheel of a vehicle and kill some innocent person, the charge is automatic—it isn't vehicular homicide, it's murder. We've had three drive-by shootings in the SUSA. The people who did the shootings were hanged. The investigation, arrest, trial, and execution took about ten days in each case. We're not interested in niceties or legal technicalities in the SUSA. Burn a cross on someone's yard in the SUSA and that property owner will step outside and shoot you and everybody gathered there with you. And nothing will be done to the person who pulls the trigger on the trespassers. My rights end at your property line, your rights end at mine."

Three couples shook their heads, got up, and left the group.

Ben waited until they had left the meeting area and said, "Our laws are few, but they are set in granite.

Don't come down there expecting to change them, because you'll fail. We take care of the very old, the very young, and the infirm. We love our pets and we take care of them. If you don't like animals, you better stay out of the SUSA."

Two couples got up and left. Ben watched them go with a slight smile on his lips.

He said, "If you're a whiner or a complainer, stay out of the SUSA. If you want a free ride, go somewhere else. If your neighbor has an unwanted pregnancy and chooses abortion, that's her business, and none of yours or mine. We don't have strikes or work slow-downs in the SUSA. Everyone is on an equal footing there, so we don't have such things as affirmative action programs. You will not be promoted simply because of your race or gender. Any position in the armed forces is open to qualified people. As you have probably already noticed, women serve in combat positions in the Rebel Army— and no bullshit about it is tolerated. Our schools teach fact, not fiction. We stress education, not who can run the fastest or throw a ball the hardest or farthest. In the SUSA, we know the difference between a hero and an athlete. Games are fun to play and watch. But they are just games. Not important. Anyone who would fight over the outcome of a game or a referee's call is an idiot and we don't want them in the SUSA."

Four men sitting together got up and walked away, their backs stiff with indignation. "Jockstraps," Ben heard Jersey mutter. "Good riddance."

A number of women in the gathering heard Jersey's comment and smiled. Several men grinned, looked sheepish, and nodded their heads in agreement.

"Don't misunderstand me," Ben said. "We have all

sorts of games in our schools in the SUSA. We just know and stress their level of importance.''

He looked over the faces of the crowd. He guessed about thirty people had left the gathering; about seventy-five remained. Ben pointed to a group of Rebels standing off to one side. ''Those are political officers. They can answer all your questions about the SUSA and the laws we live under. Thank you for listening to me.''

Doctor Lamar Chase fell into step with Ben. ''When did you get here, Lamar?''

''This morning. Early. Ben . . . dammit, you're doing it again.''

Ben stopped and faced him. ''Doing what, Lamar?''

''Don't hand me that, Raines! You're going to repopulate the SUSA with the cream and leave the rest for somebody else to worry about. The slackers and whiners can't or won't live under our laws. Those with a jockstrap mentality can't even understand our laws. And even if they could get it through all that mush in their brains, somebody would shoot them before the first week was out.''

Ben chuckled at the expression on Lamar's face, but said nothing. He knew there was more coming from his old friend.

''Ben, I understand what you're doing. But we can't heal the country this way.''

Ben moved them over to the shade of a huge old tree. ''Lamar, for forty-odd years the liberals had control of this nation. They fucked it up seven ways to sundown. They fucked it up so bad it was beyond the point of repair. If the world had not blown up in our faces, millions of American people were on the verge of armed revolution. I will not be a party to that occurring again.

The SUSA will not be inhabited by whiners and second, third and fourth generation welfare families who lay up on their asses and breed like field mice and expect the government to take care of them and their kids. I know that sometimes people are in need of help, and we've never hesitated a second in seeing that they got that help—"

Lamar held up a hand. "Ben, don't get wound up on me. I know that everything you just said is true. But you're talking isolationism."

"That's right, Lamar. But only after we visit every state that is humanly possible to visit and try our damnedest to prop these people up and get them functioning again. And you will have to agree that from what we've seen thus far, that's going to be damn near impossible."

"You know, of course, what they're waiting for."

"Sure I do. They're sitting around with their thumbs up their asses waiting for the *government* to come in and take them by their pretty little hands and make everything all better again. Just like the fucking liberals conditioned them to expect for forty fucking years! The only problem is that there *is* no government."

"Except for us," the doctor said softly.

"That's right, Lamar. Us. And like the old fellow said one time: Us'ins is gonna look out for us'selves."

Ben turned away and walked off.

Ben watched as forty-eight families packed up their meager possessions and headed south, accompanied by a team of Rebels to insure their safe passage into the SUSA.

Ben split his battalion and sent two companies east

to Marion and Harrisburg, while he took two companies and went west to Murphysboro and Carbondale.

Ben did not travel over to his birthplace, just a few miles south of Marion. He did not want to see the burned-out ruins of the house where he and his brothers and sisters had been raised, and where his mother and father had died during the chemical part of the Great War. He had buried his second brother and family in Springfield, and had buried his sister in her backyard in Normal, Illinois. Ben had been forced to kill his older brother in a shoot-out up in the Northwest, after his brother joined a Nazi Party movement and tried to kill Ben.

In both Carbondale and Murphysboro, the survivors had come together and were slowly rebuilding. Only a few families were interested in relocating to the SUSA. The Rebels who had gone to Harrisburg reported the same. And not all the people would allow the Rebel doctors to treat and inoculate them.

"What the hell is the matter with these people?" Ben questioned Doctor Chase.

"They don't trust us," the doctor replied. "But they seem to love the rhetoric put out by Simon Border. I've seen a lot of copies of his newspapers."

"Then let Simon Border come in and give them vaccines," Ben said. "Screw 'em."

The Rebels pulled out. Most of the people in that area seemed glad to see them go. Ben ordered all battalions to split and begin working in a Z-pattern, in order to hit as many towns as possible. Batt coms reported meeting no resistance of any kind as they traveled.

Ben took his two companies and angled over to get a look at what remained of East St. Louis. It was a ruin.

Scouts reported back from working their way close to St. Louis.

"This Issac Africa has troops all along the west side of the river." The Scout smiled. "They do appear to be a mite jumpy. We deliberately let them spot us."

"Let's get out of here," Ben said. "We'll head straight up 55 and investigate the towns that are located no more than twenty or thirty miles east and west of the interstate. Second section get on Interstate 57 and do the same. Continue working the Z-pattern. There is no way humanly possible to hit all the towns, but we'll visit many of them this way. Corrie, get on the horn to Buddy and have his special ops people drop in and clear the airport in Springfield for traffic. We've got to be resupplied. Our Scouts are reporting no signs of any major resistance are expected. But there might be a few creepies around. Those bastards love airports."

"We're going to be in Wisconsin when winter comes," Jersey said, a not-too-happy tone in her voice. "Does it snow much in Wisconsin?"

"Does a bear shit in the woods?" Cooper fired back.

"Wonderful," Jersey muttered. Jersey's early years were spent on a reservation in the Southwest. Winter was not her favorite time of year.

"What's the matter, my little cactus flower?" Cooper asked. "Do you miss your rattlesnakes and gila monsters?"

"No, Cooper. I've got you."

Ben and his two companies began working west to Highway 67 and east to Highway 51. The second section worked from the Indiana state line over to Highway 51. Many of the people refused to receive the inoculations or allow their children to receive them.

"Don't they realize they're putting their children's lives at risk?" Ben asked Chase one evening.

The Rebels were bivouacked in a tiny town about thirty miles south of Springfield, just off Interstate 55. The second section of Rebels were bivouacked about twenty-five miles south of Urbana/-Champaign, just off Interstate 57.

"I believe the further north we go, the cooler the reception is going to be," Chase replied. "Both from the majority of the people and the weather."

"But we'll see more and more of the people working together to rebuild," Ben added. "And that's good. That's what I want. Keep them out of the SUSA."

Lamar laughed. "These are good people up here, Ben. Good, solid, hard-working people."

"Democrats," Ben said sourly.

Lamar had a good laugh out of that.

"It was split pretty even in the last two elections before the Great War, boss," Beth said.

Ben grunted. "The Democrats still carried those states."

"You're impossible, Raines!" Chase said, standing up. "Hell, I voted for the Democratic ticket occasionally."

"So did I," Ben said. "Once."

Chuckling, Doctor Chase left the small house Ben was using for the night.

"This is a fool's errand," Ben said. "Many of the people won't even let us inoculate them. Some run off when they see us. I ought to turn the whole damn business around and head back to the SUSA. Bunker ourselves in and let the rest of the country go right straight to hell. Ungrateful bunch of semi-Socialists."

That got his entire team laughing at him.

Corrie turned to her radio and listened for a moment. "Buddy reporting in, boss."

"Buddy?" Ben stood up and walked to the radio. "I told him to send some special ops people in, not go himself." He keyed the mic. "Go, boy."

"The airport is secure, Eagle. There were a few creeps. We took care of them. Those people left in what remains of the city are in pretty rough shape."

"Any organization?"

"Not that I could see."

"Country people will survive and city people will struggle," Ben muttered. He keyed the mic. "OK, boy. We'll see you tomorrow, late."

"That's ten-four, Eagle."

"We'll drive straight through to Springfield, Corrie. We've got to be resupplied. Bump the others and tell them to start cleaning up the airport at Champaign. When they're resupplied, they're to pull out and check everything east of Highway 51 and north up to Interstate 80, and east to the Indiana line. But stay clear of Chicago. I think we're going to find some crap and crud among the ruins."

"The way we hammered that city, how could there be anything left?" Jersey asked. She shook her head and answered her own question. "But there always is. With the creepies feeding on them," she added with a shudder.

Then Cooper asked what every Rebel had asked at one time or the other. "What the hell is the matter with these people? Why don't they pick up a gun, get organized, and fight?"

Ben smiled. "Because they're waiting for the government to come in and do it for them."

Chapter Seventeen

Buddy met his father's columns on the outskirts of the ruined city, just south of Lake Springfield. "I figure at least five thousand people in the city, Father. And I'm probably short by five thousand."

"And they're doing what, as if I couldn't guess?"

"Nothing. But in areas all around the city, out in the country, people are wrapping up this season's harvest, getting the last produce from their gardens, and are getting ready to kill and butcher hogs. They've organized into groups."

Ben sighed. "OK, gang. Let's go see what we've got in the city."

It was depressing . . . even to Ben. Hundreds of people gathered around the trucks and tanks and Hummers. They were people of all ages and genders and races.

"Shit!" Ben muttered. "Corrie, get our people unassed and push these crowds back so we can set up."

Tanks rumbled up and surrounded Ben's vehicle,

forcing the crowd back. Ben got out and hopped up on a tank. Cooper tossed him a bullhorn.

"Back up," Ben told the crowds. "We'll take care of you all, but you've got to give us room to set up. Now back up, please."

Slowly, grudgingly, the crowds began backing up. Rebels quickly formed a line and began moving them further back. It took the better part of an hour before order was established and the Rebels began setting up medical tents.

"We're going to be here for a few days," Chase said to Ben. "At least."

"Get ready, boss," Beth said. "Here comes Janet House-Lewiston."

"Wonderful," Ben muttered.

"With the reporters," Jersey added.

"I'm overjoyed," Ben said.

"Oh, these poor, poor people!" Janet cried, bursting onto the scene.

"I think I'm going to be sick," Jersey said sarcastically.

"Don't you dare be sick," Ben told her. "And that's an order. I need you here."

"Planes coming in," Corrie called. "ETA ten minutes."

Ben looked at Chase and grinned. "Have fun, Lamar. I'll be out at the airport."

The doctor gave him the finger.

"Everything is shaping up just fine down home, General," one of the pilots told Ben. "Things are pretty much getting back to normal. We're screening and processing about fifty families a day and settling them in."

"President Jefferys's 22 Batt?" Ben asked with a smile.

The pilot laughed and refilled his coffee cup from a thermos. "Now that bunch, General, defies description. I really wouldn't want to mess around much with those ol' boys and gals. They may be getting a little long in the tooth, but they're still rough as hell. They wiped out the last pocket of punks found in our area. And they didn't take any prisoners."

There were six of the big transport planes parked on the tarmac, each plane capable of carrying tons of supplies. Deuce-and-a-halves were lined up, receiving the boxes and crates.

Ben spotted his son, Buddy, and waved him over. "Why don't you round up your special ops people and hitch a ride back with these guys?"

"Oh," Buddy said with a smile. "I think I'll stick around for a while, Father."

"I could order you back," Ben told him.

"Then that would put me in a hard bind, Father."

"How so?"

"Because I'm acting under direct orders from the President, that's why."

The pilot had backed off, away from the father and son. He wanted no part of this family squabble.

"Cecil order you to bird-dog me, boy?"

"Let's just say he asked that I stay close in case you needed my people."

"I see. How many people did you bring with you, boy?"

"Two companies."

Two companies of the most highly trained personnel in the Rebel army. Buddy's special operations people received training equal to the Navy's SEAL teams, the

Marine Corps Force Recon, the Army's Special Forces
and Ranger, the Air Force's Air Controllers and Com-
mandos, the French Foreign Legion, and the British
SAS. For the most part, they were young, in the peak
of physical condition, and per person, had a higher kill
average than any other unit.

"Aren't you afraid of getting bored tagging along
with us?" Ben asked.

"Oh, I think not," Buddy said with a smile. He took
a map from his pocket and spread it out on the fender
of a truck. He put a blunt finger on the area around
Chicago. "Full of creepies, Father. From the ruins of
Chicago all the way up to the Wisconsin line." He moved
his finger over to Rockford. "And that is where Ray
Brown and his gang have settled in for the winter."

Ben looked at the map for a moment, then lifted his
eyes. "Well, now. This might prove to be interesting,
after all."

Buddy smiled. "I thought you might say that, Father."

"The people want to know how they're supposed to
live through the winter," Ben was informed.

Ben sighed and ran his fingers through his graying
hair. "There are hundreds of vacant homes in this area.
Most with fireplaces. Have any of these people given
any thought at all to using an axe or a crosscut saw to
lay in a supply of firewood for the winter?"

"Apparently not," Buddy told him.

"I think they want us to do that for them," Jersey
said.

"Well, we're not going to do it," Ben said. "As far as

I'm concerned, thus far this 'nation healing process' has been a dismal failure.''

It was late fall, and a fire was crackling in the fireplace of the home Ben was using for a CP. Doctor Chase was sitting in an old overstuffed chair in a corner of the room.

"The people who are going to do for themselves have done it," Ben continued. "Those who want somebody else to do it for them have gathered and are waiting for that to happen. We're not going to do it for them . . . and that's final. Corrie, issue those orders to all batt coms.''

"Right, boss." But she did not immediately turn to the radio.

Ben looked over at Lamar. "Go ahead, Lamar. Say it.''

"Say what? What do you want me to say, Ben? Hell, I know what we're up against. We can't go into every community in twenty or more states and prop people up, knowing they're going to fall down as soon as we leave. At the rate we're going it would take us years, it would exhaust our own resources, and in the end, accomplish nothing. Right now, we've covered only half of one state and I can clearly see the so-called 'healing process' is not going to work. The plan looked very good on paper. It just didn't work in the field." He fell silent and sipped his whiskey and water.

"So far," Ben said.

"What do you mean, Father?" Buddy asked. "What are you thinking?''

"At first light, round up all the survivors that are milling around waiting for us to do everything for them.

Round them up at gunpoint and bring them here. I don't know how else to do this."

"What are you going to do, Ben?" Chase was sitting up straight, his whiskey and water forgotten. "Shoot them?"

"No," Ben said with a smile. "But they might think that's what I'm going to do."

"Seven-thousand-nine-hundred-forty-two men, women, and children," Beth said, reading from a clipboard.

"How many children under the age of thirteen?" Ben asked.

"Seven-hundred-fifty-two."

"They have been separated from their parents?"

"Right, boss. They're being served a hot breakfast as we speak."

"PA system working?"

"Affirmative."

"Tools and cleaning equipment rounded up?"

"Right, boss," Cooper said. "Rebels worked all night sifting through the rubble. We've got hammers and boxes of nails and brooms and handsaws and so forth. All stacked and ready to go."

Janet House-Lewiston stood with the three reporters, off to one side, all of them looking at Ben. "What is that man going to do?" she whispered.

"Whatever it is," Cassie said. "You can bet he's going to be uncommonly blunt about it."

Ben walked over to the raised platform and climbed up, walking over to the microphone. He tapped the mic and the sound popped out of the huge outdoor speakers. He looked down into the hundreds of faces, most of them registering undisguised fear. He said, "You people are the laziest, most irresponsible and worthless pack of assholes I have ever seen." His voice boomed out over the heads of the crowd.

The crowd gasped in shock and so did Janet. Nils, Cassie, and Frank smiled.

"I know from reading the questionnaires you filled out that most of you men and women have at least a high school education, many of you have some college and about twenty percent of you are college graduates. You ought to be ashamed of yourselves." Ben's voice was thick with scorn. "You're behaving like worthless rabble. Well, that is about to come to a halt. Right now." He looked down at the clipboard. "Mr. Scott Turner. Front and center. Right now! Move it, goddammit!"

A man with a very frightened look on his face pushed through the crowd and stood in front of the platform.

Ben looked down at him. "You stand right there, mister. And don't you move." Ben called out twenty more names, men and women. When that group had gathered in front of the platform, Ben said, "Before the Great War and during the first rebuilding process afterward, you men and women were successful in your chosen fields. You cover the spectrum. Businessmen and women, contractors, plumbers, electricians—you twenty-one people cover the whole nine yards. You did well at your chosen professions, but now you just want to give up and roll over. Well, you're not going to do that. I'm not going to let you because the nation needs you. You, Mr. Turner, are now the leader of this pack of pricks and pussies. You and these other men and women I've chosen are going to oversee the rebuilding and setting up of a very clean and prosperous and smooth-running community. Do you know why you're going to do that?''

The men and women looked up at him and shook their heads.

"Because if you don't, I'm going to come back and shoot every goddamn one of you, that's why!''

"Oh, my God!'' Janet hissed. "He can't mean that!''

"He means it,'' Nils whispered, hiding his smile.

"And while your bodies are cooling on the ground,'' Ben continued, "I'll pick twenty or so others and see what they can do. And if they fuck up, *I'll shoot them!''* he roared, the speakers rattling.

All the men and women in the huge crowd were scared, and made no attempt to hide it.

"We're going to stick around here for a week or so,'' Ben said. "But we won't be doing the work, you people will. We'll just supervise the operation. This community is going to shine. It's going to be an example. This litter and rubble is going to be picked up, hauled off, and disposed of properly. Homes are going to be swept out and floors mopped until they shine like a barracks before inspection—''

"Fuck you!'' a man shouted from the crowd. He pushed his way through to stand in front of the raised platform. "You can't make me do a goddamn thing I don't want to do. You can take your goddamn orders and stick 'em up your goddamn ass, you goddamn tin soldier son-of-a-bitch!''

Ben shot him.

Coldly, dispassionately, and without any visible sign of emotion, Ben shot him between the eyes.

"Oh, my God!'' Janet whispered in shock. "I can't believe I'm witnessing this.''

"I can," Frank Service said. "This nation's future is at stake. And Ben Raines knows it."

Ben held the pistol at his side. "Anybody else?" He spoke calmly into the microphone.

No one in the crowd uttered a sound or made a move.

"Get to work," Ben said. "Right now!"

Chapter Eighteen

"Just as busy as a bunch of little bees," Ben remarked, as he drove around the suburbs of the city. "The place is beginning to look like something again."

"I can't believe you shot that man, Ben," Lamar said. "I was there, I saw it, but I can't believe it."

"You still don't get it, do you, Lamar?" Ben questioned.

"What is it I'm supposed to get, Raines?"

"Fear, Lamar. Pure and simple fear. That's what these people were waiting on—fear. That's what the liberals conditioned a certain number of Americans to live under. *Fear*. Fear of the government. If you don't pay your taxes, we'll seize your property or put you in jail, or both. If you don't toe the line, no matter how petty and ridiculous the law, we'll punish you. We—the government—are your masters. You don't have enough sense to run your own lives, so we'll do it for you. They made rules and regulations and forms so complex, complicated, and so filled with gobbledy gook, about half of the American people caved in and became nothing more than puppets. The fucking liberals cut the heart and the guts out of millions of people. They based their government on fear. I just used that still-lingering fear to get the people back to work. That man I shot may have been a good man, a decent man. And I'm sure the Almighty will make me pay for what I did . . . among other sins too numerous to mention. But I *will* put this nation back together again.

"The SUSA will survive and prosper and grow powerful under Rebel rule. Up here, these frightened little rabbits now cleaning up the streets and homes will, eventually, get some steel in their backbones and start once again legislating themselves into a maze of rules and regulations and complexities, because that's the way the fucking liberal government of the past conditioned them to live. And in their own way, they will prosper. They'll bog themselves down building prisons and halfway houses and public housing and basketball courts for worthless goddamn punks, and tax themselves to the breaking point trying to be all things to all people all the time. In a few years, they'll have bars on their windows and twenty-nine locks on their doors, and car alarms and home security systems and they'll piss and moan about the crime rate and will never understand that it's all their fault. But . . . that's the way they want to live, Lamar. So be it. I'll help them return to that."

Lamar stared at Ben for a full minute. Then he said, "Well, I'll just be goddamned!"

*   *   *

The Rebels pulled out one week after Ben laid down his ultimatum to the people. During that week, blocks and blocks of the suburbs had been transformed into clean streets and neat homes. Water and electricity had not yet been restored, but that wasn't far off.

Ben met one last time with Scott Turner and the group. The men and women were neatly dressed and had a lot of their former pride back. "You're on your own now," Ben told them. "It's doubtful I'll be back, but Rebel patrols will be checking in until the Midwest is brought back from the ashes. After that, what kind of government you install is up to you. But I have a pretty good idea what it will be."

"You don't think much of us, do you, General?" a woman asked.

Ben shook his head. "I'll pass on that question, lady, since it's doubtful our paths will ever cross again. Maybe you folks were knocked down so hard, twice in a row, you forgot how to get up on your own. But you're up now. And whether you stay up or go down for the count is now entirely in your hands. You'd better form up some sort of home guard for defense, and appoint people as peace officers. I'm not ordering you to do that. It's just a suggestion. I'm not going to waste my breath telling you about letting criminals get the upper hand or how to deal with them. That's up to you people now. Good-bye and good luck." Ben walked out of the newly cleaned up and repainted community building. "Mount up!" he hollered. "We're outta here!"

And that was the way the Rebels began ramming some steel into the backbone of a twice demoralized American populace. From the Mississippi River east to the Atlantic Ocean, the Rebels rolled into community after community and, using threats, fear, coercion and intimidation, they started the long and tedious job of propping up America . . . one more time.

Ben took his people west and crossed the Illinois River, heading for Quincy, spending a week there. Then he turned to the northeast and headed for Peoria. Over to Galesburg and up to Moline. By this time the weather had turned bitterly cold. The Rebels began inspecting each house they came to, looking for blankets and clothing. When they were found, they were carefully laundered and given to the people. The Rebels rounded up cattle and hogs and sheep. They repaired fences and chicken coops. By the first of the new year, the people they were helping got into the spirit of the thing and began struggling to stand on their own two feet before the Rebels arrived. No one likes to be browbeaten and threatened and belittled.

"By God, Ben, it's working," Nick Stafford, commander of 18 Batt radioed from the East Coast.

"It was a desperation move on my part, Nick," Ben said. "I just didn't know what else to do. If this had failed, I was going to turn us around and head on back to the SUSA."

On the fifteenth of January, a major winter storm slammed into the nation and Ben ordered everybody to shut it down and wait it out. Ben and his 1 Batt were on the outskirts of Rockford, ready for a fight, but Ray Brown and his gang had pulled out, leaving behind them a dead city—gutted, looted, destroyed and utterly devoid of people.

"Simon Border has probably given them sanctuary," Ben said.

"I thought he was such a fine, upstanding Christian person," Beth remarked, a smile playing at her lips.

"Simon Border is a prick," Ben said. "He's playing both ends against the middle. He's shaken hands with the devil in an attempt to get rid of us."

"Ray Brown and all the other gang leaders just might decide to turn on him," Cooper said.

"They might," Ben agreed. "But not for a while. I suspect that Simon has justified what he's doing by telling his followers he's using mercenaries against us. Any means to an end. Come the spring, we'll have a real fight on our hands. And you can all get ready for it."

"But won't the people we've helped pitch in to help us when push comes to shove?" Anna questioned.

"I doubt it," Ben said. "Oh, some of them will, sure. But not the majority. We're like the gunfighters of the Old West, gang. It's all right for us to come in and clean up the town, but once the killing is done, the outlaws buried or run out, and the streets safe, the people don't want us around. We give them a guilty conscience."

Anna, now sixteen (or maybe seventeen, she wasn't sure), shook her head and walked off, muttering about people in general and certain types of people in particular.

The weather had brought the Rebel push to an abrupt halt, trapping Lamar Chase with Ben's 1 Batt in Northern Illinois, just a few miles south of the Wisconsin border. The old roads were impassable and were going to remain that way until the storm broke and the weather warmed.

When Ben started studying aerial recon maps of the

ruins of Chicago, his team knew playtime was over and they were about to get down to the serious business of war.

What was left of Chicago was under the control of gangs and creeps. For several years, the gangs and the creeps had been ranging out of the city, into the country-side, looting and pillaging and kidnapping victims for slavery or whoredom . . . or for dinner.

Ben alerted Ike's 2 Batt and Dan's 3 Batt to get ready to move against the thugs and the creeps as soon as the weather warmed. The runways were cleared at Rock-ford's airport and planes began coming in, bringing supplies for a major push.

Ike's people began clearing the main runway at an old airport just south of Gary, Indiana and the transports came roaring in. Dan began moving his people across the line to a position south and west of the city and began receiving supplies at an airport there.

In Chicago, the thugs and punks and creeps geared up for a fight.

Buddy pulled his 8 Batt in and positioned them west of the city on the old East/West Tollway.

Lamar Chase began stockpiling medical supplies.

The winter storm abated, the sun broke through, and the temperature warmed, melting the ice and snow. The highways were clear.

"Chicago is a festering boil," Ben said. "And we're going to lance it."

Two

Revolutions are not made; they come. A revolution is as natural a growth as an oak. It comes out of the past. Its foundations are laid far back.

—Wendell Phillips

Chapter Nineteen

"There are people living all over what is left of the suburbs," Scouts reported to Ben. "But they're living there of their own free will. They've aligned themselves with the gangs and the creeps."

Ben looked up at the sky. Clear blue with not a cloud to be seen. The temperature was in the low forties. "Order the planes and the gunships in, Corrie."

Over the years, the Rebels had worked this out to perfection. Artillery and planes and gunships would hammer the target for hours, sometimes days, reducing everything to burning, smoking rubble. Then the ground troops would move in, slowly searching every pile of rubble. And they rarely took prisoners. The enemy had been warned many, many times; surrender or die. Once the Rebels entered a free-fire zone, they would shoot on sight.

It took the Rebels four weeks to clear the ruins of Chicago of most creepies, gangs, and other assorted crud. After talking with what few prisoners they took, Rebel estimates were that they had cleared perhaps ninety percent of the criminals who had occupied the ruins of the once great city.

The ten percent remaining were hiding amid the rubble and the ruins. They would probably continue their way of life, preying on the innocent, but the backbone of the gangs was broken, with the heads chopped off.

The Rebels made plans to move on.

"Wisconsin," Beth read from a worn old tourist guide she had found somewhere, "comprises just over fifty-six thousand square miles. Before the Great War, it had a population of five million."

"Thank you, Beth," Cooper said. "I really needed that information."

"Talk to me, Beth," Jersey told her. "Cooper's level of comprehension stops at Mickey Mouse."

Ben was sitting at a portable desk, going over a list of supplies they would need before they shoved off. He paused, listening to his team talk.

"Did you ever get to see any of the Disney parks, Jersey?" Corrie asked.

"Only the ruins," she replied. "You?"

"Somebody took me to one when I was real little," Corrie said. "But I can just vaguely remember it. I can't even remember who took me."

"I remember just after the Great War," Jersey recalled, "gas got my whole family. I wandered around for about a week, just looking at all the dead bodies. Then I came up to the casino on the reservation. Huge place. It was all deserted, except for the dead. I must have gone into shock. For a long time after that, months, things are just a blur. How in the hell I wound up two states away is still a mystery to me.''

Many of the younger Rebels had similar stories; only vague memories of wandering, hiding from gangs, fighting for survival after the bombs and the deadly gas covered the land.

''There is an airport here in Southern Wisconsin large enough to handle our transports,'' Ben said, standing up. ''Let's get moving.''

Ben left Ike and Dan to sift through the ruins of Milwaukee and clear it of gangs. He took his 1 Batt and moved west, into the southern part of Wisconsin. Almost in the geographical center of the state, about twenty miles north of the Illinois state line, Ben and his people began getting the main runway in shape to receive the transport planes. About five hundred people were living in and around the town that once boasted a population of some fifteen thousand. Many of them did not receive the Rebels with welcoming arms.

''We're not here to bother you,'' Ben tried to assure them. ''We're here to bring you up to date on your shots, to see if we can be of any assistance, and then we'll move on.''

''We don't care for your form of government,'' the spokesperson told him. ''We want no part of it.''

''We're not here to force our philosophy on you,'' Ben told him. ''We're here to offer medical treatment, help in fixing up your community, setting up a communications link to the outside—things of that nature.''

But the townspeople weren't buying that . . . at least not at first. They were suspicious and very wary of the

Rebels. In their minds, the Rebels were just too well-fed and healthy, their equipment first-rate.

After a few more moments of decidedly one-sided conversation, Ben came within a breath of telling the local to go get screwed. Then he got his temper under some degree of control and stared at the man for a moment.

"Mister, let me tell you something. I really don't want to be roaming all over America, trying to pull this country back together. That is something you people should be doing. You people don't even like the Rebel form of government. But yet, here we are, trying to help, and all we're getting from you is guff. Mister, in our society, people help people. Maybe you don't feel that way—if that's the case, I'm sorry for you—but helping each other is the Rebel way."

The local stared at Ben for a few seconds. Shook his head. When he spoke, his tone was softer. "It's nice of you folks to come all the way up here to lend us a hand. I'll get the people together, General. It's been a long time since any of us had a real doctor look at us."

Had the Rebels stayed longer, the people might have really warmed up to them. But the Rebels didn't have the time. They did what they could to help, then moved on, pushing further and further north.

The Rebels strung telephone wire, got water and sewerage systems working. For the first time in a long time, they were more teacher than soldier, friend rather than warrior. They hit no resistance as they moved north. Ike reported that the dead city of Milwaukee had held few gangs and no creeps.

"Hell, Ben," Ike radioed. "It's *boring!*"

"Where have the punks and the gangs gone?" Ben asked Mike Richards one late afternoon.

The chief of Rebel intelligence shook his head. "I don't know, Ben. But you can bet they didn't change their spots overnight."

"Is it possible they slipped across the river into Simon Border's territory?"

"I think some of them did, yes. We talked about this earlier. My personal opinion is that they've broken up into small groups and just faded into the landscape. They've finally gotten it through their heads they don't have a chance meeting us head-on. Every time they try that, we crush them like bugs."

"All right, fine. I'll accept that. But what about the rabble—for want of a better word, and there must be one—that we chased out of the SUSA? What the hell happened to them? There were thousands of them."

"You want a personal opinion, Ben? One that has no proof behind it?"

"Might as well."

"I think the Rebels scared the living shit out of them. I think when they saw that we would shoot to kill, they finally saw the light, so to speak. I believe many of them have found a spot to roost and settled in."

After Mike had left, Ben sat for a long time, deep in thought. If what Mike said was true, and Ben had no reason to doubt it, the Rebels were, for the most part, through with their purge of the states east of the Mississippi—with the exception of the far northeast part of the country.

It was a strange feeling.

Corrie broke into his thoughts. "Boss, there is someone here to see you."

Ben looked up. "Who is it?"

"Some man by the name of Paul Altman."

"Senator Paul Altman?"

Corrie shrugged her shoulders. "I guess. Who is that?"

"A moderate Democrat, if you can believe it. I thought he was dead."

Corrie smiled. "He looks alive to me."

"Show him in, Corrie."

It was Paul Altman. Older, grayer, but then, Ben thought, so were they all.

Ben shook hands with the man and waved him to a chair. Beth brought in coffee and the senator from Michigan—or the ex-senator from what had once been Michigan—accepted it gratefully.

"Real coffee," Altman said. "It's been a long time."

"I thought you were dead, Senator. You haven't surfaced in years."

Paul took a sip of coffee and sighed contentedly. "When I saw the group that Homer was putting together a couple of years back, I decided to stay out of sight. That was the biggest pack of nitwits ever to assemble in one spot."

Ben smiled. "I will certainly agree with that without reservation."

Paul smiled and took another sip of coffee. "So now the Rebels are on the move, claiming everything in sight?"

"Not a chance, Senator. No way."

Paul's eyes widened in surprise. "Then . . . ?" He let that trail off.

"The Rebels are going state to state, doing what needs to be done to prop up the people, and doing it as best we can with what we have. Simon Border has claimed nearly all the states west of the Mississippi River. The Rebels control the SUSA. The rest of the states are up for grabs. We don't want them, Senator."

The senator cocked his head to one side and gave Ben a very curious look.

"We don't want them, Senator," Ben repeated.

"Then what happens to those states and the people in them?"

"I don't know."

"You're very cavalier about it, General."

"They aren't my responsibility, Senator." Ben smiled. "You want them, take them."

Paul laughed, being careful not to spill his coffee. "It isn't quite that simple, General."

"Sure, it is, Senator. It's a whole new world out there now. It's real easy. The biggest kid on the block rules the block. You get you a following, arm them, and take over. You do it community by community, county by county, state by state. The more territory you claim, the larger your army will be. See how simple it is?"

"If you don't care what happens to the people in these other states, then why are you here?"

Ben sighed. "Well . . . to tell you the truth, because it's probably the right thing to do, Senator. Right . . . because unless we get a lot of people inoculated, a plague is likely to spread across the land. Right . . . because without somebody coming in and helping the people rid themselves of gangs, twenty states are likely to become a wasteland. Right for a number of reasons, Senator. Why don't I want to lay claim to these states? Because the SUSA is just the right size to govern. Because the cry-babies of this nation need someplace of their own to piss and moan about the rights of baby-rapers and murderers and muggers and car thieves—" Ben held up a hand. "Remember, don't let a good boy go bad, Senator, always take the keys out of your car."

Paul Altman burst out laughing. He wiped his eyes and said, "I always did like your sense of humor, General. Albeit on the dark side."

"I'm sure you were in the minority among your fellow party members," Ben said, very drily.

"Oh, come on, General! There were always many moderate Democrats and quite a few conservative Democrats. But domestic terrorism became such a threat in this country, we had to pass many restrictive laws."

"Horseshit! You'll never convince me of that. But let's save the arguments for a later date. You didn't come out of hiding to debate political dogma with me."

"Frankly, I couldn't believe you and your Rebels were in the area and had yet to fire a shot. I thought there must be some mistake."

Ben had to smile at the gently-spoken sarcasm, offered with a straight face. He stood up and refilled the senator's coffee mug. "There were no criminals or creeps in the area, Senator," Ben said, returning to his chair.

"There are very few criminals or Night People left *anywhere*, General."

"We are thorough, Senator."

The two men sat and stared at one another for a moment. Suddenly, Ben thought, *Hell, why not? He's a good man . . . for a Democrat.* Ben put his elbows on the desk and smiled. "I have an idea, Senator. How would you like to go back to work?"

"Doing what, General?"

Ben's smile widened.

Chapter Twenty

"It's the wildest thing I have ever heard of," Homer Blanton said to Cecil, after listening to Ben on the short wave. Then he smiled. "But it might work. Paul Altman is certainly a good, decent man." He shook his head. "But those states are filled with gangs and outlaws."

"They won't be if Altman agrees to Ben's plan," Cecil said.

"I wonder what Paul thinks about it?" Homer pondered.

Hundreds of miles north of Base Camp One, the senator said to Ben, "You have just got to be kidding!"

"Why?" Ben asked. "Don't you think you're up to the job?"

"Don't be insulting, General. That isn't the point. The twenty-odd states we're referring to are in chaos."

"They won't be for long, if you agree to my plan."

"You will actually agree to the concept of civilian police?"

"For you people, sure. Liberals have to be told what to do. You people don't have the foggiest idea about how to live under a system where the individual actually controls his or her own destiny. The Rebel form of government wouldn't work up here. And I don't mean to be insulting or demeaning when I say that. So what is your reply, Mister-Almost-A-Candidate-For-President-of-the-Northern-United-States-of-America?"

"How are we going to count the ballots?" Paul asked. "How will we get the ballots to the people and how will they return them to us?"

"Don't worry about it," Ben assured him. "You'll win."

Paul stared at Ben. "Why does that statement fill me with such uneasiness?"

"Just roll with the flow, Paul. Roll with the flow."

Rebel pilots began dumping campaign literature out over three states, Illinois, Wisconsin, and Indiana, and in parts of several other states which bordered the SUSA. The literature exhorted the virtues of Senator Paul Altman and asked everyone to vote for him as the new president of the Northern United States of America.

"Who else is running?" Paul asked Ben.

"No one," Ben told him. "That's why you'll win."

"But . . . but . . . but . . ."

Ben walked off, leaving the man stuttering.

Special teams of Rebels either drove in or jumped in to help with the elections and to count the ballots.

By the time the election was held, Ben and his 1 Batt had advanced into the north-central part of the state of Wisconsin. Ben's CP was at the old Wausau airport.

"Find a judge of some sort," Ben told his Scouts. "We're going to need one to swear in Paul."

"I thought a Supreme Court Justice was supposed to do that?" Ike questioned.

"They're all dead. Hell, any judge will do. If we can't find a judge, I'll swear him in."

A judge was found, a former federal judge. Knowing how Ben Raines felt about federal judges, the man was scared almost out of his wits and had to be forcibly taken to meet Ben.

"Are you going to shoot me?" the man asked.

Ben blinked in surprise. "Shoot you? Hell, no, I'm not going to shoot you. I want you to swear in the next president of the Northern United States of America."

"I can't do that!"

"Well, you're going to. Beth, where is that oath of office?" Beth handed him the oath of office she had found in an old civics book and typed up. Ben gave it to the judge. "Hold on to this. Tomorrow, you're going to have a new president."

"Is this election legal?" the judge questioned.

"Of course, it is. Why wouldn't it be? The people voted, didn't they?"

The judge only nodded his head. He wasn't about to argue with Ben, but he did wonder about the constitutionality of the election. However, he kept his mouth shut, remembering that for years before the Great War, Ben Raines had been quite vocal about the government moving away from the original intent of the Constitution and the Bill of Rights.

Naturally, Senator Paul Altman won the election. He was the only one on the ticket. And the number of people who took part in the election surprised everyone, including Ben.

Cecil and Homer flew up from Base Camp One to witness the swearing-in of the new president of the NUSA.

The judge beat a very hasty retreat immediately afterward.

At a small reception after the swearing-in, Paul asked, "Where is the capital going to be located?"

"Anywhere you want it to be," Ben told him, drinking champagne out of a coffee cup.

"I feel sort of guilty about this," Paul said.

"Guilty about what?" Ben asked.

"Drinking champagne and eating all this nicely prepared food while millions of people are hungry."

"Oh, don't start with that crap!" Ben said sharply. "Please spare me that. The people you speak of have had several years to get organized, plant crops and gardens, get factories and shops running again, and do all the things necessary to get a workable society going. Instead, many of them have sat on their asses waiting for somebody else to do it for them. Well, Mr. President, you are the government now. Good luck."

"Does the NUSA want to borrow some money from the SUSA?" Cecil asked innocently. "We can set up a line of credit for you right now."

"I've heard that your currency is very strong."

"The strongest in the world."

"Backed by . ... ?"

"Gold," Ben told him.

"Gold? In the south?"

"Trillions of dollars of it," Cecil replied. "Also diamonds, other precious gems, and tons of pure silver."

"Where in the world did you get it?" Paul asked.

"Oh, we stole it," Ben said matter-of-factly, as he poured another cup of champagne. "From all over the world."

Paul almost choked on a finger sandwich.

"Want to borrow a hundred billion?" Homer said, clearly enjoying himself.

His wife gave him a somewhat dirty look. But not too dirty, since she was finally beginning to understand just what made the world go round and especially how the Rebel government worked.

"As a matter of fact, I do," Paul said quickly.

"Fine," Cecil said. "Have you given any thought to a cabinet?"

"Well, ah, yes, actually."

"Good, good," Homer said.

Ben backed off a few yards and looked at Corrie. "Politics bores me, Corrie. Get the troops together. We're outta here."

Ben and his 1 Batt were moving toward Michigan within the hour.

The Rebels backtracked down past the still-smoking ruins of Chicago, turned east, and headed into Southern Michigan.

"Boss," Corrie said, "we've got four battalions that are bogged down in West Virginia. They're meeting lots of resistance there."

"Tell them to pull out and bivouac in Western Maryland and stay the hell away from the D.C. area. We'll make a sweep through Michigan and then turn east for the next push. Tell Ike to come up and join me here in Michigan. He is to take everything east of 127, but leave Detroit alone until we can tackle it together. I'll take everything west of 127. Tell all other battalions to hold what they've got.''

Michigan was a mess. The Rebels hit stiff resistance the day they entered the state. Ben sent Buddy and his 8 Batt over to work the highway along Lake Michigan while Ben and half of his 1 Batt headed up Highway 131; the other half of 1 Batt would work up Interstate 69 toward Lansing.

They all encountered heavy fighting immediately upon entering the state.

''I guess we know now where the gangs went,'' Ike radioed to Ben on the afternoon of the second day in the state.

''We damn sure do,'' Ben said. ''I hate to think what we're going to find in Detroit. Or what's left of it, that is.''

''But why the hell did they come here?''

Before Ben could reply to that, he heard mortar rounds fluttering in. ''Gotta go, Ike. Incoming. See you.''

Ben hit the floor just as a round hit the front of the house and blew that part of the structure all to hell. Another round dropped into the center of the roof and the whole damn thing came crashing in.

Ben was shaken but unhurt as he crawled to his boots and stumbled through the debris to a window. Of late he'd been using a CAR, leaving his Thompson in the wagon. He grabbed his CAR and headed for a window— the door to the room he'd been using was completely blocked by the caved-in roof. The magazine pouches on his battle harness were all full, and he had several grenades and two canteens of fresh water. He jumped through the window just as several mortar rounds struck the old house and took it down. Ben rolled to his boots and started running for a ditch. He jumped for the ditch just as several mortar rounds exploded behind him and flipped him. He felt the sting of shrapnel on his legs as he was being propelled through the air. Luckily, the ditch was full of water so he had a reasonably soft landing, but the wind was knocked out of him, he had lost his helmet flying through the air, and he banged his head on something.

"Shit!" Ben said, then faded into blackness.

The gangs had counter-attacked, throwing everything they had, which was considerable, at the Rebels. The Rebels were forced to withdraw. When the counter-attack came, Buddy and his 8 Batt were in Benton Harbor, and they were shoved back some ten miles. Ben and his 1 Batt were just south of Kalamazoo, and forced back just about ten miles. Ike and his 2 Batt were on the outskirts of Jackson and they were forced all the way back to the junction of Highways 12 and 127.

As night spread darkness over the land, Ben lay unconscious in the ditch.

Cooper had pulled Jersey from the wreckage of the house. She was unconscious and bleeding from a head wound. Beth and Anna had gone back to the rear on an errand for Ben and had been cut off. Corrie had stepped outside for a breath of air just moments before the mortar rounds came in and she had been standing on the sidewalk, talking to a friend. Both of them had been knocked down and addled by the concussion. They had been picked up by friends and tossed into the bed of a truck to be taken to the rear to a MASH unit. In the confusion, it would be almost half an hour before someone realized that Ben was missing.

Ben came slowly to his senses. He opened his eyes to a world of darkness and hurt. From long experience, when he opened his eyes, he lay still. From the waist down, he was in water. He listened intently, but could hear no voices. Slowly, he turned his aching head to the left. Nothing. Then it all come back to him. The mortar rounds exploding. The sting of shrapnel in his legs. Sailing a few feet in the air and impacting against the ground and into the old drainage ditch. He lay still and tried to think things through, sort matters out. His head hurt and that made thinking difficult.

First things first, Ben, he concluded. Get out of this damn wet ditch. Moving as silently as a snake, Ben crawled out of the ditch and onto dry ground. Just that made him feel better. Then he heard voices. Faint, but very real. He could only catch a few words.

"Didn't kill as many of them as . . ."

"Taught 'em a lesson, though, by . . ."

"Get all their equipment and leave the bodies where . . ."

Then the voices faded away.

Ben felt around for his helmet but could not locate it. He got his bearings and crawled over to a shed and slipped inside, closing the door behind him. The shed was windowless and still snug. It had been well built. He pulled his trousers down and, using his flashlight, he doctored the puncture wounds on his legs, picking out one piece of shrapnel with his fingers. There was a knot on his forehead where he'd hit whatever the hell it was he'd landed on.

He pulled up his pants and stood. No dizziness, but his legs hurt somewhat. He took a couple of painkillers from his small aid kit and sat down on an overturned old wheelbarrow. Obviously, the gangs had counter-attacked in such force the Rebels had been forced to withdraw. But they wouldn't stay withdrawn for long. And when they did advance, they would first use artillery and air support. So that meant that Ben had best get the hell gone from this area, before the incoming started.

Ben smiled in the darkness. He'd pull out, all right, but it wouldn't be in the direction that was expected.

He'd do some head-hunting.

Ben checked first his CAR then his sidearm. Neither weapon had been damaged. He slipped out of the darkened shed and squatted for a few minutes outside, letting his eyes adjust to the night.

There was no point in attempting to search the ruined house for any of his team. If they were wounded or dead, they were buried under several tons of debris. He put them out of his mind and started moving toward the north.

He saw the motionless body of a Rebel on the ground, half hidden by brush. He walked over to the body and pulled off the Rebel's battle harness, taking the full magazines and the four grenades.

"All right, you sons-of-bitches," Ben muttered. "Now it's my turn to play."

Chapter Twenty-One

Ben slipped past the darkened old houses, staying in the shadows as he worked his way north. He saw several small groups of punks and gang members, but did not attempt to engage them in any fire-fight. He wanted a larger group, all bunched up in some house. Then he would announce his presence.

He stepped to one side and flattened against the side of a home when he saw half a dozen shadowy figures moving toward him, all carrying weapons.

"I heard one of them bastards talkin'," the voice came to him. "On an open frequency. Ben Raines is missin'."

"I don't believe it!"

"Me neither," another said.

"It's true. They think he's dead. Killed when we attacked."

"We couldn't be that lucky."

The group stopped about forty feet away from Ben,

standing in the raggedy yard of a long abandoned house. Four more walked up to join the original six.

Ben smiled and slipped a fire-frag grenade from his battle harness. The fire-frag was perhaps the deadliest grenade ever invented; indeed, it was a mini-claymore. Ben pulled the pin and chunked the pineapple, tossing it underhanded with a high arc before the drop. It came down right in the center of the dozen punks and exploded about three feet off the ground.

Ben was moving two seconds after the blast, leaving behind him men whose flesh was peppered with shrapnel, about half of them dying from the wounds.

Punks and thugs and assorted human crap and slime came running toward the sounds of screaming, running from all directions. Ben changed directions and joined in with a group of punks, jogging along with them for a few seconds; just long enough to take another grenade from his harness, pull the pin, and pop the spoon. He tossed it over the heads of the running group, then ducked in between two houses.

The group ran right over the grenade and when it exploded, it took out half of them, shredding flesh, breaking bones, and blinding and maiming.

Ben jumped up on what had once been a screened-in back porch and slipped through the long-looted old home. He squatted down and smiled as he listened to the sounds of confusion.

"It's mortars!" someone yelled.

"Run!" another yelled.

But before they could run, Ben raised up and emptied a thirty-round magazine into the knot of punks.

Ben ejected the empty and slipped in a full magazine before jumping out a side window and vanishing into the darkness. He did not realize it, but he was smiling. He was having more fun than he'd had in a long time.

Both Corrie and Jersey were in bed and challenged by Doctor Chase to just try to set one foot on the floor. Both of the women were suffering from concussions. Jersey's head wound had required half a dozen stitches and she was going to be out of action for about a week. Corrie's shoulder had been dislocated when she hit the sidewalk, and she also suffered cuts on her face and arm that had to be stitched.

Ben's second in command took over and ordered Anna, Beth, and Cooper not to even think about going back to look for Ben.

"Communications is reporting that someone is raising hell up in the area we just left," a runner told Doctor Chase and those standing close to him. "But we don't have any special ops people there."

Cooper smiled and winked at Jersey. "Oh, yes, we do."

"Oh?" Chase questioned.

"Yes, sir." Jersey smiled as she spoke from her bed. "And his name is General Ben Raines."

Ben had stumbled upon two more dead Rebels that the punks had not found and stripped them of their weapons and gear. Ben knew one of them personally, and he paused for a moment, saddened. He shook away the grief and quickly took the men's ammo and grenades before slipping away into the night.

Ben figured he had about seven more hours of darkness before dawn would force him to hunt a hidey-hole. He intended to make the most of the cover of night.

Ben slipped through the darkness, looking for groups of punks to attack. Quite by accident, he stumbled on what appeared to be someone's communications center. Peeking in through a crack in the boarded-up window, he could see that for punks, it was quite elaborate. He smiled as he took a grenade from his harness. It sure as hell wasn't going to be elaborate for very much longer.

Ben slipped around the house until he found an open window. He popped the spoon and blew the radio operator and his equipment into blood and junk.

"What the goddamn hell is goin' on here?" a man yelled, stepping out of a house to stand on the porch.

"We think it's Rebel mortars, Fred!" the answering voice sprang out of the darkness.

Fred LaBelle, Ben thought, one of the major gang leaders. *'Bye, Fred.* Ben lifted his CAR and put a burst into Fred's chest. The impacting .223 rounds knocked the punk leader off the porch and sent him dead and cooling to the ground.

Ben got the hell gone from that area, slipping from house to house. He found a five-gallon container filled with gas sitting by the side of an old pick-up truck and grabbed it, moving on until he came to a house that had portable lanterns burning inside. He peeped in through a window. A number of punks lay sprawled in sleep on the floor in many of the rooms.

Ben took a fire-frag, wired it to the gas can and took off the cap. He pulled the pin and then hurled the full five-gallon container through a window just as hard as he could.

Then he took off running.

The fumes from the gas must have been just right, for the explosion nearly knocked Ben off his boots. Recovering from the concussion, he glanced back. The center of the house was in ruins, the side that he could see blown completely away, and the wood frame structure was in flames.

Ben ran past a back porch that was rapidly filling with men and women and gave the crowd a full magazine of .223 rounds as he loped past.

"Team one!" Ben yelled. "Take the south side. Team two! Attack from the north. Teams three and four, scatter and hit them hard!"

Then Ben ran into the darkness, just as far away as he could get from the burning house.

The punks bought the false commands. A man yelled, "The bastards are counter-attacking!" His voice was filled with panic. "Get everybody up and to their posts. Hurry! The Rebels are all around us."

An army of one, Ben thought with a grin.

He tossed a grenade through the window of a house that had lamps burning in it and kept on running, cutting to his left. He ran right into a man who was carrying what appeared to be an old Russian RPG-16 and struggling with a pouch filled with six-pound rockets. Both of them went down to the ground from the impact. Ben slammed the butt of his CAR against the man's head and heard the skullbone pop under the smashing blow. Grunting with the effort, Ben slung his CAR, grabbed up the RPG and the heavy pouch and moved away from the scene as quickly as he could, considering the heavy load he was toting.

I'm sure as hell not getting any younger, Ben thought, as

he paused for a moment to catch his wind and rest the straining muscles in his legs.

But I'm doin' pretty good for a man my age, he amended.

Ben moved on until he found himself in what he guessed was the punks' version of a motor pool. He squatted down and rested for a moment, a slow grin creasing his lips as an idea began forming in his mind.

He stashed the RPG and the pouch of rockets and began moving from vehicle to vehicle, removing the gas caps from as many vehicles as he could safely reach. In the back of half a dozen pick-up trucks, he found many full five-gallon gas cans and began pouring the gas all around the cars and trucks and motorcycles. Then he moved back to his stash and moved away about five hundred yards. He fitted a rocket into the RPG and smiled.

"Have fun, boys and girls," Ben muttered, then fired the RPG.

The entire motor pool went up in a whooshing roar, the heat concussion reaching Ben in a blast of hot air. Ben moved further back as the cars and trucks and motorcycles began exploding, sending hot steel flying in all directions.

Ben hummed a few bars of the old song "In the Heat Of The Night," and then moved further back into the night as a dozen or more figures came screaming out of the inferno; moving balls of fire staggering about in the parking lot.

Several thousand yards away from the burning motor pool, in the shelter of an empty house, Ben counted the rockets left in the carry pouch. Six 6.6-pound rockets left. He knew the weapon was accurate up to about nine hundred yards . . . providing no wind was blowing with any intensity.

Resting, Ben ate a thoroughly disgusting emergency ration bar and drank some water. The ration bar tasted like sheep shit smelled. Ben knew it was packed with nutrients and vitamins and other stuff essential for the human body to survive—but he didn't have to like the damned thing.

He rinsed his mouth out with water from one of his two canteens and felt better. Just as he was standing up, an old Michigan National Guard APC came rolling up the street. The words painted across the front of the armored personnel carrier brought a smile to Ben's lips: Big Tommy.

That would be Tommy Monroe, more than likely. Ben hoped the gang leader was inside.

He fitted a rocket into the slot, lined it up, and let it bang. The APC went up like a Roman candle; obviously the APC was an older model, for many of the newer models would not have exploded in that manner.

Ben grabbed up his gear and took off.

He was looking for a hidey-hole, for he had been working full-tilt for hours, the adrenalin pumping hard, and he was getting tired.

He began making his way more cautiously now, working his way toward the northeastern edge of town. He damn sure did not want to be in this immediate area when the Rebels opened up with artillery at dawn. He stayed in the alleys and back streets, occasionally looking back toward the punk motor pool, which was still blazing, lighting up the sky.

Ben walked for what he guessed was about four miles before stopping. He had put most of the city suburbs behind him before he found a half-burned-out house that looked as though it was dangerously close to falling in. That would make a perfect hidey-hole. Punks being what they were, they would not think of looking for him in a ruined home when so many perfectly good homes were available.

He took a leak in a ditch and then walked into the weed-grown yard. Ben circled around to the back and slipped inside, working his way under some fallen timbers in what had once been a cathedral-ceilinged dining room. He made himself as comfortable as possible, and drifted off to sleep in a matter of minutes.

He awakened stiff from the hard floor just as daylight was beginning to sift through the holes in what remained of the roof. Ben rinsed his mouth out with water and wished he could brush his teeth. He ate another of those awful emergency ration bars and day-dreamed about a breakfast of bacon and eggs, hash browns and toast, and a tall cold glass of milk.

Ben was screwing the cap back on his canteen when the first rumble of artillery reached his ears. He crawled out from under the fallen timbers and stood up, stretching until his joints popped and his muscles were straining.

He had just worked the kinks out of his muscles when the muzzle of a rifle was jammed against his back.

"Well, well," the voice said. "Another Reb soldier. But you're a little old for the field, ain't you, Pops?"

"Yeah, I am," Ben said. "And I'm hungry, too. You got any food with you?"

"Don't try to be a comedian, Pops. I ain't got shit with me except this rifle. Turn around."

Ben thought of spinning around and slapping the

rifle from the punk's hand, but rejected that almost immediately. His muscles were still stiff from the cool night on the floor. He slowly turned around to face the punk.

His captor was about twenty-five years old, Ben guessed, and he'd been wounded in the side. The left side of his shirt was bloody and his face was pale from shock and pain and loss of blood.

"I've got a first-aid kit," Ben said. "Let me took at that side of yours."

"Huh? You gotta be shittin' me, man. Where's your rifle?"

Behind the wall and under the timbers with the RPG and the rockets. "Lost it during the battle."

"Yeah? Gimme one of them canteens. I'm real thirsty. Do it slow, Pops."

Ben slowly pulled one canteen free and handed it to the wounded man. Keeping his eyes on Ben, the younger man drank deeply, draining the canteen.

"Good," he said, handing the empty canteen to Ben. "You got any food?"

"No. That's what I asked you."

"Oh, yeah. You did. Gimme that pistol, Pops. Do it slow, now."

Ben slowly pulled his 9mm from leather, reversed it, and handed it to the punk, butt first.

"You givin' up awful easy, Pops."

"What else is there to do? You've got the gun pointed at me."

"For a fact. The Rebs is gonna attack, ain't they?"

"Yes. That thunder is artillery. Next will come the planes and gun ships. Ground troops will follow."

The punk squinted his eyes and stared at Ben. Ben suspected he needed glasses. "What rank are you?"

"Sergeant."

"Yeah? What am I gonna do with you, Sergeant?"

"You go your way, I'll go mine. Unless we both want to stay here until we fall over from exhaustion. You're not going to go far with that wound. It needs attention."

"For a fact." He lowered the rifle and laid Ben's pistol on the floor. "I give up," he said, his voice sounding very tired. "I quit. I don't wanna fight no more. I hurt." He pushed both rifle and pistol toward Ben.

Ben holstered his pistol and then checked the M-16. It was dirty. "You have a name?" he asked the wounded young man.

"Jerry. What's yours?"

"Ben Raines."

Jerry's mouth dropped open and his eyes widened as sudden recognition filled them. "Oh, shit!" he whispered.

"Relax. You're out of the war. I'll see that you live."

"You might not live long enough to see to that, man. Not if Ray Brown learns where you are."

"Ray Brown is here?"

"Sure. He's runnin' this entire operation. His headquarters is about two, three miles from here. He hates you."

"The feeling is mutual, I assure you. You been with Ray long?"

"Naw. 'Bout two months or so. I come down from the upper peninsula just before winter. Me and my sister. She died and I linked up with Ray's bunch. Bunch of crazy fuckers, you ask me. I was pullin' out, gettin' away from them, when I seen this house and decided to rest for a spell. I am so tired.''

"Then go to sleep. I'm going to go look around.''

"Man—I mean, General, sir, don't do that. Ray's got people out lookin' for you. He wants you real bad.''

"Not nearly as bad as I want him, I assure you. You want me to take a look at that wound?''

"Naw. I'll be all right. I'm goin' to rest for a time. I don't recall ever bein' this tired.''

"How long have you had that wound?''

"'Bout a week, I think. One of Ray's men shot me. He said it was an accident, but I don't believe that. He meant to shoot me. I didn't fit in with that crowd.''

Jerry was asleep on the floor when Ben retrieved his RPG and pouch of rockets and his rifle. Ben knew from the way the wound smelled that Jerry was not going to make it. Gangrene had set in.

He stood for a moment, looking down at the young man. Jerry's face was shiny with fever-sweat.

Ben shook his head and walked out of the house. He was going to find Ray Brown.

Chapter Twenty-Two

Ben walked for several miles, heading in a northeasterly direction, paralleling old Highway 43. There was no way that the punks could head south, for the Rebels had that area blanketed. Ben had a hunch that Ray and his punk army would try for Detroit and a last-ditch stand and then over into Canada.

If Ben had anything at all to say about it, Ray's days would end right here in what used to be called Michigan.

But as fate would have it, Ben had nothing at all to say about the future of Ray Brown, at least not this time. Before Ben could get into a good defensive position along the old road, the Rebels smashed into the looted city of Kalamazoo and put the punks to rout, scattering them in all directions. Several hundred surrendered and the rest let the wind take them. Ben had aced several fleeing punks with his CAR and set two APCs blazing with rockets from his RPG before a team of Rebel Scouts found him on high ground in a stand of timber.

"Shit!" Ben said, as the Scouts quickly threw up a defensive circle around him and radioed in.

Ben was hustled back to a MASH unit and doctors went to work, checking him out.

"I'm fine!" Ben said.

"Shut up," Chase told him. "And sit still until we clean out these cuts."

"I can't have any fun anymore," Ben bitched.

"Raines," Chase said, disgust in his voice, "you are a middle-aged man. Commanding general of thousands of troops. You are not Rambo."

"Right," Ben said.

"General," a Scout said. "We found that house you told us about. There was a guy in there matching this Jerry person's description. He was dead, just like you said he might be. We buried him."

Ben nodded his head.

"Hold still, damnit!" Chase thundered. "Before I stick this swab in your ear!"

"Ray Brown?" Ben asked, ignoring the doctor.

"No sign of him. But some captured punks told us they were ordered to head for Detroit . . . or what's left of it."

"Have Buddy drop some of his people outside the city. Check it out. Have the pilots start gearing up for an air assault on the city."

"Yes, sir."

"I would order you placed under observation for twenty-four hours, Raines," Chase said, "but you'd just bitch and shout and give orders to anyone who had the misfortune to come close and in general make life miserable for all my people. So get the hell out of this facility. Once again, you lucked out."

"Skill, Lamar," Ben said with a smile. "Skill."

"Horseshit," Lamar countered.

The bridge was blown and the tunnel blocked leading from Michigan to Canada. If the punks were stupid enough to go into the ruins of Detroit, there would be no escape for them and nothing for them to do but die. After some thought, Ben just couldn't buy the gang leaders ordering their people into the rubble of the once-great city. Even a punk would have enough sense to know that would be like signing his own death warrant.

Ben ordered fixed-wing aircraft up for high-altitude aerial recon, and it didn't take them long to get a fix on the punks.

"They're heading north," Ben was told. "Into the timber."

"Shift 7 and 8 Batts over here to beef up Buddy's 8 Batt and go after them. Ike, you, me, and Dan will concentrate on the ruins of Detroit."

"It's full of creeps," Ike reminded him.

"Yeah," Ben replied, disgust evident in his voice.

Ben's team was back together, although Corrie's left shoulder was still a little sensitive. The battalions had gathered in Eastern Michigan for the assault against Detroit. Ben had been in contact with President Paul Altman of the NUSA and assured him that Michigan would be cleared of punks, thugs, and creeps by early fall.

"And then what am I supposed to do with it?" Paul asked.

"I'm sure you'll think of something," Ben told him. "How's your cabinet coming?"

"Slowly, very slowly. General, I'm thinking of making Indianapolis, Indiana the new capitol."

"Whatever. Say hello to Dan for me."

Paul waited patiently until Ben had stopped chuckling before asking, "Could I borrow a team of your engineers to start work?"

"Sure. Give Cecil a bump. We'll be glad to help. The sooner we can find a place for all the liberals to gather, the better off the rest of us will be."

"Thank you," Altman said, very very drily.

Ben looked through long lenses at the smoking ruins of what had once been Ann Arbor. At first glance, there didn't appear to be much left and absolutely no sign of life.

Ike McGowan stood to Ben's left, Dan Gray to his right.

"Three battalions won't be enough, Ben," Ike said, lowering his binoculars.

"I know it, Ike. But we'll just have to make it enough. We'll split our battalions into six battle groups. Each group will have twice the normal number of tanks. The last of them should be arriving midday tomorrow. We'll start the push at 0600 the next day."

"The punks have been cornered," Corrie said, after listening to her headset. "The old Michigan Militia has surfaced and blocked off any further escape to the north. Buddy is coming up fast from the south."

Ben glanced at her, surprise in his eyes. "I thought the

federal government destroyed them before the Great War?''

"They tried," Corrie said. "But Beth has just learned that a lot of the militias went hard underground after the liberal government grab. They've kept their areas as clean as possible since the balloon went up. Mike has just learned that the Montana Militia is waging a guerrilla action against Simon Border's people. And the Wyoming Militia has surfaced and is doing the same in their states. Constitutionalists all over the Northwest, that were forced hard underground years back, are surfacing to align with us and fight Simon Border. And all these groups have people of all races in their ranks. Mike's spooks have confirmed that.''

"Well, I'll just be damned!" Ben said.

Corrie said, "The Michigan Militia, or at least an offshoot of it, whatever they are, have spread out along Highway 10, east to Saginaw Bay. They're holding, but badly need ammo and medical supplies." Corrie had been a small child when the civilian militias, concerned about the federal government's interference in the lives of citizens, sprang up all across America. Some of the militias were blatantly racist groups, some were filled with kooks and nuts, but many were just law-abiding citizens very much afraid of the direction the government was taking.

"See that they get anything they need," Ben told her. "Arrange for air drops."

"Including the western states under Border's control?" Corrie questioned.

Ben smiled. "Let's see if we can't supply them a bit more covertly."

"Right, boss."

Ike and Dan exchanged glances and smiles at that. Like all the batt coms, they knew that the Rebels would someday have to fight Simon Border's army.

"Have all battalions reported in?" Ben asked.

"Affirmative, boss. They are holding and resupplying for the next push north and east."

Ben nodded his head. "All right, people. Let's gear up to take this city."

Thousands of miles away, Bruno Bottger carefully read the latest reports on Ben Raines and the Rebels. Bottger hated Ben Raines, but he had to grudgingly admire the man. Raines was going to put America back together again. There was no doubt in his mind about that. There was also no doubt in his mind that once Raines turned his attentions west of the Mississippi River, toward Simon Border and his followers, it would be the beginning of the end for Simon Border.

Bruno wondered again if Ben would someday turn his attentions toward Africa.

"The militias have surfaced, sir," an aide told Simon Border. "Obviously the government did not succeed in destroying them all before the Great War."

"And you think these groups have kept their heads down all these years?" Simon questioned.

"Yes, sir. That is exactly what our intelligence thinks."

"Then they were much better organized than we originally thought."

"Yes, sir."

"Ben Raines?"

The aide knew what Simon meant. "Steadily advancing against the gangs and the Night People. They've already cleared half a dozen states."

"Our people in Michigan?"

"Most of them have been ferreted out and either shot or hanged. Those left are keeping out of sight."

"Did the Rebels execute them?"

"No, sir. The militia did."

Simon felt like cursing. But of course, being a very devout Christian, he didn't. He dismissed the aide, waited until the door had closed behind the young man, then he cussed, long and low.

Mostly he cussed Ben Raines.

Additional tanks had been brought in from other battalions to beef up those battalions standing ready to launch the final assault against the ruins of Detroit.

Ben had decided against air strikes, for air recon had showed the creeps and the punks were underground, in basements and storage areas and bunkers. Air strikes would be a waste of explosives. The Rebels were going to have to go in and take the ruins by land search and destroy. And to a person, they all knew it was going to be down and dirty work.

On a gray morning that was threatening rain, Ben glanced over at Corrie, standing patiently, waiting for orders. "How's the shoulder?"

"Oh, it's fine now. Not tender at all."

Ben nodded. He no longer had to give orders for everyone to be buttoned up in body armor; those were standing orders and any Rebel, regardless of rank, found without body armor could expect a chewing out.

To complicate matters further, the Rebels knew the creeps would have underground storage areas, or holding pens, for their human food supply, fattening them up to eat later. The Night People, or creeps, as they had been nicknamed, were held in complete contempt by the Rebels. They were they most disgusting people the Rebels had ever encountered.

And the Rebels never took any Night People prisoner. At first they did, and tried to rehabilitate them. Not one creep had ever been successfully rehabilitated.

Doctor Chase walked up, a grim expression on his face.

"Get into body armor!" Ben snapped at him. "You're not three hundred yards from the front, Lamar."

A Rebel quickly found body armor and helmet for the doctor. Lamar struggled into the protective gear and looked at the weapon in Ben's hands. An old M-14 (7.62×51), .308 caliber.

"Loaded for bear this trip, eh, Ben?"

Ben smiled and patted the old Thunder Lizard. "I drag it out from time to time."

"We're set to receive wounded," Chase said quietly. "I have six MASH units set up in a semi-circle on the outskirts of the city."

Ben nodded his head.

"Don't bring me any creepie wounded, Ben. Man, woman, or child."

"I understand, Lamar." And he did, but like most Rebels, he did not have to like that knowledge.

The Rebels had found out the hard and bloody way that the children of Night People were even more savage than the adults. But most Rebels could not bring themselves to shoot a child, unless that child was shooting at them. They usually just ran them off, knowing full well that someday, they would, more than likely, have to fight them again.

"Everybody in position, Corrie?" Ben asked.

"Set to go, boss."

Ben motioned to a Rebel. "Escort the doctor back to his HQ, please."

Lamar offered no objections to that. "See you, Ben."

"See you, Lamar."

When the doctor was gone, Ben said to Corrie, "Let's do it."

Corrie spoke into her headset and the tanks surged forward, the Rebels right behind them.

The final battle for Detroit had begun.

Chapter Twenty-Three

The Rebels had to slog through several miles of suburbs before they even reached the small cities that surrounded Detroit. Ben and his split battalion were going straight in, first on Highway 14, then switching over to Interstate 96, or what was left of it.

They hit stiff fighting just west of the ruins of Plymouth and the advance was slowed to a crawl.

Some of the thugs and punks who had gathered in Michigan had fled to the city, and they were fighting a last-ditch stand in the suburbs. Most of the creepies had retreated to the city proper.

"They'll be dug in deep by the time we get there," Ben said to his battalion and company-level commanders. "Hard underground. They'll have all sorts of nasty surprises waiting for us. Everything we touch is going to be booby-trapped and blow up in our faces." Ben smiled a warrior's smile as he turned to Corrie. "Get on the horn. I want every combat engineer we can spare up here. Have Cecil start loading the transports with all the explosives he can get his hands on and crank up the munitions factories. I can play just as dirty as the creeps can."

"Dirtier," Ike said with a smile.

The Rebels continued to beat back the hundreds of punks that had gathered in the suburbs. With dozens of MBTs spearheading, their 155 and 120 main guns spitting out HE rounds, literally disintegrating the ruined buildings the punks had taken refuge in, the criminal element was slowly driven back toward the city.

But the thugs and punks apparently had no stomach for aligning themselves with the creeps. On the fifth day of the Rebel advance, the gangs of criminals began surrendering in droves, walking or staggering out of the buildings with their hands held high in the air.

POW camps were set up on the outskirts of the city and the prisoners trucked to the camps. Ben went to see some of the punks captured in his sector.

They were a sorry-looking, sullen, unwashed and unshaven pack of rabble. They were also stark naked, for the Rebels had ordered them stripped, their stinking clothing burned, and they were being lined up for very close haircuts and then the de-lousing program.

Somehow, Janet House-Lewiston had managed to wrangle a ride to the battle zone; after one look at the lines of naked men and women, she quickly fled to the safety of Doctor Chase's main MASH unit. That action was prompted when one of the prisoners shook his dick at her and made some rather lurid and really quite inventive suggestions concerning what a lovely time they could have together. What really set her boots to flying was when another prisoner said she had a mouth perfectly shaped for sucking cocks.

Janet was vocalizing her outrage to an extremely bored Doctor Chase when Ben walked in and caught the last of her venting her spleen.

"Now, now," Ben said, not wanting to pass up the opportunity to stick the needle to a liberal. "You're forgetting that these men and women probably came from broken homes and were all traumatized by some horrible act they witnessed as children. They're only venting their rage toward an uncaring society, mainly populated with what used to be called Republicans."

The look she gave him was indescribable in its disgust. Chase turned his head to hide his smile.

"And to further add to the predicament of these poor little lost lambs—" Ben wouldn't let up "—I'm sure that someone in their neighborhood had a fancier bicycle than they did, or a more expensive pair of tennis shoes, maybe the kind that have batteries in them, that light up at each step. Those were really neat . . ."

Chase had to put a hand over his mouth to stifle his chuckle.

". . . And I'm sure that the teachers picked on them, as did the police. For no reason at all, certainly. They probably got spanked, too. Oh, my word, what terrible traumas that must have caused . . ."

Janet stared at Ben through narrowed eyes.

". . . And to make matters worse," Ben continued, "they probably didn't have a new car all their own to drive around in when they were young. And since the liberal left of the Democratic Party never could get wealth redistribution passed in Congress—other than through huge increases in personal income tax by the

IRS, that is—the punks just went out and stole them-selves a car. And when they got caught, why, some judge—probably some old meanie who belonged to the Republican Party—actually had the gall to sentence a few of them to prison for stealing. Not many, mind you, but a few.''

Janet stared at Ben. If looks could kill . . .

Doctor Chase was quietly edging away.

"Now, let's see, what else?" Ben began. "Oh, yes. We must not punish those poor, poor unfortunate people. For they—''

Janet held up a hand. "General Raines?"

"Yes, Ms. Janet House-Lewiston?"

"Fuck you!" She wheeled around and stalked off.

Lamar Chase burst out laughing at the expression on Ben's face. "Oh, boy! She got you that time, Raines." He pointed at Ben. "You look like you just bit into a green persimmon, Raines."

Ben smiled. "I love liberals. I think they're all full of shit, but I love to be around them . . . for very brief periods of time," he added.

"What the hell do you mean, General Raines, what do I want done with the prisoners you've taken?" President Altman asked over the horn.

"It's your nation," Ben replied. "We're just here doing a bit of clean-up for you." Ben's eyes twinkled and he smiled. "You want us to shoot them?"

"No!" Altman shouted. "Hell, no. Just . . . wait a minute. Let me think."

After a moment, Ben keyed the mic. "I have another suggestion."

"I hope it's better than the first one."

"We can't stay here and guard the prisoners. That's out. What we can do is transport them to the edge of the NUSA and run them over into Simon Border's territory. Let him take care of them."

"Won't they just return and continue a life of crime?"

"Sure. *Then* we shoot them."

Hundreds of miles south of Ben's location, President Altman looked at Cecil. "Is he kidding?"

"I assure you he is not."

Altman sighed. "I suppose I have no choice but to turn them loose in Border's territory. What does Ben plan on doing with Detroit when he's finished with those damn cannibals?"

"Destroy what is left of it. As much as possible."

"He's not leaving me with much," Altman said wistfully.

"Better than what you had before the Great War," Cecil said drily, and that got him a very startled look from President Altman.

Ben walked the long line of prisoners. There was no hooting or cat-calling or derisive remarks from the ranks of captives. They knew to a person that Ben Raines would not hesitate to shoot them. And most of the prisoners knew, too, whether they would admit it or not, that if Ben Raines, or someone like him, had been in power, laying down the law before the Great War, more than likely none of them would have turned to a life of crime.

The prisoners had all been photographed, and blood had been drawn for DNA testing.

Ben's speech to them was short and not very sweet. "We're going to transport you all to Simon Border's WUSA eastern boundaries and shove you across. Let him deal with you. But I give you this warning—if you ever come east of the Mississippi River again, you're dead men." Ben looked at a Rebel sergeant. "Get them out of here."

Ten minutes later, Ben was busy pouring over maps of Detroit, the prisoners forgotten.

The Rebels threw a noose around the ruins of Detroit. They stretched out east to west along Highway 102, north to south along Highway 39 to the river. The creepies were in a box, with absolutely no place left to run.

The Rebels began retaking the city, block by block, and as they went the combat engineers began leveling the city with explosives. When the creeps went underground to their tunnels and bunkers and basements, the combat engineers sealed them in their stinking lairs forever by bringing tons of rubble down on them, blocking entrances and exits.

It would have taken years to blow every building left standing in the city, but the Rebels knew what signs to look for to determine where the Night People lived . . . usually by the foul odor of their unwashed bodies. A few creeps did try to escape; they were shot by Rebel snipers positioned on the roofs of buildings purposely left standing for that use.

By the first day of September, Detroit was declared a dead city—if the many square miles of rubble could be called a city.

And as was their custom, the Rebels took everything

that could be used, cleaned it up, loaded it on trucks and shipped it back to Base Camp One. Commodes, sinks, bathtubs, cooper tubing, vehicle parts, bricks . . . *anything* that might later be put to use.

Buddy, Rebet, and Danjou had linked up with the militia and Northern Michigan was declared clean and free of criminals and creeps.

The battle for Michigan was over and another state could be added to the growing list of President Altman's NUSA.

Simon Border's aides and advisors came to see him, and from the expressions on their faces, he knew what it was all about. Simon waited behind his desk.

"You had better start thinking about some sort of peace agreement with Ben Raines," his senior advisor told him. "Some sort of written co-existence plan. It is our unanimous opinion that there is no force on the face of the earth that can stop Raines and his Rebels."

Simon sighed and leaned back in his chair. "I remember when Ben Raines and the Rebels first surfaced," he said, almost in a whisper. "Immediately after the Great War. No one took them seriously. They were considered to be just another right-wing nut group. What a mistake that was. Draw up the plan," he said very softly. "I'll sign the damn thing."

Not all the people who were part of Issac Africa's inner circle were extremists or kooks. Many of them were rational, educated, reasonable men and women, and they could all clearly read the writing on the wall. The message they read was decidedly grim.

"You'd better start talking peace with Ben Raines, President Altman, and Simon Border," they urged Issac. "And do it very quickly. We're in a box with no way out. We are completely surrounded with little brushfire wars all over the state. We cannot last."

Issac's generals immediately disagreed, of course, but for once, Issac waved them silent. He had given it much thought. He supposed he might be able to take his people say, oh, up to Maine and make his dream work. He shuddered at just the thought. But *Maine!* Good God, who wanted to spend the rest of their life in *Maine?*

"All right," Issac said softly. "So far, this year has been a disaster. We plant one field, the damn guerrillas burn two more. It's obvious we can't continue like we have. Perhaps we were fools to even think we could make this work."

"Are we just going to give up?" General Mobutomomba asked, defiance in his eyes and tone.

"We can't win," Issac said, resignation behind his words. "In a year's time, Raines will have control of very port and every major highway east of the Mississippi River. Even if we could manage to produce a crop or enough manufactured goods to sell, he wouldn't let us through."

"We could kill the son-of-a-bitch!" General Cugumba suggested.

Issac smiled. "That's something that a lot of people have tried over the years. No one has ever succeeded— obviously. And should we try that, Raines' Rebels would invade this state and when they were through, none of us would be alive, or any of our followers. The Rebels would annihilate us down to the last person. Put killing Ben Raines out of your mind.''

Colonel Zandar, and Generals Cugumba and Mobuto-mamba, exchanged glances and nods, then rose as one. Zandar said, ''We're pulling our people out. We will never surrender to Ben Raines.''

''Ben Raines is not asking for our surrender,'' Issac corrected. ''Just that we not have a closed, racist society. And before any of you start spouting a lot of words that are false, let me stop it before it begins. The SUSA is neither closed nor racist, and you all know that. Now, I don't like Ben Raines. As a matter of fact, I hate the bastard! But I won't accuse him of being something he isn't.''

''We're leaving, Issac,'' Cugumba insisted.

''Then leave,'' Issac replied with a shrug of his shoulders. ''But if you're leaving to wage war against the Rebels, you're going to lose.''

''We have thirty thousand men under arms,'' General Mobutomamba boasted.

Issac smiled. ''And no planes, and not much in the way of supplies, except what you can carry with you. You will have no supply lines. For every tank you have, Ben Raines has thirty. For every Howitzer you have, Ben Raines has fifty. For every bullet you have, Ben Raines has a million. You can't beat him. I urge you all to reconsider. Just think rationally for a moment. That's something I hadn't done for a long time until quite recently and I assure you, it's refreshing. Think about this—if we sign a pact with the SUSA, we'll have markets for our goods, we'll have the strongest ally in the world beside us, and we can stand down at least half our army and live like normal people.'' He shook his head. ''I listened to that idiot Rita Rivers and her nitwit cohorts for too long. They poisoned my mind. I have more years behind me than I have in front of me. I'd like to live them in relative peace."

"We're taking our people out and fight Ben Raines," Zandar said.

Issac lifted a hand in farewell. "Take those idiot twins, Yahoo and Yazoo, with you. And don't come back here begging for assistance or sanctuary," he warned. "Once you leave, you're on your own."

"We could just take over this state, you know," Colonel Zandar said with a smile.

"Try it," Issac's voice turned very cold and menacing.

Cugumba put a restraining hand on Zandar's arm. "Stop that kind of talk." He looked into Issac's eyes. "When we return, we shall come back as victors, Issac."

Issac shook his head. "Not when, General. *If.*"

Chapter Twenty-Four

"Cecil just touched base," Corrie told Ben. "Both Simon Border and Issac Africa want to talk peace with us."

Ben looked up and smiled.

"That's the good news," Corrie said. "Now comes the bad."

Ben's smile faded.

"Three of Issac's commanding officers have broken with him and left the state to fight us. Cugumba, Mobutomamba, and Zandar. They have officially declared war against the Rebels. They have approximately thirty thousand men and women under arms."

"Are they moving toward the SUSA?"

She shook her head. "They are moving toward us. Intelligence says they plan to engage us in Ohio."

"Why? Why would they declare war against us? We haven't bothered them."

Corrie spread her hands in a "who knows?" gesture.

"Very well. Get me one of those break-away command-ers on the horn. Before I launch any attacks, I want to hear the declaration of war from them."

It took only a moment to connect with the break-away troops. "Colonel Zandar, boss," Corrie said, handing Ben the mic. "But I think, despite his rank, he runs the whole show."

"This is Ben Raines, Colonel Zandar. Why have you declared war against us?"

"Because you are the enemy," Zandar responded without hesitation.

Ben had to think about that for a moment. He keyed the mic. "Why am I your enemy?"

"Because you refused to recognize our state."

"I recognized your state, Colonel. I just said I wouldn't trade with you as long as your philosophy was based on racial hatred."

"Whites are our enemy."

"Only if you make them your enemy, Colonel. People of all races live and work together in the SUSA without a problem."

"Uncle Toms and Oreos."

"Oreos?" Cooper questioned.

"Black on the outside, white on the inside," Ben told him, then once more keyed the mic. "Colonel Zandar, don't tangle with us. It's a fight you cannot win."

"We shall be victorious, Raines. You're a dead man."

"And you're a fool," Ben replied, then tossed the mic to Corrie. He looked at Beth. "Fuck him."

"No thanks," Beth said, straight-faced.

Ben burst out laughing.

* * *

0700 hours.

"Thirty thousand troops make for a very long convoy," Ben said to his squadron leaders. He pointed to a map. "As of one hour ago, the enemy was here, moving toward us on Interstate 70, in Indiana. You boys and girls see how much grief you can cause this column."

Two hours later, the souped-up P-51E's hit the miles-long column of Cugumba, Mobutomamba, and Zandar with rockets, cannon, bombs, and machine-gun fire. They came in out of the sun at 500 mph, right on the deck, leaving behind them dozens of blown-up, burning, and destroyed vehicles, and hundreds of dead and wounded soldiers.

Then the planes circled around and hit the column again, catching the soldiers as they were coming out of ditches and timber, heading back to the burning convoy to offer assistance to the wounded.

When the planes headed back to Ohio, they left behind them a convoy in ruins, and a thoroughly pissed-off Colonel Zandar.

Generals Cugumba and Mobutomamba were at the rear of the miles-long column, and did not arrive at the front of the convoy until some forty-five minutes after the attack.

"This was a warning to us," Mobutomamba said, after looking around and assessing the damage and the deaths, which were both considerable.

Cugumba nodded his head. "I agree."

"So?" Zandar asked belligerently.

Mobutomamba and Cugamba exchanged glances.

Zandar picked up on the looks immediately. When

he spoke, his tone was contemptuous. "I know you've been talking behind my back. And I know what you've been saying. You want to quit. You want to go back to New Africa and break up your armies and grovel at the feet of Issac and Kenyata. Well, go on. Leave. Some of your men will return with you. But most will follow me. Our dream of a New Africa will never have a chance as long as Ben Raines is still alive. I am going to kill Ben Raines."

The two older men shook their heads. Cugamba said, "You will not kill Ben Raines. You probably will never get close to Ben Raines. And we have not been speaking ill of you, Zandar. You are a brave man. But you are also an angry man; you are a rebel with no cause. Issac saw that Ben Raines is not our enemy. Then Mobuto-mamba saw it, and finally I realized it." He waved a hand at the smoking wreckage. "Ben Raines has planes enough to have finished this. Yet he did not. He's giving us a chance, Zandar. And I for one, as is Mobutomamba, will take his warning and return to a life of peace and productivity. We shall open our borders and live in harmony with men of all colors."

"Cowards," Zandar spat the word. "Both of you."

Cugumba cut his eyes to Zandar and smiled grimly. He had been a soldier before the Great War. A full bird colonel in the United States Army; an infantry officer. "Watch your mouth, young man," he warned. "I am no self-appointed officer. I earned my rank the hard way. I was first an enlisted man, then went to OCS and climbed upward on my merits. Don't you ever call me a coward. I am going back to the state of Missouri, not New Africa—Missouri. And I am going to ask Issac to forgive my rashness. As for you, Zandar, I hope you will find your peace in the grave. For when you attack Ben Raines, that will be your future.''

The two older men spun around and walked off.

"About half of Zandar's people have turned around and headed back west,'' Corrie called to Ben. "Eyes in the Sky estimates some fifteen thousand troops have broken up into small units and are heading our way.''

"They'll be picking up black punk gangs as they move toward us,'' Ben said. "Incorporating them into the ranks ...'' He paused. "Or using them for cannon fodder.''

"Probably the latter,'' Ike said.

Ben looked at his son, Buddy, commander of 8 Batt, the special operations battalion. "Get your teams together, son. Dan Gray is already forming his people up. Then check with operations and work out where you'll be. Start harassing Mr. Zandar and his people.''

The ruggedly handsome and muscular Buddy pulled out a double-edged dagger, held it up, and smiled.

"Yes,'' his father said. "Fear is an excellent motivator.''

Zandar had split his thousands of people up into company-sized groups and sent them in all directions, with orders to regroup once they reached the Ohio line. It was a bad mistake on Zandar's part. While the Rebels were a mighty fighting force *en masse,* they had first begun as down and dirty guerrilla fighters, fighting unbelievable odds ... and winning. The Rebels had perfected guerrilla fighting down to an art that few people could ever attain. The Rebels were at their best operating in small, highly lethal groups.

"Forget it, Raines," Doctor Chase told Ben as he stood in the doorway to Ben's office, located in a home some twenty-five miles south of Toledo. He had caught Ben pacing the office like a caged animal.

Ben slowly turned to face his old friend. "Do you now have the ability to get into my mind, Lamar?"

"No." The doctor poured a cup of coffee and sat down. "I just know you too well. You want to be out there with Buddy and Dan and all the other special ops people, slithering around on the ground with your face painted and a cammo rag around your head, cutting throats." He pointed a finger at Ben. "If you try it, Ben, I'll order you into the hospital, and I mean it."

Ben smiled and sat down. He knew Chase meant it. In any army, anywhere, the doctors had the last word, and it made no difference if one was a general or a private. If Chase ordered him into the hospital, Ben would have to go. "Yes, I'd like to be out there, Lamar. But I'm not going. That isn't to say I couldn't do a good job. But this time I'll leave it to younger fellows."

"Even that old fire-breathing warhorse Dan Gray is staying back overseeing the operation," Chase said. "And he's a few years younger than you."

Ben chuckled. "I'll admit something, Lamar—I really don't mind being middle-aged. I thought I would hate it, but I don't. I think because I really haven't slowed down that much. I'm a step slower. But I've learned to compensate for that."

"We were a couple of firebrands when we first met those long years ago, weren't we, Ben?"

"A couple of revolutionaries with a wild dream and two dozen or so followers."

Both men chuckled for a moment, recalling memories that went back over a span of a dozen years.

Anna stuck her pretty head into the office. "Reports coming in from the field, General Ben. Buddy's people really raised some hell last night. They killed about a dozen of Zandar's personal troops, cut off their heads, and stuck them up on poles."

"Jesus, Ben!" Chase said.

Ben shook his head. "You know I didn't order that done, Lamar." He looked up as Corrie joined Anna in the doorway. "Are you in contact with Buddy?"

"Negative. His last transmission said he would be out of pocket for about forty-eight hours."

"He planned that well," Ben remarked sarcastically. "That devious—" He bit that off.

"I wonder where he got it from?" Lamar questioned drily, getting to his feet and moving to the door. He paused and looked at Ben. "I meant what I said, Ben."

Ben smiled. "You can't prevent me from inspecting my own troops, Lamar. No matter where they might be. That is any commander's right."

"Raines," the doctor said, knowing Ben had him on that point. "You're a prick!"

At the time, Ben really had no intention of visiting Buddy, or any of the other special ops troops. He just wanted to stick the needle to Lamar. But the more he thought about traveling over to Indiana, the better the idea sounded.

Zandar had approximately four divisions of twenty-five hundred troops per division. Eyes in the Sky reported that about two thousand of Cugumba and Mobutomamba's troops had stayed with Zandar. Twelve thousand troops spread out north to south over about three hundred miles, along Highway 31.

"Let's end it," Ben muttered. "Zandar is not going to quit." He called for Corrie. "Pull in Ike, West, and Georgi. Get the tanks rolling. Put all fixed-wing and chopper gunships on alert. Order Dan and Buddy to cease immediately all guerrilla action, form up their battalions, and start gradually falling back. Prepare to throw up a defensive line along Interstates 69 and 65. Buddy's 8 Batt at the top, Georgi's 5 Batt to the extreme south end. The placement will be Buddy, Dan, us, Rebet, Danjou, Ike, West, and Georgi. I'm tired of dicking around with this guy, Corrie. Let's go bump heads."

Zandar had ordered the guards tripled at night—and still the infiltrators were slipping through and doing their deadly work. But it was not demoralizing his people. Zandar personally saw to that. Then the throat-cutting abruptly stopped.

Zandar was filled with hate, but he was far from being a stupid man. Actually, his IQ was very high. He just never did much with that intelligence . . . except hate white people.

But the ceasing of the infiltrators puzzled him. Why go to all that trouble, and then suddenly pull back?

His forward teams had reported that the Rebels were pulling back. They had withdrawn to Highway 15 and were still falling back toward the east.

Why?

Was Raines giving up?

Despite his shining arrogance, Zandar considered that highly unlikely.

An aide broke into his thoughts. "Sir? Ben Raines has made contact with us. He wishes to speak to you."

Zandar stared at the aide for a moment, then stood up and walked to the communications room.

"Hey, Zandar! Are you there, asshole?" The voice of Ben Raines sprang out of the speaker.

Zandar froze in shock. *Nobody* spoke to him in such a manner.

"Hey, prick-face." Ben's voice was taunting. "Pick up the damn mic and speak. Oh, you have to press that little button on the side to talk, in case you haven't figured it out yet. And as stupid as you are, you probably haven't."

Zandar snatched up the mic and shouted, "This is Colonel Zandar!"

"Colonel?" Ben's voice was filled with sarcasm. "Colonel? Hell, boy, you wouldn't make a pimple on a real colonel's ass. You're nothing but a goddamn sleazy street punk."

"What do you want, Raines?" Zandar shouted.

"Your black ass, boy."

Hundreds of miles away, Issac was listening to the transmission. "He's deliberately taunting you, Zandar. And you haven't got enough sense to understand that. You're a damn fool if you fall for this trick."

"You honky son-of-a-bitch!" Zandar shouted.

"I have about a hundred acres of cotton down south that needs pickin'. I figure that's about all you're good for. I'll feed you lots of greens and fatback and corn-bread."

"Fuck you, Raines!" Zandar was livid with rage.

Cugumba and Mobutomamba were also listening to the transmission. They exchanged glances and both shook their heads. Ben Raines was playing Zandar like a puppet on a string.

"I'll kill you, Raines!" Zandar screamed out his rage.

"How?" Ben responded. "You gonna hit me with a chitlin', boy?"

Zandar finally got it. He had almost fallen for Ben's taunting. He took several deep breaths and calmed himself. He keyed the mic. "Very good, Raines. Excellent. You had me going there for a time. But I won't fall for your race-baiting. You are not a racist, Raines. I know that for a fact. I hate your guts, but you are not a racist. Now what do you want?"

"Very well, Zandar, or whatever the hell your name is. We can do this easy, or hard. It's up to you. Lay down your arms and disband your army. Make a life for yourself and your followers. Live a long time. This is the only warning I'm going to give you. Butt heads with me, and you're a dead man. You understand all that?"

"Raines, go right straight to hell. I'm going to destroy you."

"Then you really are a fool, Zandar. Better men than you have tried that. I'm still around."

"I will meet you in combat and defeat you, Raines."

"OK, sucker. Come on."

Ben broke the transmission.

"Arrogant son-of-a-bitch!" Zandar said.

Ben handed the mic to Corrie and winked at Jersey.

"Kick-ass time!" Jersey said.

Chapter Twenty-Five

Zandar was soldier enough to see that if he pulled his troops together *en masse* and smashed through any part of the Rebel line, Ben's troops would just fall in behind him and he'd be no better off than before. Ruefully, Zandar realized he had to meet Ben Raines on his terms.

Both armies were now facing each other in company-sized groups, or smaller.

Ben had placed his heavy artillery well back from the several miles of No Man's Land that separated the two armies, and the Rebel tanks were close in and carefully placed and camouflaged.

The Rebels waited for Zandar to make the first move.

But Zandar had turned suddenly cautious. Ben Raines had called his hand and was waiting for him to either bet his cards or fold.

It was purely unintentional, but Zandar and Ben were facing each other at the junction of Interstate 69 and Highway 18, just east of Marion, Indiana.

"That's Zandar facing us," Corrie said to Ben. "Scouts just confirmed it."

Ben nodded his head then checked his watch. "Wonder what he's waiting on? It's well past dawn."

Zandar was pacing the ground. His people were in place, waiting for his orders. The time was *now*. He could not wait Ben out; he didn't have the supplies for that. Many of his people were living off the land as it was and supplies were critical. The realization came to him in a rush: Ben Raines knew all that. The Rebels were well-fed, well supplied, and waiting like a fat cat for a mouse to come out of its hole.

"The son of a bitch!" Zandar cursed.

Another hot rush of realization flooded Zandar. If he ordered his troops forward, it would be suicide. The Rebels would chop them to bloody pieces. Zandar looked up into the blue of the Indiana sky. No planes, no helicopter gunships. Oh, hell, no. Raines was holding them back until Zandar ordered his people across the three miles of empty, then they would swoop down like huge mechanical carrion birds, spitting out death.

Zandar was many things. But he was no fool. There was no way for him to win. Just . . . no . . . way . . . at . . . all.

Zandar sat down on a camp stool and put his face in his hands. He just could not give the orders to sacrifice his troops. The punks and thugs he'd gathered along the way had vanished like smoke in a breeze when the Rebels started their murderous nighttime guerrilla tactics. Those bloody death-grinning heads up on poles had really done it for the punks. They had disappeared in a rush after one look at that hideous sight. Just recalling it left Zandar with a queasy feeling in his stomach.

Zandar finally admitted something else, too: from the moment he first saw those bloody heads stuck up on poles, he had known the war was lost, had realized then he was not going to defeat the Rebels. All his talk had been just that: so much hot air from the mouth.

"When do we attack, sir?" An aide broke into his thoughts.

Zandar looked up at the young man. He shook his head. "We don't," he whispered.

"Sir?"

"Order all troops to stand down. I'm not going to turn this ground red with our blood. It's pointless. Get me Ben Raines on the horn."

"Zandar on the blower, boss," Corrie said, handing Ben the mic.

"Colonel," Ben said.

"General Raines. If we lay down our arms, will you let us surrender in dignity?"

"Of course, I will. I'll do more than that. We'll help you get settled in somewhere and help you out with food for the coming winter."

"You would help us with all that?"

"Sure. Why not? We're no longer enemies, are we?"

Zandar felt his eyes burn with a mist. He keyed the mic. "No, General Raines. No. We are no longer enemies."

"Good. Have you had breakfast?"

"Why . . . ah, no, I haven't."

"I'll send a Hummer over for you. We'll talk about getting you folks settled in over a hot meal."

"I'll be waiting." After Ben had signed off, Zandar stood for a moment. Finally, he shook his head. "I just don't understand that man. I wonder if anybody really knows what Ben Raines is all about?"

In the span of twenty-four hours, the state of Missouri was reborn and became a part of the SUSA, Zandar and his troops began making plans to resettle all over the Midwest (with many of them expressing a desire to relocate in the SUSA), and a major battle was avoided without having to fire a shot.

Indiana was declared clean and another state was added to President Altman's NUSA.

"Ben Raines can do more in three months than the entire federal government could do in three decades," Paul Altman remarked.

The western third of Ohio had been purged of the criminal element (for the most part) but the eastern two-thirds was quite another matter. The punks and thugs and assorted human crud, including the Night People, were running out of places to hide, as the advancing Rebels were slowly pushing them back into the northeast corridor.

"It's been relatively easy so far," West, the mercenary and commander of 4 Batt, remarked at a meeting of batt coms. "But now comes the hard part."

"What about West Virginia?" Jim Peters, commander of 14 Batt asked. "It's a damn battleground."

"I don't want to get bogged down in that state," Ben said. "That's the last thing I want. Old blood feuds erupting, race wars popping up all over the place, old union members against old non-union factions shooting at each other. It's madness. I know there are thousands of good, decent people living there—existing is probably a better word. But we'll just avoid that state for the time being."

"How about this winter, Ben?" Ike asked.

"We'll keep going as long as we can. But our meteorologists are predicting a bad winter here in the north. Shifting over to a more pleasant subject, Cecil tells me he's received documents from Simon Border detailing a non-aggression pact and an agreement of cooperation and trade between our two nations. North America just might be headed toward the road to peace after all."

"You always did predict we would break up into nations within a nation," Jim Peters said. "Even before the Great War, that was the way you said we'd eventually go."

Ben smiled at that. Those books he'd written before the Great War had gotten him into trouble with the federal government. The FBI had put him on their subversives list and launched an investigation on him that had still been on-going when the Great War toppled every government on the face of the earth. That investigation had the FBI snooping and prowling into every aspect of his life, from the cradle on. One friend who had been interviewed several times by the Feds told Ben the Bureau had a dossier on him that was about six inches thick. Such was the paranoia of the liberals in power at the time. At one point in the investigation, the Bureau strongly suspected that Ben was the leader of a huge underground army of guerrillas, whose goal was to undermine and finally overthrow the government.

When Ben learned of that, he was amused for days.

With the nation awash in every type of crime imaginable, the government had spent several million dollars investigating a writer of popular fiction.

Ben had once pointed out the absurdity of that to the FBI agents who visited him.

The Bureau had not been amused.

The Rebels began their march toward the Northeast, but now it was much slower going. The thugs and punks knew they were being pushed up into a box from which there was little chance of escape, and they were fighting like cornered wildcats.

Cecil had the ring of missiles around the SUSA fully operational and the home guard was once more built up and ready to defend the SUSA should the rabble try again to overrun their borders—something no one believed would ever again occur. He released the battalions that had been stationed in the SUSA and Batts 16, 17, and 21 joined the Rebels in the field.

Just as Ben's 1 Batt and four other battalions were getting into position to strike against the ruins of Cleveland, Akron, and Canton, winter reared up several weeks early and laid a blanket of ice and snow over the land.

"Dig in and stay warm," Ben told his troops. "It'll warm up before long. This storm is a freak of nature. It's far too early for it to last."

But Ben also knew the punks would take the opportunity to split. The gangs they were dealing with now were the more intelligent ones: smarter, tougher, larger, better-equipped. They had lasted for years, and for most of the gangs, that was not based on luck, but on brains. Ben knew that most criminals, had they applied their intelligence to legal and legitimate endeavors, would be highly successful men and women.

"From now on," Ben said to his team one freezing

cold day in late October, "it's going to be down and dirty. Scouts are reporting the three cities are virtual ghost towns. Except, of course, for you all know who."

Mass groans greeted that.

"That's right," Ben said. "Our old friends, the creepies. We can always count on them to be very predictable."

Cincinnati, Dayton, Columbus, Springfield—all had been deserted cities when the Rebels pushed through—except for bands of creepies.

"Ben," Ike stood up. "What's this about you and your 1 Batt heading down south and pushing east through Wheeling?"

"That's my plan. Why?"

"Well, Ben, in case you haven't looked at a map lately, Wheeling is in West Virginia. And Wheeling, according to Scouts, is a battleground." Ike was one of only a few officers who could talk to Ben in such a manner.

Ben laughed at the expression on Ike's face. "I'm going to Pittsburgh, Ike. And I'm going to come up from the south. Dan is going straight in from Weirdton, and Buddy is coming in from the north. If the bands of malcontents in Wheeling want a fight, we'll give them one. Right now, let's start clearing out the creeps in Cleveland."

Corrie stuck her head into the room. "We got a problem, boss. Emil Hite is missing."

"Missing? He's supposed to be inspecting playgrounds. What'd he do, get tangled up in a swing?"

"He probably wishes he had. Seems as though Emil found a bunch of his old followers, among others. They decided that we might need some help up here—"

"Oh, shit!" Ike muttered.

"The last anyone heard from him, he and his . . . ah

. . . well, followers had crossed the border into West Virginia. By the way, the group is about two hundred strong and call themselves the Rainbow Warriors.''

Dan Gray groaned at that.

Ben sighed. "OK, Corrie. See if you can find out how well armed the, ah, Rainbow Warriors are.''

"They're very well armed, boss. They tried to steal some tanks, but no one could figure out how to drive them. But they did leave in APCs and Hummers and deuce-and-a-halves, and they took plenty of supplies.''

Ben smiled. "There are any number of punks and thugs and assorted trash who made the mistake of not taking Emil and his people seriously. We helped bury a lot of them. Emil and two hundred followers could put up a hell of a fight. I sort of feel sorry for anyone who tangles with them. Corrie, try to get a frequency fix on Emil. All right, let's revamp our schedule. Here's what I'm going to do . . .''

"Where in the name of all that's holy are we?" Emil asked.

Emil and a dozen of his Rainbow Warriors were standing in the middle of the cracked old highway, looking at maps. Not that the maps would do them much good, for all the highway markers were long gone.

"Lost," one of his followers said mournfully.

"Well, I *know* that!" Emil said. "But does anyone know *approximately* where we might be?"

"West Virginia," another of his people said.

Emil looked heavenward and shook his head.

Emil and his Rainbow Warriors were deep in West Virginia. How they had managed to get that far without someone taking a shot at them would forever remain a mystery. But all that was about to change—abruptly.

The men and women of the Rainbow Warriors had started out with good intentions: to assist Ben Raines in clearing the country of hoodlums and criminals. Getting hopelessly lost in West Virginia was definitely not part of the plan.

"I think someone should climb a tall tree and take a look around," a man suggested.

Emil turned slowly to stare at the man. "Climb a tree? What a brilliant idea, Rolf. Superb. Why don't you do that? I mean, take your choice of trees. We're surrounded by millions of them. Might I suggest that one." Emil pointed toward a high mountain. "It will only take you a week to get up there. Now shut up with this tree business. What happened to all the damn road signs?"

Emil, a former con man who had linked up with Ben some years back, always meant well. Even when he was running a scam, professing to be a holy man in perfect harmony with the Great God Blomm . . .

"I'm cold," a woman said.

"Go sit in the truck, dear," Emil told her.

Emil then drew himself up to his full height, which was only a few inches above five feet, and looked all around him. Never one to conform to Rebel dress codes, for this foray into the unknown Emil had chosen low quarter shoes, a nice dress suit with matching tie, and a snap-brim 1940s-style Bogart hat. He wore a trench coat over the suit. But while Emil looked just about as ridiculous as a person could look—considering the time and place—he was far from being stupid. He had survived on his wits for years, getting out of more jams than Dick Tracy.

"Mount up," Emil told his people. "This damn high-way has to lead somewhere."

It did. It led to a small town located in a long and wide valley between two mountain ranges. The decent people of the small town had long departed for safer ground, leaving the town in the hands of one Lukey DeFray and his small army of thugs.

Lukey had long been the Bull of the Woods around those parts. Six feet, six inches tall, two hundred and sixty-five pounds of mean. What Lukey wanted, Lukey got—one way or the other. Lukey was the stereotypical bully; if he had anything even resembling a conscience, no one had ever seen it exhibited. Lukey had gathered together some three hundred of the most worthless men and women to ever walk the face of the earth. They were the absolute bottom of the dregs of humanity

"Army vehicles a-comin' in from the south, Lukey." The voice sprang out of the speaker of the CB radio.

"Looks lak Ben Raines and his soldier boys and girls has arrived," Lukey said, standing up. "I been lookin' forward to this moment. I'm a-gonna whup that son-of-a-bitch until his toenails curl up. I been hearin' for years how tough the Rebels is. Now, by God, we'll just see how tough they is." Lukey picked up the mic. "Is they any women in that bunch, Ashford?"

"Some."

"Good. I need me some strange pussy. Maybelle's 'bout all wallered out. Time to give that some rest." He picked up his M-16. "Let's go give Raines' Rebels a proper greetin,' boys."

Chapter Twenty-Six

"Pilots reported what appeared to be a military convoy heading north on this highway," Corrie told Ben, pointing to the map spread out on the hood of a pickup truck. "Right there."

"We're still a good two or three days from there," Ben said.

Ben's batt coms had put up quite an argument about his heading off by himself in search of Emil, but the boss was the boss, and Ben prevailed.

"All sorts of gangs operating all over this state," Cooper reminded Ben.

They had crossed the Ohio River and were just inside what used to known as West Virginia. For a very brief period of time, the capitol of the United States had been located in the state. It had been looted and destroyed by gangs. Most of the good, decent people had either fled the state, bunkered themselves deep in the mountains in heavily armed communities, or turned small towns into forts against the many roaming gangs of human predators.

As Ben had predicted, the sudden and unexpected cold snap had abated and the weather had turned warmer, melting the snow and ice. The air was still crisp, holding the promise of full winter, but for now, it was not uncomfortable.

Jersey looked around her at the unfamiliar country. "Emil is a pain in the ass," she said.

Ben chuckled. "Yeah, you're right, Little Bit. But he's *our* pain in the ass. Let's go find the little bastard and his intrepid band of followers."

"Pain in the ass," Jersey muttered.

"Just hold it right here," Emil said, lowering his binoculars. "I don't like the looks of this."

"What's wrong with it? It's a lovely little town," a woman said.

"Not really," Emil contradicted. "The streets are full of trash. Store windows have been smashed out. And there is a body on the sidewalk in front of that old drug store."

"This is the best highway we've been on in two days," a year-long friend of Emil's said. "And it goes right through that town. Either that or we backtrack for fifty miles."

"I have no intention of backtracking through that dismal area," Emil said, looking back in the direction they'd just come.

Actually it wasn't dismal at all, but it was almost winter, the trees were stark in the cold sunlight, and the area was all but devoid of human life . . . decent human life, that is.

Emil could be a clown when he wished to be, and that was most of the time. But he was also a pretty savvy soldier, with a nose for smelling out trouble. And his nose was sending him some alarming signals about the peaceful-looking little town.

"APCs button up and edge on down to that town," Emil ordered. "I want every gun ready to go."

The APCs that Emil had taken from an unguarded depot down in the SUSA were actually Bradley Fighting Vehicles. They carried a squad of five and a crew of three: driver, gunner, and commander, the driver and commander positioned in the turret. Its weapons were a 25mm chain gun that was awesome when put into action, a coaxial machine gun and an M-60 machine gun. It could also fire TOW missiles with deadly accuracy up to about three thousand yards.

Lukey DeFray was about to come head to head with modern, Rebel re-worked and re-armored machinery of war.

"Let that armored thing come on in," Lukey ordered. "Everybody stay down and don't fire at it. We want them folks to think we're nice and friendly. What do the boys up on the bluffs say?"

The boys on the bluffs were using CB radios to communicate and Emil and his people were listening to every word being said.

"They's about two hundred or so of them folks. 'Bout half of 'em women. But they don't think they's soldiers, they all dressed sort of funny."

"How funny?" Lukey asked.

"Sorta like hippies. 'Ceptin' that little bandy rooster

that 'pears to be runnin' the show. He's all duded up in a suit and tie.''

"Well, he ain't no hippie then. I never knowed no hippie to wear no Sunday clothes.''

"For a fact.''

"Well, we'll sucker them in and then kill all the men and fuck all the women.''

"Sounds good to me.''

"Cretins,'' Emil muttered. "Worthless trash.'' He grabbed up a mic. "They're unfriendly,'' he radioed to the Bradley. "Be ready for anything.''

"That's a big fat ten-four,'' the commander of the Bradley said. The commander had been a Rebel for years, until getting wounded and forced out of the field. Then he went back to being a hippie, enjoying the laid-back life-style. But he definitely was not a member of the peace-and-love bunch. "You hear all that, Cornpone?'' he asked his gunner.

Cornpone, another Rebel who'd gotten a bit long in the tooth for the field and went back to a hippie life-style, shifted a wad of bubble gum and said, "Shore did. That's plumb discouragin',' too.'' Cornpone had been born and reared in rural Alabama. "Makes me sad when people ain't friendly.'' He reached over and flipped a switch, activating the all-weather speaker he had installed outside the Bradley. He hit another switch which turned on a tape recorder. The sounds of Bobby Blue Bland singing "Share Your Love With Me'' filled the street.

"Gawddamn nigger music,'' Lukey bitched. "I hate nigger music.''

Lukey had never served in the military, and did not know a Bradley Fighting Vehicle from a banana. He'd never been more than a hundred miles in any direction from the area in which he had been whelped. Lukey had been twenty years old when the Great War struck the globe a decade back—and he was not going to see another birthday.

The Bradley stopped in the middle of the street, Main Street. The fifty thousand-pound fighting vehicle squatted on the cracked old street like some prehistoric beast. Inside, the six firing-ports were opened.

"Hey, you inside that there machine!" Lukey hollered. "Why don't y'all get out and show yourselves. If you don't, we liable to think you don't like us and have to pull y'all out of there and whup your asses."

"The man is an idiot," Cornpone remarked.

"And hush up that gawddamn squallin' coon music, too," Lukey added.

"Now he's beginnin' to get on the wrong side of me," Cornpone said. He reached over and turned up the volume. The voice of Ray Charles singing "What'd I Say" blared over the street.

Lukey lifted his M-16 and gave the speaker a full burst of 5.56 rounds, blowing it apart and stilling the music.

"Fire!" Emil shouted into the mic.

The turret swiveled and the 25mm chain gun began yammering. The rounds blew out the front window of the store, tore the door off its hinges, and demolished the interior of the store, sending dust and wood and plaster flying in all directions, decapitating three of Lukey's followers and blowing great smoking holes in the chests and belly of several others.

"Gawddamn!" Lukey bellered, from his suddenly attained position on the dirty floor. "Git the fuck outta here, boys!"

Up on the bluffs, Emil jumped into his HumVee and shouted, "Charge! Forward into the fray, Rainbow Warriors!"

The driver floorboarded the pedal, the 8600-pound vehicle, powered by a V-8 6.2-liter engine surged forward, and Emil wound up in the back seat in a sprawl of arms and legs.

"Lukey!" the spotter on the bluffs shouted into his CB mic. "They's a-comin',"

There was no reply, for the CB base station had been blown into a thousand parts, and Lukey was in the alley behind the store, pickin' 'em up and puttin' 'em down just as hard as he could.

The Bradley leaped forward, made a hard left at the intersection and came to a halt at the mouth of the alley. The turret swiveled and the chain gun began belching out 25mm high explosive rounds. The alley turned into a slaughterhouse.

A dozen more of Lukey's followers were blown into oblivion. With a squall of pure terror, Lukey leaped through an open door, rolled on the floor of what used to be a dress shop and came to his feet, looking wild-eyed all around him, just as six more Bradleys rolled up outside. Six more chain guns began firing in all directions and thirty M-16's began firing from the ports of the vehicles.

"Oh, Lordy!" Lukey hollered, curling up in a ball on the littered floor.

That was the last thing he ever said, as the second floor of the old building, built in the early 1920s, collapsed, burying the gang leader under a dozen tons of brick and wood.

Emil Hite and his Rainbow Warriors had taken the town. What was left of it.

"Victory is ours!" The speaker, located about a foot from Ben's head, screamed out the words. Ben spilled a cup of coffee all over himself and Jersey fell off her camp stool.

"It's Emil," Corrie said, struggling to keep a straight face.

"No kidding?" Ben replied.

"We have fought in the hedgerows and in the alleys and the streets," Emil's voice rang out. "We shall never surrender!"

"I'll personally strangle that crazy son-of-a-bitch!" Jersey said, getting to her feet.

"The forces of darkness and evil have been conquered!" Emil continued his harangue. "Good has prevailed. Though outnumbered at least a hundred to one, the Rainbow Warriors were victorious, fighting valiantly. Although wounded—" Emil had a bump on his forehead from impacting against the floorboards of the back seat "—I led my people in battle. West Virginia is ours!" A short pause. "Well, a small part of it, anyway," he wound down.

"Corrie," Ben said, mopping himself with a towel given him by Anna. "See if you can find out the location of that little bastard. And tell him to stay put!" Ben went off to change into dry BDUs.

Two days later, Ben and his 1 Batt rolled into Central West Virginia and hooked up with Emil Hite and his Rainbow Warriors.

* * *

Ben just couldn't stay mad at Emil. Somehow, despite himself, Emil always managed to come out on top. Ben stared at him for a moment, then shook his head. "Emil," he said, drawing upon all his patience, "do you realize that we are in the middle of a state that is crawling with gangs and malcontents, people who have been feuding with each other for a damn century, and God only knows what else?"

"Never fear, my general," Emil said, tugging at his hat brim. "The Rainbow Warriors will lead you to safety."

"Oh, shit!" Jersey muttered.

"I'm sure you will," Ben said, just as sarcastically as he could, which was considerable.

The sarcasm bounced right off the little con artist. Nothing could hurt Emil's feelings.

"What do you have in mind, Emil?" Ben asked. "About leading us to safety, that is," he was quick to add.

"Well . . . to tell you the truth . . ." Emil hedged. "I mean, we've been so busy here, I really haven't had the time to give that much thought."

"I see. Then I'll tell you—mount up. We're getting the hell out of this country before hard winter sets in and we're trapped in here. And yes, Emil, you're going with us. I can't very well send you back."

Emil snapped to attention. "You will not be sorry, my general."

Ben just stared at the man for moment before turning away, softly muttering under his breath.

Ben put Emil and his people in the center of the column, thus insuring their safety and more importantly, effectively nullifying any chance of Emil screwing up.

The long column angled and snaked around on worn and cracked old state roads for a day before coming to a major U.S. highway. The column headed north, with what used to be the Monongahela National Forest to their east.

They passed through several small towns that were deserted, after having been looted.

"There is life in Elkins," Corrie said, after receiving a report from recon. "And they are not hostile."

"That has a nice sound to it," Ben said.

A town of nearly ten thousand before the Great War, there were now about seven hundred people living in and around the town. And they welcomed the Rebels.

"We get the news on shortwave out of your Base Camp One, General," the spokesman said. "Is Paul Altman really the new president?"

"That he is," Ben assured the man. "And I believe he's going to be a good one. I personally saw to it that the election was on the up and up." Ben said it with a straight face; Jersey rolled her dark eyes, Beth almost choked on a fresh-baked muffin, Anna left the room before she could burst out laughing, and Corrie and Cooper exchanged glances and then ducked their heads to hide their grins.

"We've got a pretty good communications system here, General," the appointed leader of the townspeople said. "We monitor a lot of chatter. And I feel I have to warn you that from here on east and north, it's a damn battleground."

"We know. We'll deal with them. For the moment, let's talk about this state."

The local's expression changed. "From what we've been able to pick up from your open frequencies, you don't plan on cleaning out this state any time soon, General."

"I changed my mind about that, Mr. Thomas. But we're going to have to have some help in doing so."

Those locals gathered around applauded and cheered. "That's the best news we've heard in months," Thomas said. He sighed and shook his head. "There are a lot of good people left in this state, General. West Virginia had some bad press for years before the Great War, and unfortunately, some of it was deserved. Now some of those same factions are shooting at each other. But we don't know the solution. Do you?"

Ben cut his eyes to Jersey and she smiled. "Oh, yes," Ben told the man. "We sure do."

Chapter Twenty-Seven

Ben ordered Buddy and his 8 Batt to come south and cut into West Virginia at the first standing bridge around Huntington. Dan was to come into the state at Parkersburg, and Rebet to enter the state at Wheeling . . . after cleaning out that city.

Ben set up his CP at Elkins.

Ben had learned that West Virginia had an active militia before the Great War, but had been forced hard underground by the government, before and during the gun-grab that disarmed most Americans. The great gun-grab, brought on by hysterical liberals and members of the left-leaning press, didn't do a thing to curb crime, but it did turn a lot of law-abiding American citizens into criminals, because the citizens, instead of turning in their guns, carefully sealed their weapons and buried them.

Those that survived the Great War promptly dug up their weapons and used them to defend themselves against the hundreds of thousands of thugs and punks that immediately began roaming the land.

Ben started pulling the West Virginia militia back together. He sent out political teams to explain the Tri-States philosophy to all who were interested in learning about it—and most were.

"Get me President Altman on the horn, Corrie. And get ready to listen to him squall."

Ben explained what he was doing to Altman and there was a long moment of silence from the newly elected President of the NUSA. Finally, Altman exclaimed, "You've done *what?*"

"I made the West Virginia militia the new state police," Ben repeated.

"Jesus Christ!" Altman shouted. "That bunch of wacko gun nuts!"

"Even if that statement were true—which it certainly isn't, now or in the past, not for the most part—can you think of a better group to enforce the law? That is, considering the time and place?"

Altman was silent for a moment, conscious of Cecil looking at him, a faint smile on his lips. Altman slowly sighed, shook his head (which was graying rapidly since the "election") and pressed the talk button. "No, I suppose not, Ben. Tell me, which side is West Virginia going to come under?"

"The NUSA, I assume. We're explaining the Rebel philosophy to the people at town meetings. But that's just in effect while we are here trying to help. After we leave, the laws they choose to enforce will be up to the people. You do plan to let the people have the final say, don't you?"

Cecil's smile widened.

"Of course, I do," Altman said. "That's what a democracy is, Ben."

"Paul, don't try to disarm the people this go-around," Ben warned. "That's a warning offered in a friendly way."

"I will abide by the majority will of the people on that issue, Ben."

"Then you're asking for trouble, Paul. For you know perfectly well the NUSA will be filled with hanky-stomping liberals. Eagle out."

Ben looked at the several dozen spokespeople, representing communities from all over the state, gathered around him in the large room. He shook his head. "Paul still clings to the belief that fifty-one percent of the people can rule the remaining forty-nine percent."

"He will never disarm us, General," Thomas said. "That won't happen, ever again."

"It won't come right away. But it will come eventually."

The men and women exchanged glances. "Then we'll align with the SUSA, General," Thomas said.

"Your decision," Ben said. "Welcome abroad."

Paul Altman came into Cecil's office just before official closing hours and sat down. Cecil fixed them both drinks of bourbon and water and they sipped in silence for a moment.

"I am quite upset about West Virginia." Paul broke the silence.

"The old ways won't work, Paul. You've got to understand that. Maybe fifty years from now, when the nation has healed and the scar tissue is no longer sensitive.

Maybe then, after all the roaming gangs of criminals have been dealt with, the factories are once more running full-tilt, the airports are busy, the highways are filled with cars and trucks carrying people and produce and goods, when people are working and able to enjoy the small pleasures of life and home and family and cook-outs—maybe then whomever is in power can question the need of civilians to own M-16's and Uzi's and M-60's and so forth, but not now, Paul. My God, not now! Not when the nation is still reeling and staggering about from a world war followed by a civil war and total collapse. If you can't see that, then I fear you're in for a long rough haul over very rocky roads.''

"I've hated guns all my life," Paul said softly. "I've never even fired a gun. There was no draft when I was of draft age, so I didn't serve in the military. I don't even like to kill roaches. I want a society that is free of guns, Cecil.''

"Good luck," Cecil said, very drily.

The spokesman from Elkins had been elected governor of the state of West Virginia. It had happened so fast—and just as Paul Altman had thought (and still did)—Thomas wasn't quite sure it was all legal. But Ben Raines had assured him it was.

"But I was the only candidate on the ballots you had printed up," Thomas had protested to Ben.

Ben smiled. "If you don't want the job, tell me now."

"I didn't say that. Oh, what the hell! It's strange times we live in, right?"

"That's right, Governor. Now let's get you settled in. My people have just finished mopping up around

Clarksburg. You have any objections to that being the state capital?"

Governor Thomas smiled, and then laughed. "No, General Raines. No objections at all."

"Fine. Now, I have a surprise for you."

"Another one?"

Ben led him outside and they made the relatively short drive to Clarksburg, stopping and getting out at an office building that had been cleaned out and renovated. Governor Thomas hadn't even been aware it was being done—the Rebels moved so damn fast and got so much done in such a short time! The governor was stunned to see about fifty men, most in their forties, standing in line, at attention, dressed in the uniform of the old West Virginia State Police.

"I've had people scouring the state, and this is all that is left of the state police. Two-thirds of them will go on patrol immediately, the rest will fan out and hand-pick candidates for training. The militia has agreed to work with them and when the ranks are filled, they'll step down at your orders."

"How . . ." Governor Thomas shook his head. "How in the hell do you get things accomplished so quickly, General?"

"We don't fuck around, Gov. We don't have fourteen committees and thirty-nine sub-committees and five hundred-and-fourteen staffers running all over the goddamn place, and all the rest of that bullshit from past governments. And if you want this state to move forward, I suggest you adopt the same tactics."

"It is constitutional?"

"It works," Ben said. "Even my sworn enemies will agree with that."

* * *

Rebel law was simple; so simple that many people either could not or would not comprehend it.

Jersey brought it all down to a list that anyone could understand. She sat down behind a typewriter and wrote:

IF YOU BEAT YOUR WIFE OR GIRLFRIEND OR ABUSE YOUR CHILDREN, YOU WON'T MAKE IT IN ANY STATE THAT SUBSCRIBES TO THE TRI-STATES PHILOSOPHY.

IF YOU ARE CRUEL TO ANIMALS, STAY THE HELL OUT OF ANY AREA UNDER REBEL CONTROL.

IF YOU ARE A SMART-ASS, A BULLY, ENJOY INSULTING PEOPLE OR BROWBEATING EMPLOY-EES, PRACTICE RACISM, POACH GAME, CHEAT OTHERS IN BUSINESS, SELL DRUGS, RESENT AUTHORITY, DELIBERATELY MISREPRESENT THE TRUTH IN ORDER TO SELL A PRODUCT, DRINK AND DRIVE, FAIL TO RESPECT THE PROPERTY AND THE RIGHTS OF OTHERS, EXPECT SOMETHING FOR NOTHING, DON'T KNOW THE DIFFERENCE BETWEEN CONVERSATION AND MALICIOUS GOS-SIP . . . DON'T EVEN THINK ABOUT LIVING UNDER THE REBEL PHILOSOPHY.

Ben looked at the list and nodded his head. "That pretty well sums it all up, Jersey. If we've forgotten anything, I think everybody will still get the message."

Governor Thomas had slipped away from his office and driven down to Elkins. He tapped the short list of rules. "There are going to be some unhappy people in this state," he said, sitting in Ben's CP.

Ben finished cleaning and reassembling his old

Thompson. He snapped in a magazine and smiled at the governor. "They won't be for long."

"What do you mean?"

"Want to take a ride?"

"Better judgement says no, but curiosity overwhelms it. Sure, why not? I'm caught up on paperwork for a change."

"Come on."

They drove a few miles out of town and Cooper turned onto a county road. Thomas immediately tensed. "Do you know where you're going, Ben?"

"Sure do."

"I wonder. This is Wilcott territory."

"This is a public road and anybody has the right to drive on it."

"The Wilcotts don't see it that way. They never have."

"They will very shortly. Those that are left, that is."

"They're throwbacks, Ben. Back to the bad old days. They've been in their glory since the government collapsed. Ben, the Wilcotts are—"

"I know exactly who they are. My people found where the chief of police and the sheriff hid their records when the country started blowing up around them. That whole family is nothing but trash. And they love what they are. They don't want to change. They're bullies, thieves, poachers, murderers, rapists—you name it, they've done it, and they're proud of it. The Wilcotts are exactly what you don't need in this state."

"You can't just kill them."

"You want to bet?" Ben said, and that shocked the governor into silence.

"Roadblock up ahead," Cooper pointed out. "Right where the Scouts said it was."

Ben lifted his handy-talkie, set to the frequency of the MBT that was traveling right behind them. "Blow it," he ordered.

The main battle tank swung around the big wagon and lowered the muzzle of its main gun. Five seconds later, the roadblock was reduced to smoking, burning junk.

"Push it out of the way," Ben radioed, and moments later the short convoy rolled on.

The governor twisted in his seat and looked behind him. "That's Reverend Neely behind us."

"Yeah. I invited him along. There will probably be some need for his services in a very short time."

"You're going to have church services at the Wilcotts?"

"Sort of."

Governor Thomas got it then. "Oh, hell, Ben! You're talking about a *funeral!*"

"Could be. Damn sure will be if the Wilcott clan doesn't want to listen to reason. There are two state police cars behind the preacher."

"Ben—"

"It's got to be this way, Gov. The people have to know that you're the boss. And they have to understand Rebel law. Most already do. But people like the Wilcotts will never obey any type of law. Believe me when I say we had people like the Wilcotts all over the SUSA. The Wilcott types were even more of a pain in the ass than ultra-liberals."

"I have to ask, even though I'm not sure I want to know the answer—what happened to those people?"

Ben smiled. "Liberals or Wilcott types?"

The governor sighed patiently.

"Some of the bully-boys saw the light and turned into good, productive, law-abiding citizens. Others packed up and pulled out. Still others were buried."

"And Wilcott and his clan?"

"I suspect some them will be buried here, Gov. It isn't that they can't change to conform with the few laws the Rebels have on the books. The Wilcott types *won't* change. We'll soon see."

Cooper turned off the county road onto a gravel road, following the MBT. Patches of snow remained in the shadowy, cool spots on both sides of the road.

The column stopped in front of a large, two-story house that immediately brought to mind Tobacco Road—for those old enough to remember the motion picture or to have read the book.

There were smaller houses located on each side of the big house, each of them in just about the same condition as the bigger house, the yards equally filled with all sorts of trash: rusting hulks of cars and trucks, old worn-out tires stacked about, motorcycles in various stages of repair and disrepair, machine parts scattered all over the place.

A large man stepped out onto the front porch, just as Ben was unassing from the wagon. Ben recognized him as Wade Wilcott, the Big Daddy of the Wilcott clan.

"That's Wade Wilcott," Thomas whispered. "The He-Coon of the family."

"Yeah," Ben replied, raising his voice so all could hear. His voice carried in the cold, late winter air. "Ugly son-of-a-bitch, isn't he?"

"Harry Thomas!" Wade yelled to the governor from the porch. "You'll pay for tearin' up my roadblock."

"You can't block a public road, Wade," the governor called.

"I'll do anything I damn well choose to do, you little white-collar piss-ant!" Wade shouted. He cut his eyes to Ben. "You'd be the head honcho of the army, right?"

"That's right, Wilcott. And I have a few things to say to you. So haul your fat ass off that porch and get over here."

Wade Wilcott blinked at that. Been a long, long time since anyone dared to speak to him in such a manner. "You got a lot of brass on your ass, solider boy, to speak to me lak 'at. I run this part of the county. Me and my kin do."

"Yeah?" Ben questioned. "Your brother's name was J.C. Wilcott, right?"

"Was?" Wade asked, stepping forward to the yard. "Did you say was?"

"Yeah. He's dead."

"Dead? My brother's dead? You a damn lie!"

"Your brother and some of his kin made the mistake of ambushing a Rebel patrol early this morning, over at a place called Cutter's Ridge." Governor Thomas cut his eyes at Ben. First he'd heard of that. "When I'm finished here you can claim what's left of the bodies. If you're still alive, that is," Ben added, very matter-of-factly.

Wade's eyes bugged out. "Why wouldn't I be alive?"

"Oh, well, I suspect I might have to kill you in a minute or two," Ben told him. "Because you're not going to like what I have to say."

"Kill me? Kill me! Hey, he threatened me!" Wade hollered to the state troopers standing off to one side.

"I want that man arrested for threatenin' my life. Y'all heard him do it. Now, go on and do your duty."

The faces of the troopers remained impassive. They did not move.

"The way I see it, Wilcott," Ben said, "you have but three choices. You can either change your ways and start obeying the law, you can pack up and move out, or you can die, right here, and right now, your entire miserable, worthless, slovenly, good-for-nothing family with you. Now what's it going to be, Wilcott?"

Wade Wilcott let out a roar of rage and charged Ben, big booted feet slapping the muddy ground.

Chapter Twenty-Eight

Ben side-stepped at the last possible split-second and slammed the butt of his Thompson into the man's belly. The air whooshed out of him and he sprawled on the ground, sliding for a few feet in the cold mud.

One of his sons jerked a rifle to his shoulder and aimed it at Ben. Jersey shot him in the face, the 5.56 round punching a hole in the center of the man's forehead and knocking him backward. He stopped at the outside wall of the house and slid down, dead with his eyes wide open.

"I guess you want to do this the hard way, Wilcott," Ben said. "Suits me."

Wilcott slowly rose to his knees, his face a mask of mud. He wiped the mud from his eyes and looked back toward the house. "That there was my youngest boy. He was a good boy, you son-of-a-bitch!"

"No, he wasn't," Ben contradicted. "He was a thief, a bully, an extortionist, a rapist, and a murderer. The state police have warrants for his arrest. I just saved the public the expense of a trial and a hanging."

Wade Wilcott, still on his knees, glared up at Ben. He was having trouble catching his breath after being stroked by the butt of the Thompson.

"They don't hang folks no more in this state, soldier boy," he panted.

"Oh, they do now," Ben corrected. "This state is now part of the SUSA. We give you a choice. We'll either shoot you or hang you."

Wade cussed Ben, loud and long—but made no attempt to get up off the cold, muddy ground.

"Get your crap packed up, Wilcott. My people will escort you and your family and what is left of your kin to the border of your choice. Leave and don't ever come back here."

Wade came up off the ground like an enraged bull. But Ben had been expecting that. He hit him in the mouth with the butt of the Thompson and Wade went down like a rock, landing on his stomach, all his front teeth gone and his lips pulped and bleeding. Wade groaned once, managed to turn over, and his eyes rolled back in his head. He was out cold.

Ben motioned to a group of Rebels. "Throw him in the back of the first pick-up you find that will run." He turned to the others of the clan, all looking at their unconscious father (or uncle or cousin or whatever), their eyes wide in shock. "Get your shit packed up," Ben told them, his voice hard. "And do it quickly. In half an hour, these stinking hovels will be reduced to rubble."

The Wilcott clan stood and stared at Ben.

Ben lifted his Thompson and blew half a clip into the late winter air. *"Move, goddammit!"* he shouted.

They moved.

"Shame about the kids," Governor Thomas muttered, as the hurried packing was getting under way.

"You want them?" Ben asked.

"I beg your pardon?"

"You want the kids, take them. I'd hate to see another generation of white trash being raised."

"You can't do that!"

"We've been doing it for years, Harry. Under eight years old is best. But I warn you, it doesn't always work out. And with these kids, I'd be careful. Our scientists in the SUSA—and we have the best in the world—have recently proven that the bad seed theory is no longer a theory. It's a fact."

"I never doubted it, Ben. I've believed in that all my adult life."

"You goddamn rotten son-of-a-bitch!" Wade yelled at Ben, as he sat up in the bed of the pick-up truck. His mouth was swelling and dripping blood and his words were badly slurred.

But Ben got the general drift.

"You have no one to blame but yourself, Wilcott," Ben told him. "Now just shut up."

Two newspapers had reopened since the Rebels came to town: the local paper in Elkins, and another in the new capitol. The two reporters had been a few minutes late arriving on the scene—they had laid back several miles in following the governor—but they got the general idea of what was going on.

Ben had met the reporter from the local paper and

had found him to be fair in his writing. He did not know the second reporter.

Governor Thomas caught the direction Ben's eyes had taken. "He's all right," he assured Ben. "He doesn't agree with everything we're doing, but he's fair."

"This ain't constitutional!" Wilcott bellered. "Y'all ain't got no right to do this!"

"You and your kin have thumbed your thumbs at the law around here for years," one of the state troopers surprised Ben by saying. "You've terrorized travelers and assaulted people on a whim. You've shot at hunters on public lands and shot at cars traveling on highways. You've burned down the houses of people who dared to speak out against you and your kin. You've assaulted police officers and threatened to kill judges who dared to put your kin in jail. The list of laws you have broken is as long as my arm. It's over now, Wade. If General Raines had not moved against you and your kind, I was going to kill you myself."

Wade Wilcott wiped the blood away from his mouth with his sleeve. He opened his mouth to speak, then thought better of it and remained silent. He sat in the bed of the old pick-up truck and glared hate at the state troopers.

The family members loaded their suitcases and cardboard boxes and trunks into the beds of trucks and climbed on.

"I got me kin over in the hills and hollers of Missouri," Wade shouted at Ben. "I'll take my people to Missouri and set up there."

Ben smiling, thinking of Zandar and Cugumba and Mobutomamba and Issac Africa. "Oh, I think that's a splendid idea, Wilcott. Yes, indeed. We'll even give you ample supplies to reach that destination. Have fun in Missouri, Wilcott."

"You're an asshole, Raines!" Wade screamed at Ben. "When I get to Missouri, I'll gather up my people and we'll take over that damn state."

"Good luck," Ben called. Then, under his breath, he muttered, "You're damn sure going to need it. 'Bye, now." Ben waved as the trucks began rattling out onto the road.

Wade Wilcott gave Ben the finger.

Ben gave him two in return and the line of state troopers could not contain their laughter at his gesture.

"Drag that dead man off the porch and bury him. Then burn these houses to the ground," Ben ordered.

"How do you know Wade won't get a few miles out and then turn around?" Governor Thomas asked.

"Because he knows I won't hesitate to shoot him if I ever see him again," Ben replied. "You can forget about Wade Wilcott. He won't last long in Missouri. You've seen the last of the Wilcott clan."

"Thank God for that," one of the senior troopers said.

As the first warm breezes of early spring blew in, the Rebels began making plans to pull out of West Virginia. They all knew their toughest job lay ahead of them, in the northeast.

Cecil had approved and signed a non-aggression and cooperation pact with Simon Border . . . but even as he signed it, he knew it wasn't worth the paper it was written on. He knew that someday, the Rebels would have to fight the army of Simon Border and the WUSA.

President Paul Altman and his staff and cabinet left the SUSA and moved into the new capitol of the NUSA, located in Indiana.

The once most powerful nation in all the world was now split into three nations . . . with the entire northeast section of the country up for grabs.

Hundreds of miles to the south, Mexico, Central America, and South America had exploded into violent civil war. No one really knew what was happening in China, but much of Europe was settling down and digging out of the ashes of war and unrest and beginning to rebuild.

Parts of Africa were ablaze in civil war, as was India and Pakistan.

On an unusually warm day in early March, Ben shook hands with Governor Harry Thomas and climbed into the wagon. He looked back at Jersey.

"I'm not going to say it," Jersey grinned.

"Aw, come on, Jersey!" Ben urged.

She laughed and shouted, "Kick-ass time!"

And the convoy pulled out, to write another page in the rebuilding of America.